A Wedding
RENEWAL

IN SWEETWATER, TEXAS

A Wedding

RENEWAL

IN SWEETWATER, TEXAS

KIM O'BRIEN

© 2012 by Kim O'Brien

Print ISBN 978-1-61626-737-7

eBook Editions:
Adobe Digital Edition (.epub) 978-1-62029-048-4
Kindle and MobiPocket Edition (.prc) 978-1-62029-049-1

Cover design: Faceout Studio, www.faceoutstudio.com

Published by Barbour Publishing, Inc., P.O. Box 719, Uhrichsville, Ohio 44683, www.barbourbooks.com

Our mission is to publish and distribute inspirational products offering exceptional value and biblical encouragement to the masses.

 Member of the
Evangelical Christian
Publishers Association

Printed in the United States of America.

Dedication

For my family with love and thanks
for all the support and encouragement.

Chapter 1

The phone rang Friday morning at 7:45 a.m.

"Help!"

Sylvia Baxter squeezed the phone between her shoulder and ear as she filled two cereal bowls with Froot Loops. "Eat," she whispered to her sons who were shooting a Matchbox car down the center of the table.

"Eat?" Rema repeated. "I call on the verge of collapse and all you can say is 'eat'? What kind of help is that?"

"Oh Rema, I was talking to the boys." Sylvia deftly steadied the gallon jug of milk before Tucker accidentally dumped its entire contents on his cereal. "What's the matter?"

"I'm married to the world's biggest jerk, that's what." Rema's voice drilled into Sylvia's ear. Her best friend had a flair for the dramatic, which made it hard at times to accurately judge the true depth of the crisis. "You aren't going to believe what he did this time."

"Tell me."

"It's a long story. Honestly, Sylvia, every time I think that guy has lost the power to hurt me, he proves how wrong I am."

Sylvia sighed sympathetically. Rema sounded genuinely distressed. She glanced at the clock. This morning she was dressing up as Mr. Slice at the boys' school in order to boost sales for the weekly pizza fund-raiser. She also had to go to the craft store, grocery shop, unclog the bathroom sink, and run a couple loads of laundry.

Calculating quickly, Sylvia figured if she skipped breakfast, ignored the house, and made all the green lights on the way to the elementary school, she'd have an extra hour.

"Don't worry." Sylvia spotted one of Tucker's sneakers beneath the table. Where was the other? "Whatever it is, we'll fix it. Come on over. After I get the boys off to school, we'll hop in the spa and have a soda. You can tell me all about it."

By the time Sylvia returned from taking the boys to school, Rema had arrived. She'd let herself in through the back gate and was sitting on one of the deck chairs, staring into the turquoise depths of the pool. Waving, Sylvia opened the back door. "Let me change into my suit and I'll be right out. Why don't you get the sodas?"

"Okay." Rema's kitten heels clicked on the tile as she followed Sylvia into the coolness of the air-conditioned kitchen. Opening the refrigerator door, she reached for the drawer Sylvia kept stocked with sodas. "I might need something stronger than soda. My head feels squeezed, like I have a migraine coming."

"Don't worry." Sylvia peeled off her jeans and slipped into a well-worn one-piece bathing suit, purchased because it advertised the kindest cut on the market. "I have a whole new bottle of Excedrin."

Stepping back outside, Sylvia tossed her towel on the back of a lounge chair, considered going back in the house for sunglasses, and then decided against it. The March sunlight was bright, but it was impossible to have a good conversation with someone without seeing his or her eyes.

At eight thirty, sunlight already bathed the kidney-shaped pool. The temperature was in the low eighties and promised to get even warmer. It never failed to amaze Sylvia, who had grown up in Ohio, how fast summer came to Texas. The water felt cool at first, and then deliciously silken as she settled herself into the spa.

"So what did Skiezer do this time?"

Rema handed her a soda and popped the other open. "Family game night strikes again."

"Uh-oh." Sylvia set her soda can on top of the stone rim around the hot tub and leaned back against the jets.

"Our game of Sorry turned nasty. Skiezer tried to get the boys to gang up on me." Rema frowned. "Talk about low. Who tries to convince a five-year-old and a nine-year-old that their mother is mean and deserves to lose?"

"He probably was only teasing you," Sylvia suggested hopefully.

The topic of marriage was as familiar as the taste of soda on Sylvia's tongue. How many hours had they sat in this same spot and swapped confidences? Ever since she and Rema had met at the Methodist church's preschool, they had been fast friends. She studied the lines of worry in Rema's face. Beneath the artfully applied makeup, Rema looked truly discouraged. Her heart ached in sympathy.

"What happened next?"

"I called him a big, fat cheater then stormed out of the room. I had to sit for thirty minutes in my closet just to calm down."

Sylvia laughed. "Thank heaven for closets."

"What is it about men?" Rema sank to chin level in the water. "Just for once, I want to be with someone who stares into my eyes and isn't about to accuse me of something."

"I know what you mean." Sylvia also sank deeper so she was eye level with her friend. "I love Wilson and all, but sometimes I read these romances and my heart just aches. The guys in those books never spend their evenings doing e-mail."

"Or inspecting the walls to see if any of the kids have left fingerprints." Rema's gaze turned thoughtful. "Or snapping their fingers when they're on the phone to get your attention."

Rema fired off a series of finger snaps, rolled her eyes, and jerked her head around as if she were having some sort of seizure. Sylvia laughed so hard she almost swallowed a mouthful of water.

"Let's face it," Rema said, a grin replacing her earlier worry lines. "Our husbands are never going to star in a best-selling romance." She snorted. "If Skiezer's going to star in a book, it'd definitely have to be something by Stephen King."

"Wilson would be perfect for *The Invisible Man*," Sylvia confessed. "I never see him anymore." She shook her head a little sadly. "He used to be romantic, but now all he does is work, work, work."

"Skiezer, too. His Bluetooth is permanently attached to his left ear."

"Rema, don't you wish, just for once, that somebody would come crashing through your front door and sweep you up in his arms and carry you off somewhere really romantic?"

"I'd settle for someone who greeted me when he came home from work as warmly as he did the dog." Rema's thin, arched eyebrows drew together. "Sylvia, I don't understand why Skiezer has to be so—so controlling."

"Maybe because he feels insecure."

Rema seemed to mull this over for a moment. "So insecure that he wanted to annihilate me over a game of Sorry?"

"Did you beat him last time?"

"I don't remember. Maybe." A pause. "Yeah. By a mile."

Sylvia waited.

"So what do I do? Throw the next game? Because if I have to let him win at everything, what kind of marriage is that?"

"I don't know," Sylvia said. "Maybe you should talk to him. Tell him how you feel."

"Talk about feelings?" Rema snorted. "He'd rather undergo a root canal."

"You could explain that women need to feel cherished by their husbands." Sylvia looked off into the privacy fence that surrounded their small backyard. She found herself more than a little bit relating to Rema's problem. "We want our men to be strong enough to sweep us off our feet and gentle enough never to hurt us with an unkind word. And we want them to spend even more time during the day thinking about us than we do about them."

Rema groaned. "Oh Sylvia, you've been reading those romance novels again. There's a reason they call that stuff fiction."

"I don't care," Sylvia stated, no longer sure if they were discussing Rema's situation or her own. "What's the saying? That art imitates life, or something like that."

"Only if it's good Chick Lit."

Chuckling, Sylvia craned her neck for a peek at the kitchen clock. "Oh darn it," she said. "I've got to get to the school. Do my Mr. Slice thing."

"How come they don't call you Mrs. Slice?"

"I'm not sure," Sylvia admitted, "maybe because pizzas aren't supposed to have breasts?"

Rema laughed. "I don't think pizzas are supposed to have arms and legs—or other parts either."

"Well, I may be Mr. Slice, but it's the moms who are buying the pizza." She rose dripping from the spa. "I've got to go. You going to be okay?"

"Yeah, I knew this wasn't a crisis, but it just helps to talk sometimes."

Sylvia smiled and wrapped herself in a towel. "Yeah, I know what you mean. I still think you should talk to Skiezer about opening up more, but if that isn't going to work, maybe you should try family movie night."

"Yeah," Rema agreed. "I will. Now you get going. I've made you late enough as it is."

Later, dressed in black leggings and the foam pizza costume, Sylvia peered at the world through strategically placed slits in the pepperoni. The air smelled old and stale, and a trickle of sweat rolled down her chest. *It's all for a good cause,* she reminded herself as she walked down the kindergarten hallway. The school would receive money from every pizza sold that evening.

"Hello, Mr. Slice," a little boy with a crew cut and chunky black-rimmed glasses called out.

"Hello there!" Sylvia replied, trying to sound like the world's friendliest pizza. "Are you going to see me in the box tonight?"

"You bet." The little boy grinned. His eyes grew round with wonder, and his voice assumed a deferential tone as if he were in the presence of royalty. "You're really cool."

"Well thank you." Sylvia grinned back, although she knew the boy couldn't see her face.

As she reached the first classroom, she paused. Apparently she made a pretty cool slice of pizza—but what about herself as a woman? Reaching for the doorknob with her pepperoni hands, she thought how easy it was to get lost in a marriage, to become a mom and wife and lose that piece of herself that had nothing to do with fixing healthy meals, doing the laundry, or shuttling the kids around. Not that there was anything wrong with those things, she assured herself.

It was just, well, lately it felt like she and Wilson were more roommates than soul mates. Just this morning, hadn't he called her *Mom*, as in, *"Hey Mom, have you seen the power cord to my PC?"*

Her advice to Rema rang in her ears with alarming clarity. If she wanted something more from Wilson, she'd have to do more than just wish for it. She needed to take action.

Chapter 2

Three days later, Sylvia leaned over the bathroom sink to study herself in the mirror. Her brunette hair, freshly cut and colored, now had highlights and lowlights. She turned her head and admired the caramel-colored streaks that had taken three hours at the beauty salon to put there. She liked the way the layers framed her face, maybe even took off a year or two. She couldn't wait to show Wilson. Hopefully he'd like it and not ask how much it had cost.

The chirp of the door alarm announced Wilson's arrival. Smoothing her fingers over her new black capri pants, she took one last deep breath for courage. *Okay,* she thought. *Here we go.*

As she stepped into the kitchen, the first thing she saw was Wilson holding Tucker upside down by the legs. The little boy's fingertips just touched the tile floor, and he was yelling, "I am Upside-down Man." Simon was clinging to Wilson's back like a small monkey. All three Baxter men were grinning from ear to ear.

"Wilson, put Tucker down," Sylvia ordered. "He just ate

spaghetti about ten minutes ago. Do you want him to throw it all up?"

Wilson lowered Tucker and shot her an apologetic glance. When his gaze lingered on her, Sylvia felt a rush of pleasure. She could almost see the wheels in his brain turning as he struggled to figure out why she looked so great.

"Sorry." Wilson, still staring at her, gave Tucker a pat on the head. "I was hoping I'd gotten home in time to eat with you all tonight."

"You never get home in time to eat with us," Simon said.

"You dad works hard." Sylvia automatically defended Wilson. Besides, she didn't want the conversation going in that direction. She touched her hair in a hint that Wilson was supposed to say something nice about it.

Simon, however, beat him to it. "Mom got her hair cut."

"It looks very nice," Wilson said, but he looked more worried than impressed. This was okay with Sylvia. He was probably trying to figure out if he had forgotten an important date. They used to celebrate all kinds of things—like the anniversary of the first time he asked her out, and the day he had proposed to her.

"You sure you like it?" Sylvia casually combed her fingers through the new layers.

"Yes, but I liked the way you looked before just as much," Wilson said.

"I liked her hair better before," Tucker stated with as much importance as he could muster in his five-year-old body.

"Tucker, your mother looks beautiful no matter how she wears her hair."

Sylvia beamed. "Thank you." She almost, but not quite, missed the wink he exchanged with Tucker.

Simon frowned. Behind his glasses, his eyes blinked furiously as his seven-year-old brain focused its considerable horsepower on her hair. "How do they make it change color? Do they use paint? Does it wash out?"

"We'll ask Marie the next time I have it done," Sylvia promised. She pointed her finger in the direction of the upstairs game room. "Now scoot. *Bobsled Billy* is on TV. Do you want to go and watch?"

Usually she limited the amount of time she let the kids watch television, but tonight she was relenting in order to give herself and Wilson a little private time.

She turned in time to catch Wilson staring at her new black capri pants. Another thrill worked its way through her body, and suddenly she was very glad that she'd bought a size smaller than usual. So what if she could never wash these pants and zip them again. She purposely crossed the room to give him a view of the way the material clung to her body.

Reaching the refrigerator, she turned around, half-hoping to see that look on Wilson's face—the unblinking, hungry-for-love man gaze. However, he wasn't even looking at her. All three Baxter men had their heads bent closely together. Simon had his half-assembled balsa racer clutched in his small hand.

"You've done a good job sanding this, Simon." Wilson examined the car's triangular shape. "This is really good. I'm not just saying that either."

"How about mine?" Tucker stuck his race car so close to Wilson's face it nearly hit him in the nose. "Look at mine."

"It's incredible," Wilson assured him. "You two are going to be the hotshots at the Pinewood Derby."

"Daddy! Daddy!" Tucker shouted. "Are you going to come to the race?"

"Wouldn't miss it."

Racer derby? Balsa cars? Sylvia shut the refrigerator, forgetting why she'd opened it in the first place. *This is even worse than I thought.*

Didn't he see that she'd bought a new outfit, put on makeup, and set the table with candles? She ran her fingers through her hair and felt, well, as if she were a car and someone had let the air out of her tires. Her moment was over. Not only that, but she feared that Wilson privately agreed with the boys and liked the way she used to look much better.

Watching Wilson with the boys, she realized she didn't have the heart to send Tucker and Simon upstairs. Clearly Wilson was enjoying being with them. Her hopes of a romantic evening died. *We're a family,* she thought, *and this is how it is supposed to be.*

Yet, was that true? What about herself and Wilson as a couple? They loved each other. He told her so every night right before he fell asleep—that is, if he wasn't in his office working. Maybe though, it wasn't the kind of love she wanted from him. Maybe she was just a package deal—someone who came with the kids.

Frowning, she tried to remember a conversation with Wilson that hadn't involved the coordination of schedules, the boys, or some item of Wilson's that needed to be found.

When he'd married her nearly ten years ago, he'd promised to love and cherish her until death do us part. She still wanted that, she realized—that crazy, romantic kind of love.

It was time to stop fooling around. New hair and tight pants obviously weren't going to cut it. She needed something stronger.

She wrinkled her brow, thinking hard. A complaint session in the spa with Rema would be fun, but she didn't want fun—she wanted a plan.

Tonight, when Wilson buried himself in e-mail, she would hit the phone and call an emergency meeting.

Chapter 3

On Wednesday evening, four women gathered around Sylvia's kitchen table. Placing the bowl of potato chips next to the onion dip and the platter of double fudge brownies, Sylvia checked to make sure everyone had a drink before settling into her seat.

The minute she sat, the kitchen became utterly silent. Sylvia hesitated, straining for any noise that might indicate that Wilson wasn't safely enclosed in his study or the boys weren't asleep. This was *woman* business.

Finally satisfied, she popped the top of a diet soda. No matter what this session yielded, she was convinced it would include an edict to lose five pounds. Therefore, regular soda, which she preferred, was out of the question. Unfortunately so were the chips and brownies.

"I like your hair," Susan commented, breaking the expectant silence. "It flatters your complexion."

Sylvia patted her hair, aware that Susan could simply be being nice. With her kind blue eyes and graying blond hair, Susan was probably the least appearance-conscious person in their group. "Thanks," she said.

"The cut is terrific," Andrea Burns added, crossing one leg of an expensively cut trouser over the other. "I like the layers." Andrea's own dark hair was cut short and edgy. As a corporate lawyer, Andrea wanted to present a no-nonsense exterior, a look she had perfected down to the point of her high-heeled executive pumps.

"Are you sure the highlights aren't too red?" Sylvia asked a tad self-consciously.

"No, they're perfect." Kelly, a fragile-looking platinum blond, sipped from a stainless steel canister that contained a lime-green concoction that Kelly had been trying to get Sylvia to try. "But I don't think we're here to talk about hair color. You said it was serious. How can we help?"

Sylvia looked away from Kelly's forest-green eyes. She could see the doctor in Kelly getting ready to focus on whatever symptoms Sylvia presented, and then prescribe a solution. As if it would be that simple.

It suddenly seemed impossible to blurt out that Wilson had lost interest in her. Mortifying, really, to admit she needed help. And yet, a voice in her brain said very clearly, *If you feel this way about your marriage now, what do you think you're going to feel like five years from now?*

Taking a deep breath, Sylvia reminded herself that these were her closest friends. They would help her. She leaned forward and spoke very quietly. "Two days ago I had my hair done and wore tight capri pants, and Wilson was more interested in the boys' Pinewood Derby racers."

A chorus of sympathetic clucking noises resounded around

the table. "It's like I'm not even there anymore," Sylvia continued, gaining speed. "He comes home from work, eats dinner while I put the kids to bed, and then he settles in front of his computer while I watch TV by myself." She searched the faces around her. "I know Wilson loves me, but it's so *lonely.*"

Rema squeezed her arm sympathetically. "Marriage can be a lonely place, Syl."

"But it shouldn't have to be," Sylvia argued. "That's why I've called all of you here tonight. You all are my closest friends. With our combined years of experience in marriage, I was hoping we could come up with a solution."

"If we could," Andrea said, "we'd be millionaires."

Susan placed warm fingers on top of Sylvia's cold ones. "Wilson adores you. I've seen the way he looks at you."

"He'd be lost without you," Kelly added. "Seriously, Sylvia, I've always admired your relationship with Wilson."

"That's awfully nice, Kelly," Sylvia mused, "but my marriage is far from perfect."

"Everyone struggles." Susan's round face reflected supportive concern.

Sylvia sighed. "I know that—and it's not like anything is really wrong. I mean, we don't fight or anything. And I still love him." She glanced around the faces of her friends and took heart in the sympathetic expressions. "It's more like there're two worlds—my world, which is the house and the kids; and his world, which is work. I feel like there isn't a lot of overlap."

Andrea pulled a legal pad out of her briefcase and uncapped an expensive-looking gold pen. She wrote the date then the number one. "This could be a tough one," she said after a moment.

"So what do I do?" Sylvia's brow wrinkled. "Just accept the fact that once the romance is gone, it's gone?" She reached for a handful of potato chips, momentarily forgetting her need to lose five pounds. Unhappily, she stuffed them in her mouth.

"How about marriage counseling?" Susan suggested. "Our church has several Christian counselors. Maybe you and Wilson need to talk to a professional."

"Wilson's too smart for that," Sylvia said. "He'd not only answer the questions correctly, but also throw in free financial investment advice. The counselor would end up on Wilson's side, and I'd end up looking like an idiot."

Heads nodded around the table. "But I'll keep it in mind," Sylvia added, not wanting Susan to think she didn't appreciate the advice.

Kelly's pencil-thin eyebrows rose. "Why not just talk to Wilson and tell him how you feel?"

"He'd listen," Sylvia said, "and he'd say he would do better, but I don't think he'd change." She grabbed some more chips and wondered if gathering the group had been a mistake. So far no one had a solution, and she felt worse than ever.

"Face it, ladies," Rema broke in, "if sensitivity was a required course in school, most men would fail it."

Susan set her teacup on the table. "You know, I did this study once on the book of Proverbs, which talks about how a woman can have an incredible marriage. A lot of the women in our group had doubts going in, but all of them ended up saying it was one of the best studies they'd ever done."

Sylvia sat up a little straighter. "An incredible marriage?"

" 'She rises and her husband and children call her blessed,' or something close to that," Susan quoted.

"Well, when I rise, I don't want to tell you what my husband and kids call me," Rema joked.

"Blessed," Sylvia repeated. This sounded awfully close to *treasured*, which was what lacked in her marriage. "What else do you remember?"

"Something about her good deeds bringing her recognition from even the leaders of nations."

Sylvia narrowed her eyes. She didn't want recognition from the leaders of nations. She wanted Wilson to love her. However, maybe she had been looking at the problem from the wrong angle. She couldn't change Wilson, but maybe she could change herself. Standing, Sylvia smiled down at them. "Ladies, we're on to something. I'm going to get my Bible."

Sylvia retrieved her Bible from its spot beneath a stack of romance novels on her bedside table. She sent a small prayer of apology to God for not thinking of this sooner.

Returning to the kitchen, she handed the heavy book over to Susan. "You're a genius for coming up with this."

Susan put on her reading glasses and flipped through the pages. "Here it is, Proverbs 31, 'A Wife of Noble Character'."

The room became so absolutely silent that Sylvia swore she could hear Wilson's fingers clicking on the keyboard upstairs. A chill of excitement ran down her arms. *This is it,* she thought, *the answer to my prayers.* "Read," she urged her friend.

Susan cleared her throat. " 'A wife of noble character who can find? She is worth far more than rubies. Her husband has full confidence in her and lacks nothing of value. She brings him good, not harm, all the days of her life. She selects wool and flax and works with eager hands.' "

"Hold on." Sylvia held up her hand. "We have a problem here. Spin wool and flax? I have trouble threading a needle."

Susan shook her head. "You're being too literal. Remember, this was written ages ago. We have to focus on the idea and *modernize* it."

"You mean she should hit Saks?" Rema leaned forward eagerly. "Syl, I'll go with you. We'll open you a charge card and buy the best wool and flax on the market."

"That's absolutely not what it means," Susan said sternly. "It's talking about character. It's saying that we should be trustworthy and think of the needs of others more than ourselves."

"Sylvia already has a great character," Rema said loyally. "She's the most giving person I know."

To the kids maybe, Sylvia thought, but what about what she gave to Wilson? Didn't he get whatever was left of her after she put the kids to bed? Maybe she was as much at fault as he was. "Thanks, Rema, but there's room for improvement. Trust me." She turned to Susan. "Do you remember enough of the study to take me through it?"

She shook her silvery blond head. "Not off the top of my head, but I could go home and try to find my notes. Basically, we looked at each verse and talked about it and how we could apply it to our marriages."

"We can do that," Andrea stated. "Give me the first verse and I'll write it down."

" 'A wife of noble character who can find?' " Susan read, " 'She is worth far more than rubies. Her husband has full confidence in her and lacks nothing of value.' "

"Well," Rema said after a moment of silence. "We all know Sylvia is completely trustworthy, which means we should focus on the 'satisfying his needs' part of the phrase." A wicked glint came into her dark eyes. "I'm thinking that maybe Sylvia needs to buy some new lingerie."

There was some laughter. Sylvia felt herself blush. "I thought we were going to talk about character."

"Sylvia's right," Susan said.

"Okay then, the key word is *needs*." Kelly looked straight into Sylvia's eyes. "What does Wilson need more than anything?"

Fighting the nervous giggle that had worked its way up her throat, Sylvia felt the intensity of four women staring at her. "He needs to lose five pounds," she blurted out. "And stick to an exercise program."

They both did, Sylvia admitted to herself. For years exercise and diet had topped their New Year's resolution list. In fact, they'd justified the additional expense of the swimming pool for this very reason. However, although the kids swam like small dolphins up and down the pool, she and Wilson rarely did anything but relax in the hot tub. They hadn't done a lot of that lately either, she realized.

"An exercise program," Kelly repeated thoughtfully. "Excellent. You need to get those endorphins flowing."

Excellent? Sylvia searched her thoughts for something else that Wilson needed. Something less strenuous. She liked Rema's shopping suggestion, but considering how vehemently it'd been discarded, didn't have the courage to suggest it.

"Was there something the two of you used to do together before you had the boys?" Kelly moved the bowl of chips just as Sylvia's fingers reached for another handful. "Keith and I love to go jogging together."

"Well, we used to do a lot of things," Sylvia said. She smiled as she remembered a particularly enjoyable date when they had hiked around Mystic Lake and then climbed hundreds of rickety stairs for a picnic lunch on the platform of an observation tower.

"We used to go for hikes," she admitted.

"Perfect," Susan exclaimed. "Don't you see? If you two start doing the things you used to do before you had kids, you'll not only get the exercise you need, but also rediscover how much fun you used to have together."

Heads nodded agreement around the table. Sylvia stared hopefully at Rema, as if her closest friend could be counted on to come up with an eleventh-hour rescue. However, Rema nodded enthusiastically. "You can start Saturday," she said. "I'll watch the boys for you."

Sylvia tried to imagine herself and Wilson hiking. At first all she could envision was two middle-aged, slightly overweight people pretending to have a good time as they dripped sweat and slapped mosquitoes. However, the more she thought about it, the more potential she saw. First, there would be no power outlet so Wilson would have to leave his computer at home. Second, they might see some kind of wildlife, preferably small, which might spark Wilson's primal instincts, and he might put his arm around her protectively. Third, if nothing else, she'd burn calories and therefore be able to wash those new capri pants and still fit into them.

"Okay, guys," Sylvia said at last. "I'll start Operation Proverbs 31 on Saturday, as planned. Pray for me, okay?"

"We will, *and*, we'll pray for you right now," Susan said.

All the women joined hands. Sylvia bowed her head and closed her eyes. She took a deep breath as Susan began.

"Heavenly Father, we ask that You be with Sylvia this week as she struggles to integrate the principles You've outlined in

Proverbs 31 into her life. Please help her understand Your words, and give her the strength to do whatever she needs to do in order to strengthen her marriage. We know all things are possible through You. It is in Jesus' name we ask. Amen."

"We will," Susan agreed. "Let's meet again, next Tuesday. You can tell us how it's going."

"Agreed." Sylvia sank back in her seat. "Thanks, everyone. I don't know what I'd do without you."

Four faces grinned back at her. Sylvia sighed, feeling better already. Something wonderful was about to happen in her life. She knew it. She could hardly wait to begin the Proverbs Plan.

Chapter 4

As Wilson lifted the mountain bikes from the roof of the minivan, Sylvia watched the muscles in his arms flex. For a forty-two-year-old man, actually for an any-aged man, she corrected herself, her husband looked pretty good. She'd always been attracted to his height and solid build. The few extra pounds he'd gained over the years only added to his masculinity.

"I pumped your tires up." Wilson wheeled her bike over to her, squeezing the front tire to confirm his words. "Here, feel how tight they are."

Sylvia squeezed the front tire and managed a grateful smile. Although she appreciated the concern, she hoped Wilson wouldn't get sidetracked. He loved bikes. Loved looking at them, loved talking about them, and most of all, making sure their bikes were in tip-top condition before he let anyone ride one. The last time they'd gone for a family ride it had taken over an hour just to get out of the driveway, and by then the boys had been tired and cranky and ready to come home.

Maybe she should have stuck to the original plan and gone hiking. However, walking had seemed too middle-aged, too complacent. Not only that, she admitted to herself, she'd been afraid Wilson would turn her down.

Wilson lifted the back tire and spun it with his finger. He stood transfixed, watching the wheel rotate between the brake pads. If it wasn't perfect, she knew he'd pull out his tools and get to work. They could stand there for at least an hour. She resolved to get the date back on track.

Sylvia cupped her hand to her ear. "The mountain paths are calling. Let's get going."

Wilson frowned. "Your back tire needs truing. I'm not a 100 percent sure, but it looks like your derailer is bent." His eyebrows drew together. "How could that have happened?"

Probably when she'd driven the minivan too deeply into the garage and smashed the bike against the back wall. She buckled her helmet. "I'm sure it'll be fine. Come on, honey."

Giving her bike's rear tire one last frown, Wilson reached for his mountain bike. For a moment, he held it at arm's length, smiling and looking at it admiringly. Sylvia sighed. Why couldn't he look at *her* that way?

However, as soon as they started down the grassy path, some of the tension eased between her shoulder blades. The sun warmed her back even as a breeze cooled her cheeks. Around her, wildflowers grew chest high. Their fluttering leaves seemed like applause as they pedaled past. *This is great,* Sylvia thought. *How beautiful God's world really is. How thankful I am to be a part of it.*

"I can't believe we're here." Wilson pedaled easily at her side. "You and me and a gorgeous day at Lotoka park."

Sylvia shot him a sideways glance. He looked so pleased that a rush of warmth spread through her body. "It's like we have the whole park to ourselves."

"All one hundred acres of preserve, twenty-five miles of dirt paths."

"We'll have a picnic lunch by the water," Sylvia added. "I made a special lunch."

She didn't add that she'd spent hours consulting countless books and magazines, searching for new recipes which would be both delicious and nutritious. She intended to follow the instructions in Proverbs 31 to the letter.

They passed smoothly through the meadow, picking up speed as the land dipped slightly. The wide tires on her bike cushioned the uneven earth. Strapped to her bike rack, their picnic lunch rode like a silent passenger behind her. She could practically feel the years slipping away. When had she last felt so young and free? Usually the boys would have been with them, and she would have been worrying about Simon, who wasn't very athletic and would be devastated if his younger brother sailed past him.

Sylvia stopped herself. This was the problem. The boys always found their way to the top of her thoughts. Today it was going to be all about Wilson.

"The trail is narrowing," Wilson pointed out. "You can go ahead of me."

Rushing toward them with alarming speed, the trail did indeed narrow. Sylvia hesitated and braked slightly. Although she felt fairly certain that from the side, her black Lycra shorts were flattering, she held no illusions about the view from the rear. She didn't want him to think that her butt was the size of Texas.

"Oh no, no," she protested. "You go first."

"Ladies first."

"Wilson, you know I have no sense of direction."

"It's okay," he replied. "I've studied the trail maps. Basically, all the paths lead to the lake. It'll be more of an adventure if you lead the way."

Sylvia swallowed her protest. The last thing she wanted was to waste precious time arguing. Besides, she had to stop worrying so much about how she looked. The important thing was to have fun together. She pedaled faster and pulled ahead of Wilson just as the meadow ended and the forest of pine trees began.

Almost immediately, the trail changed. Tree roots bulged through the earth, making her bike jostle and bump. She heard the food rattling in their soft-sided cooler and tried not to imagine her carefully prepared salads being pulverized in their containers.

After ten more minutes of this, she decided it didn't matter. By the time they arrived at the lake, her butt was going to be so sore that she wasn't going to be able to sit and would have to eat standing up. She had pictured a much, much smoother path.

"Unweight the front tire when you hit a big root," Wilson shouted from behind. "You won't get bounced around so much."

Unweight the front tire? "What do you mean?" Sylvia clenched her jaw as the bike hit a lump the size of a speed bump. No amount of padding in her bike shorts would ever make up for the amount of jostling her body was taking. She didn't even want to think about what the bike helmet was doing to her hair.

She hit another tree root and heard the cooler give an alarming thump behind her then Wilson's shout, "Pull up on the handle-bars before you hit the root," he instructed. "And lift your rear out of the seat until you land."

I'm too old for this, she thought in despair. Too old to be jumping tree roots on a mountain bike, too old to change anything about herself, much less her marriage. What was she doing?

Her despair deepened as the trail became even narrower and steeper. Thick, scabby trunks of the pines pressed closely on either side of her, and she kept pedaling unexpectedly into cobwebs.

When the path forked, she chose the one on the right because it appeared slightly less rocky. However, she'd barely gone twenty yards when the ground changed, becoming overgrown with grass. The ribbon of trail disappeared completely. "I think we've gone off-road," she shouted.

"We're fine," Wilson called back. "Isn't this great?"

Sylvia bit her tongue and kept pedaling. She tried not to think of snakes slithering in the grass or how many mosquito bites she was getting. *You're having fun,* she ordered herself. *Don't be whiney.*

"Shouldn't we be at the lake yet, Wilson?"

"Any minute," Wilson agreed, heartedly. Too heartedly.

"Are you sure?" They came to another meadow. She slowed but didn't stop. The grass tickled her leg. If the path became any more overgrown, they'd need a scythe to get through. A chorus of buzzing noises increased in volume on either side of her head as if the crickets were coordinating their plan of attack.

"Of course I'm sure." She heard Wilson smack his leg. "Ouch! Darn bugs. How come they don't go after you?"

"Because I'm coated with spider webs from blazing the trail."

"Well, why don't you brush them off?"

"If I take one hand off the handlebars, I'm going to crash." Sylvia tensed as grass wound itself into her gear and the bike slowed. "Are you *sure* the lake's just ahead?"

"As long as we're on a path, we're heading toward the lake." Wilson slapped another bug. "Go faster, I'm getting eaten alive."

Sylvia gamely pedaled harder, ignoring the long spears of grass that tangled around the gears. How long would it take before Wilson admitted they were lost?

Somehow, she must have taken the wrong path when the trail split. Moment by moment, she and Wilson pedaled deeper into the 125-acre wildlife refuge. This wasn't romantic. It was *suicidal.* She mentally calculated how much food they had and how long it would take before the park rangers came after them. She hoped it was before dark.

"Wilson, I really think we should turn around."

"Just another mile or so," Wilson stated with firm conviction. If she hadn't known him as well as she did, she would have believed he actually knew this for a fact.

Sweat stung her eyes. Huge bugs buzzed past her ears. Her butt alternated between a numbing paralysis and excruciating pain. And then, suddenly, the trail took a hard turn to the left, the meadow fell away, and a grove of hardwoods opened up in front of them. The tall grass gave way to a bed of soft pine needles, and the growth of the trees formed a perfect natural canopy above them. The temperature dropped instantly and the air smelled like pine. She barely had time to appreciate the graceful arch of the old trees before she saw the lake ahead, a glistening patch of blue surrounded by lush forest.

"I see the lake!" Sylvia risked unclenching one hand from the handlebars and gave a thumbs-up signal. "We made it!"

"It's incredible." Wilson's voice rang with excitement. He pulled up alongside her. "I love you, Sylvia."

Suddenly all the aches and pains of the ride seemed inconsequential. He *loved* her. Sylvia grinned so widely it hurt. Here they were, alone, surrounded by a hundred acres of virgin forest. With no distractions, Wilson was becoming romantic, just as she'd hoped.

"I love you, too, Wilson."

They stopped their bikes on a bank overlooking the water. Sylvia measured the lake with her gaze, pleased at the junction of sky and water. No powerboats—nothing mechanical to distract Wilson. Perfect. She unstrapped the picnic lunch from the bike rack as Wilson spread a red-plaid cotton blanket over a thin patch of grass. The silence alone was heady. No kids arguing, no telephone ringing, no noise, nothing except for the slight stir of a breeze through the pines.

She put the paper plates on the blanket and added plastic goblets. The napkins color-coordinated with the blanket, and when she added the bowl of grapes as a centerpiece, she felt certain Martha Stewart would have approved.

Wilson opened the first container. Sylvia frowned when half the potato salad stuck to the lid, no doubt thrown there from the centrifugal force of the ride. "This looks good, Syl."

Sylvia held her plate out as he served her. "It's low-fat, too. Everything is. I want us to be healthy and live a long life *together*."

Wilson smiled. "Absolutely. Did you bring the Fritos?"

Laughing, Sylvia pulled out another container. "Try these pita chips. They're much better than Fritos."

Opening the container, Wilson frowned. "Are they supposed to look like this?"

She peered over his shoulder. "Well, I guess they got a little broken up in the ride. Here, I have a special dip to go with them."

She rallied with a smile. "It's called hummus."

Wilson put a chip in his mouth. He reached for another. "These are really good."

She leaned forward, smiling. "Doesn't this remind you of the old days?"

Wilson washed down the chips with a long drink of sweet raspberry iced tea. "Yeah." He squeezed her fingers with affection. "Remember when we went canoeing? That was great."

Great? They'd capsized in the first set of rapids. She'd swallowed half the river before managing to surface, clinging to the canoe as some park ranger shouted at her to let go. Sylvia popped a grape in her mouth. Maybe recalling the past wasn't a good idea, after all. She handed him a container of cold marinated beef, sliced razor thin. Maybe after they ate they would lie on their backs and look up at the vast blue sky. He would reach for her hand, and they would lie there like teenagers and dream aloud.

The beef smelled delicious, and Sylvia added a generous amount to her plate, followed by a large scoop of tri-colored pasta salad. She decorated the edges of her plate with olives and black beans in a cilantro vinaigrette. The food really looked like a work of art.

"We should do this more often." Wilson polished off the entire container of chips and hummus. "Get away—just you and me."

Sylvia smiled. "My thoughts exactly. Starting today, you and I are on a special diet and exercise program." She stopped talking at the look of worry on Wilson's face. "Don't worry, you're going to love the turkey burgers I've got planned for tonight."

Wilson held his hand up. "Quiet." He peered somewhere over her left shoulder. "I think I hear something."

Sylvia held her breath as Wilson strained to hear in the silence.

This is exactly like I imagined, being in the wilderness is sparking Wilson's protective instincts.

"What is it?"

Wilson shook his head. "Sounded like an animal rooting around."

She smiled. "Maybe a rabbit wants some of my endive salad."

"Endive salad? Pass it over here."

For the next thirty minutes, she and Wilson polished off every bit of the gourmet picnic she'd packed. Placing the final empty container in the cooler, she mentally reviewed all the things they'd talked about: the boys' upcoming Pinewood Derby, the boys' most recent soccer game, Simon's new fascination with bugs, and Tucker's ability to eat half a pizza by himself. Not once, she realized, had they talked about themselves. It was almost as if without the boys they would have had nothing in common. The thought added to her determination to get their date back on track.

Taking her husband's hand, she urged him to lie on his back next to her. "Let's look up at the clouds," she suggested. "I see one that looks like a sheep. What do you see?"

When Wilson remained quiet, she glanced over at him. He had his eyes closed. She nudged him gently. "Are you sleeping?"

"No," he said. "Just relaxing."

She studied the rise and fall of his chest. "Let's talk."

His eyes remained shut. "What about?"

She took a deep breath. It was now or never. "Us." She turned onto her side, facing him. "Are you happy?"

Wilson smiled. "Very happy."

She waited for him to ask her the same question. However, when his hand tucked under his chin, she realized he was going into his sleeping position.

She looked up at the sky in frustration. Some great date. Wilson found her company so invigorating it required a nap; it would be days before she sat comfortably again, and the shrubbery around them looked suspiciously like poison ivy.

She heard something rustle in the distance. There was silence, and then the snap of a branch breaking. "Wilson," she whispered. "I hear something."

"The boys are fine," he muttered. "Go back to sleep."

She shook his arm. "Listen."

The underbrush crunched as something moved closer to them. The small hairs on her arms stood straight up. "Wilson, some animal is coming. I hear it."

Wilson's eyes shot open. "What?" He sat upright and stared hard in the direction of the noise.

"What is it?" Frozen in place, she watched color bloom in her husband's face.

"We're going." Climbing to his feet, Wilson pulled her roughly upright.

"What is it?" She hissed.

Wilson strapped the basket to her bike in record speed then glanced over his shoulder. "Go," he whispered with urgency. "Just *go*!"

Chapter 5

"And then what happened?" Rema leaned forward eagerly, nearly upsetting the pitcher of green tea. "What was after you?"

Sylvia looked around her kitchen table at the expectant expressions of the group. Three days had passed since her infamous date with Wilson, and she couldn't put off the truth any longer. "Well, we jumped on our bikes and pedaled as fast as we could to get out of there."

"What was chasing you?" Rema locked her gaze with Sylvia's. "A bear? A wolf? A bobcat? What?"

Sylvia swallowed. "A wild pig."

"A pig?" Rema repeated in disbelief. "You ran from Wilbur?"

"This wasn't *Charlotte's Web*, Rema. This thing had horns. This long." Sylvia gestured with her hands.

Kelly sat straighter in her seat. "He saved you from a wild boar. Sylvia, don't you see how romantic that is?"

Sylvia shook her head. "Saved me? He nearly ran me off the trail trying to get out of there." She sighed. "In short, the whole date was a disaster."

Rema patted her arm. "You did great. Who could have predicted the pig thing?"

Sylvia sighed and reached for a carrot strip. Dunking it in the low-fat onion dip, she shook her head. "I don't know what I did wrong."

Susan shook her silver-blond head gently. "You didn't do anything wrong. You and Wilson spent time together, and now you have a funny, exciting new story to tell. I think it was a huge success."

Sylvia sipped her diet soda. It wasn't nearly as good as the real stuff. "I didn't even tell you guys what the hummus did to Wilson's digestion. Let's just say it was a good thing we hustled out of the woods."

"Change always feels uncomfortable," Susan stated. "What's Pastor Rick always saying—that God loves us too much to let us stay in the same place? We need to keep growing in our faith. I think as long as you're asking God to help you understand His Word, you'll be fine."

"So what does Sylvia do next?" Rema asked. "Does she keep working on fulfilling Wilson's needs, or does she move on to the next verse?"

All heads turned to Susan, who put on her reading glasses and consulted a manila folder filled with papers. "When my group did this study, we looked at a different verse every week. But I don't think there's a right or wrong way to do this. What are you comfortable with, Sylvia?"

Sylvia shifted on the kitchen chair. The exercise part of the plan wasn't working out as well as she'd hoped. Although Wilson had agreed to take family walks after dinner, so far they hadn't gone on a single one. Every night he'd come home and worked on his laptop.

Sylvia looked around at her friends. "I think," she said slowly, "that I should keep trying to help Wilson lose weight and exercise more, but maybe we should go on to the next verse."

"That's a great idea," Rema agreed. "You need to keep the momentum. If you get bogged down in the first verse, you're never going to get anywhere."

Andrea, wearing yet another power suit, pulled out her legal pad and consulted her notes from the last meeting. "I agree. There are about twenty verses that refer to the Proverbs 31 woman. If Sylvia spends two weeks on each, it'd take her about a year to get through them all. I think she should move on to the next verse."

"It's not a race," Kelly argued. "The important thing is for Sylvia to feel better about her marriage, herself, and her relationship with God." She sipped her herbal concoction and smiled sympathetically at Sylvia. "Some things take time. I'm always telling my patients that getting better is a process."

Sylvia ran her fingers through her hair. "I know," she said. "And even though the date wasn't exactly a romantic success, I think Wilson had fun. When we got back to the car, he laughed harder than I've seen him do in months."

Rema patted Sylvia's arm. "There you go," she said. "I knew it wasn't a total disaster. What's next?"

Sylvia reached for her Bible. She opened the satin pages to Proverbs 31.

" 'She brings him good, not harm, all the days of her life.
She selects wool and flax and works with eager hands. She
is like the merchant ships, bringing her food from afar.' "

Sylvia looked up. "I'll admit it. I don't get how I'm supposed to be like a ship."

"Maybe you're supposed to be like the *Love Boat*," Rema joked and began to hum the opening theme to the show.

"You're supposed to take this seriously," Susan snapped. She pushed her glasses higher on her nose and looked at Kelly and Andrea for support. " 'She brings him good, not harm.' This is what we should be talking about."

"Well, the 'do no harm' part—that sounds like my medical oath," Kelly commented. "So if I translate that to marriage, I think it means our actions, as wives, have consequences. We need to be sure that our choices help our husbands and aren't just selfish ones."

Andrea tapped her pencil on her legal pad. "But honestly, don't our choices have to be selfish sometimes? I mean, sometimes isn't it okay to get take-out even though your husband really wants your chicken tetrazzini for dinner? And, come to think of it, why can't he make the tetrazzini? Or, when your husband turns on Sports Central, and you'd rather watch *Pride and Prejudice*, why does the woman have to concede?" She shook her dark hair. "This verse feels like we have subjugated ourselves as women."

"Andrea has a good point," Rema agreed. "If I didn't stand up for myself, I'd get run over at our house." She tapped her manicured fingernails along the tabletop. "I love Skiezer, but I could be bleeding on the side of the road and he'd drive right past me without even noticing."

"Are you so sure?" Susan argued. "I don't think this verse means you have to be a doormat, or watch Sports Central all the time." She paused and added dryly, "Or be the *Love Boat*." She glanced at

Sylvia. "What do you think it means, dear?"

Sylvia swallowed. The last time she'd blurted out an answer she'd ended up in a race with a wild pig. She'd be more careful this time. "Could someone read me the first part of it again? Not the *Love Boat* part. Just the beginning."

" 'She brings him good, not harm, all the days of her life.' "

Sylvia thought of the times in her life when she'd felt closest to Wilson. There were the big events of course, like their wedding and the births of their children. But there were other times, smaller things. Like the time she'd gotten sick. He'd taken care of her, brought her chicken noodle soup, and laid a cool cloth on her forehead. She'd felt so loved. What could she do that would be good for Wilson?

Her gaze drifted beyond the table to the front of the refrigerator, which was covered with the boys' drawings. Hidden nearly out of sight beneath a blue crayon dinosaur, she saw a tattered piece of paper containing a long list of to-do's she'd created for Wilson. She looked away quickly. *No*, she thought, *please Lord, not that*. She didn't know how to do half the chores on it, and the other things were pretty gross.

Their wedding anniversary was in May. Maybe she and Wilson could go shopping together. He could help her pick out a nice new dress. Even as this thought played through her mind, she knew it was wrong. If she wanted to have a better marriage, Wilson needed to work fewer hours, and that included the maintenance work around the house.

"Well," she began, "Wilson does need help with some things that need to be done around the house." She looked at the refrigerator unhappily. "I've made a list. Maybe 'doing good' would be tackling some of those items."

"You're going to take on your own honey-do list?" Rema's

eyebrows lifted in shock.

"Why's that so bad?" Andrea asked.

"Because she's setting a precedent," Rema stated firmly. "If she shows him that she's capable of doing man work, then he'll assume she'll do it in the future." She shook her head. "I don't see how that would help her improve things."

"You're right," Andrea agreed. "Once she assumes responsibility of the man list, the chores arguably could be assigned to her." She hesitated a moment. "You could hire someone, Sylvia. A transfer of responsibility, if you will. I've seen plenty of ads in our local paper for a rent-a-husband."

"It wouldn't be the same." Sylvia picked up a piece of celery stuffed with cream cheese, raisins, and walnuts. "It has to be personal—he has to know that I'm trying to help him."

"I think you're on the right track," Susan said. "It should be you doing something for him."

Rema's face wrinkled with worry. "Are you sure about that list, Sylvia?"

Sylvia sighed. "Yes. I've been nagging Wilson about that stuff for weeks—it hasn't helped and all it does is make me feel bad about myself." She frowned. What was on that list? Most of it, she recalled, was heavy, sweaty stuff—fertilize the lawn, clean the gutters. Well, she'd do the best she could. She put on what she hoped was a brave face. "How hard can it be to power wash and change a few light bulbs?"

Chapter 6

Wilson Baxter looked up from his computer at the discreet knock on his office door. Since the door was already open, the noise was a formality designed to get his attention, not his permission to enter.

"Got a second, Wilson?"

"Sure, Bruce." Wilson pushed his chair back from the desk as his boss shut the door behind him. The action more than anything told him the conversation was not only important but also private. His gaze narrowed on the pale, wrinkled face of the man who had control of his career.

Bruce's glossy, black cane thumped lightly as his boss crossed the gray industrial carpet. His boss was only in his fifties but had started using the cane three years ago after his hip replacement.

"They took it." Bruce's distinctive, raspy voice resonated with significance. "It's in legal now."

Although Wilson had expected this—had in fact worked on the proposal to acquire the small savings and loan bank—he was unprepared for the shot of pleasure that rushed through his system. This was his project—*his baby*. He forced himself to assume Bruce's matter-of-fact demeanor. Later, when he got home and told Sylvia, he'd allow himself to beat his fists against his chest and roar like a gorilla.

"That's great news," Wilson said calmly.

"Legal's got the signed contracts," Bruce confirmed. He smoothed his chin thoughtfully. "But we need to take another look at the merger redundancy analysis you did."

"Sure." A couple of key strokes later, he had the requested information on his computer screen. "I'll print you a copy." He knew that Bruce, although well capable of using the program he'd used to create the spreadsheet, preferred to see things in hard copy.

"Thanks, Wilson." Bruce scanned the spreadsheet. "After I've had a chance to review this, you and I are going to have a serious conversation about your future." His boss leaned forward and his deep-set, brown eyes had fire in them. "This new bank of ours is going to need a branch manager. Since you've been analyzing its operations for more than a year, I can't think of a better person for that job." He paused to let his words sink in. "Would you be willing to relocate?"

Relocate? Sylvia would kill him. Wilson heard himself reply, "Of course."

"Excellent." Bruce stood. "Of course nothing's set in stone, yet, but it's something to think about." He paused at the door. "Are you free at six? Legal should have something for us by then."

Again, he readily agreed even as he heard the disappointment in Sylvia's voice when he told her he'd be missing yet another family dinner.

Bruce nodded then followed his cane down the hallway to his corner office. From experience, Wilson knew the man would walk slowly, not because of his disability, but because it gave him an excuse to peek through the glass walls into the offices of the other bank employees and see if they were really working.

Bruce might be wily, but he was a financial genius, Wilson conceded. Not only that, but he admired the man's willingness to take risks. In an industry infamous for its conservative nature, Bruce seemed to love a new financial venture as much as any gambler on a riverboat.

Leaning back in his ergonomic computer chair, his gaze fell on Sylvia's picture on his desk. He couldn't wait to tell her that his merger had gone through, and not only that, he was being considered for the position of branch manager.

Branch manager. The word tasted like filet mignon on his tongue. He picked up the phone, smiled, then hung up. This wasn't news to share over the wire. He wanted to look deeply into his wife's beautiful brown eyes and watch them fill with pride. Tonight, after the boys went to bed, he'd suggest a private soak in the hot tub. Sylvia liked to light the citronella candles, pour them both her special batch of iced tea, and lie back in the spa. With the stars overhead, he'd reach for her hand, and—

She'd probably try to drown him. He raked his fingers through his hair then carefully flattened it again to hide the small bald spot. No way was she going to want to move. Not when she loved everything about their town. And lately she'd gotten so prickly about everything. He couldn't believe she'd dyed her hair that awful color and had started making them all eat cereal that tasted like cardboard instead of the chocolate one they all liked.

He studied her picture again, making a mental note to call her and let her know he'd be late for dinner—again. She wouldn't be happy about that either. Well, he'd make it up to her later. The wife of a branch manager was sure to have a lot of perks. He couldn't wait to lay all of them at her feet.

The next time Wilson looked up, it was seven o'clock. Groaning, he realized he'd forgotten to call Sylvia. What was wrong with him? He rubbed his tired eyes. Great. Now he'd be in the doghouse. He picked up the phone to call Sylvia, but Jen Douglas, his boss's executive assistant, sashayed into his office.

"You ready, Wilson?" She was an attractive woman, in her thirties, but her tendency for figure-hugging blouses and dresses always made him a little uncomfortable. "Bruce is waiting for you in the conference room."

"I'll be there in a minute," Wilson said, just as Sylvia picked up. He heard the boys' voices in the background.

"I know I should have called sooner, but I won't be home for a while. I'll tell you about it later, but right now everyone is waiting for me in the conference room." Out of the corner of his eye he saw Jen check her watch. "It shouldn't be too long," he continued. "I'll call you from the road."

To his surprise, she said, "It's okay, honey. Your plate's in the fridge." He heard the sound of Simon and Tucker laughing in the background, and for a moment the noise seemed to come through the receiver and grab his heart. It suddenly seemed like a very long time since he'd seen them or Sylvia. Still, he reminded himself, everything he did was for them, and he'd be home in time to tuck the boys into bed. It wouldn't always be like this, he promised himself as he hung up.

Gathering his papers and laptop, he turned the light off in his office and followed Jen to the conference room.

Sylvia gently replaced the receiver in the cradle. Another late night for Wilson. When had he last been home in time for dinner? She couldn't remember. The new norm was for him to come home just as she was putting the boys to bed.

One minute they were about to fall asleep, and the next they'd be jumping up and down with excitement at the sight of their father, who liked to swing them up in the air or wrestle. Calming them down again took at least forty-five minutes and repeating the whole go-to-bed sequence. She'd tried to explain to Wilson how tired she was at the end of a long day, but he didn't seem to get it.

"Boys," she yelled, "bath time."

"Do we have to?" Tucker shouted from the upstairs game room.

"Yes," Sylvia called back. "Come on down."

"But we're practicing for the Pinewood Derby," Simon called, his seven-year-old voice implied that nothing, especially not a bath, could compete with the importance of the event.

Sylvia climbed halfway up the stairs. All she really wanted to do was get into bed with a cup of hot tea and her romance novel. "You guys," she said, "let's get going. You can work on your racers tomorrow."

"Aw, Mom," Tucker said. "Do I have to?"

"Just five more minutes," Simon pleaded. "It takes that long to fill the tub anyway."

She couldn't argue with his logic. He'd probably turn out to be a lawyer, just like Sylvia's father. Shaking her head, she recalled losing every debate with her dad. Retreating to the bathroom, she turned the hot water spigot on full blast.

Dangling her fingers in the gush of water, she thought about her mother; how easy she had made raising children look.

Maybe it was selective memory, but she couldn't remember either she or her younger brother ever defying their parents. Her father worked long hours as a patent attorney, but it never seemed to faze her mother, who worked equally long hours taking care of her and her brother Tyler.

The water turned warm and then hot. Adjusting the flow, Sylvia remembered wearing the dresses (never jeans) her mother bought her, eating the meals put in front of her (including vegetables), and going to bed without fussing. All of this occurring without her mother raising her voice. How had she accomplished that?

It was a different world then, Sylvia decided. Kids played outside with their neighborhood friends. There weren't as many activities scheduled, so no one was always busy, always on the run. Although she knew her mother had had her share of parental challenges, it still seemed like her mother did everything much better than Sylvia did.

"Tucker, Simon," she hollered above the noise of the water. "The tub's ready."

"Aw gee, Mom," Tucker yelled. "Two more minutes?"

"No!" Sylvia shouted. "You'd better come *now* or else we're not going to have time for a story tonight." She knew this threat was guaranteed to bring them quickly. The boys loved their nightly reading time together almost as much as she did. She pictured the three of them smashed into one twin-sized bed. How could Wilson bear to miss stuff like that?

She heard giggles, the thump of running feet, and then two naked boys dashed into the bathroom and jumped into the tub. Water sloshed against the sides and over the rim.

"Hey," Sylvia warned, "take it easy. This isn't the swimming pool."

Her admonition met with a series of giggles, and then two small heads simultaneously disappeared beneath the surface. Reaching for the shampoo, she couldn't help but smile. They looked like wild sea creatures with their hair flowing like brown seaweed and their arms and legs long and fluid in the water.

Simon surfaced first. Without his glasses, and with his blond hair plastered to his small head, he looked younger, more like the toddler who had peeked out at the world from behind the wall of her legs.

She squirted his head with shampoo, and did the same when Tucker came up for air. Lathering them up, she took her time turning their short hair into horns, spikes, and antennas before swishing it clean in the water.

When she'd been a girl, her hair had been long. Her mother delighting in creating soapy hairdo's for her. Sighing, she wished for the millionth time that her mother were still alive. She needed her counsel more than ever. One thing she was sure of was her mother would have approved of the Proverbs Plan.

"Okay, guys," she declared. "You're clean."

Wrapping each boy in a fluffy towel, Sylvia hugged her sons dry. "Pajama time," she ordered.

"Is Dad going to be home soon?" Simon asked.

Sylvia knelt on the wet bathroom floor. She saw the worry in her son's eyes. "I don't know," she admitted. "But even if you're already asleep, he'll check on you."

Tucker impulsively threw off his towel and ran naked out of the bathroom, shouting to the world that he had escaped from the evil kingdom of Bathtime.

"You'd better be escaping to your bedroom," Sylvia called after him. " 'Cause Mama Dragon is on her way right now."

"How come Daddy has to work so late?" Simon asked.

" 'Cause he loves us so much," Sylvia replied.

"Maybe he shouldn't love us so much," Simon suggested.

Sylvia straightened slowly. Looking in the mirror, she saw her son's worry reflected in her own eyes. She quickly looked away. "There's no such thing as loving someone too much." She touched his nose. "Especially you and Tucker. Now hurry up and get your pajamas on."

After Simon left, she continued to stand in the bathroom. She fingered one of her curls, remembering her mother sitting at the vanity in her bedroom, carefully putting on makeup and styling her hair so she would look nice each evening when her husband came home. No matter how late that was, her parents would have dinner together, privately, in the kitchen.

Maybe this was what had gone wrong in her marriage. Sylvia didn't wear makeup. More than once, she'd even worn the same T-shirt the day after she'd slept in it. Wilson had never seemed to care, and it'd saved her a shirt in the laundry. She'd spent hours helping the boys collect bugs in the backyard instead of worrying about what she looked like, or even, she admitted to herself, if the beds had been made. Now, however, she worried that she'd been so preoccupied with being a mother that she'd let something else precious slip through her fingers.

"Are you coming, Mom?" Tucker yelled, jerking her back to reality.

Well, she decided, she might not be perfect, but she was going to do better. Giving the woman in the mirror a short, determined nod, Sylvia left the room.

Chapter 7

On Friday morning after she dropped the boys at school, Sylvia went straight to the refrigerator and pulled off her honey-do list. The first item was power washing the pool deck and driveway. She had never power washed before, but she'd seen Wilson do it a couple of times and it hadn't seemed too complicated. She'd also gone on the Internet to pick up a few tips.

She rolled the machine out of the garage (which needed organizing, also on Wilson's list) and mixed the bleach solution. Putting on a pair of safety goggles, she set to work.

The tips on the computer said to start nearest to the house, so she pointed the wand at the step next to the back door and pressed the START button. Nothing happened. She checked all the connections and tried again. Nothing.

She pressed the button a second time. It remained dead. Frowning down at the machine, Sylvia decided to treat it like the vacuum, which tended to get temperamental. "This is your last chance," she warned and gave it a third try. When nothing happened, she said,

"Okay, then," and when she turned on the machine, she also kicked it with the toe of her Keds. The power washer jerked to life with a roar that made her jump.

"That's the way, baby," she said and directed the narrow blast of water at the concrete. Almost immediately the shade began to lighten. The spray reminded her of the world's strongest Waterpiks, and she made a mental note to tell Rema, who would joke about trying it on Skiezer's teeth.

The wand had a little more kick than she'd expected, but she kept a tight grip and was careful not to leave any lines. The work was monotonous, but then most housework was. This was a nice change from vacuuming or running another endless load of laundry. It wasn't that she minded these chores—they weren't fun, but they were part of her job of caring for her family.

A job that was changing, she silently acknowledged as she widened the area again. When Simon had started kindergarten, it'd only been for half a day. She'd barely gotten him out the door before she was picking him up. But with Tucker, it was different. He spent the whole day at school. Although she had worried he might not be mature enough to handle eight hours of good behavior, Wilson had been adamant things would be fine. So far, he'd been correct. Other than a couple of times Tucker had to "sign the book" for impulsive behavior, he was doing well—solidly in the middle of his class. He wasn't as good a student as Simon, whose teacher had bragged was "scary smart," but Sylvia was fine with that. Having a high IQ came with its own set of problems. Simon was sensitive and tended to cry easily. He had a nervous stomach and sometimes had awful nightmares.

She'd finished the pool deck and was working on the driveway when Rema roared up in her black Suburban. Parking on the curb, Rema hopped out of the SUV. She wig-waggled her way up the driveway on a pair of sandals with three-inch heels.

Sylvia turned off the machine. "Hey," she said. "How does it look?"

Instead of inspecting the pavement, Rema lifted a pair of oversized dark glasses and looked Sylvia over from head to foot. A grin slowly formed on her olive-skinned face. "My gosh," she said. "Are you one hot mama or what?"

"Well, it's like ninety degrees." Sylvia wiped the sweat from her face with the shoulder of her tank top. Like the shorts, her shirt was ancient and a little tight fitting. But she'd wanted to wear something old—something she wouldn't mind getting ruined if she accidentally splashed bleach on it.

"It's the safety goggles," Rema said. "It gives you a brainy-brawny look. I ought to text Wilson a photo."

Sylvia shook her head. "Please don't. I look like a mess—and besides, I don't want to tell him what I'm doing. I think it would defeat the purpose." When Rema's brow furrowed, she added, "he'd feel guilty that I was doing something he always does."

"So you're not going to tell him?"

"Only if he notices."

Rema thought about this for a moment. "Maybe you're right. If Skiezer realized I was power washing, he'd probably have an anxiety attack. He'd think that I did something awful, like go on a shopping spree, and was trying to get on his good side before he found out."

Sylvia laughed. The shopping bag in Rema's hand was proof of her love of the mall. "I'm ready for a break. Why don't we get a soda and sit in the shade for a while? I want to see what you bought."

"Just a quick one," Rema agreed. "I have to get home before Cookie gets bored and chews up something. You know that Oriental rug in my entrance?"

Sylvia nodded and put the wand on the ground. She knew that rug—it was a lovely old wool with navy, red, and gold designs.

"Well, Cookie ate a hole in it. I have a repair person coming after lunch. If he can't fix it, I'm going to have to figure out how to hide it from Skiezer."

Sylvia wasn't surprised. Cookie, who was a black-and-white Border collie, was beautiful but full of energy. She was about nine months old and chewed like a termite. So far Cookie had gnawed down most of the window sills and the trim along the back door. Skiezer had threatened more than once to take the dog to the pound. Whether or not he'd actually do this wasn't clear to Sylvia, but it scared Rema enough that she tried to hide whatever damage the dog did from her husband.

"Is it a big hole? Maybe you can put the umbrella stand on top of it," Sylvia suggested.

"It's too big." Rema shook her head and sighed. "Skiezer's going to kill me when he finds out that I haven't been crating Cookie when I leave the house. Honestly, Sylvia, if he had to see the look in poor Cookie's eyes when he gets locked in that crate, he wouldn't be able to do it either. And it's too hot to leave him in the backyard."

"Well." Sylvia opened the back door and felt the cool rush of air-conditioning on her skin. "Next time, bring him with you when you come."

Rema slid into the chair and pushed Tucker's bowl of cereal to the side. "Thanks, Sylvia." She lifted the shopping bag onto the table. "This is for you."

Grabbing two diet sodas out of the refrigerator, Sylvia turned around in surprise. "For me? What for?"

Rema smiled. "For the Proverbs Plan. I know you're working on the honey-do list, and I just thought you should have something nice to wear." She pushed the bag toward Sylvia. "Go ahead, open it."

"You didn't have to do this." Sylvia eyed the Ann Taylor logo on the bag and wondered what her friend had been up to.

"I know. It's just my way of helping." Rema smiled. "If you don't like it, we can take it back."

Sylvia pushed aside the tissue wrap and pulled out a pair of cuffed denim shorts. "Oooh, they're cute," she said and held them up, admiring the sparkly designs on the rear pockets. Checking the tag, she saw it was the right size, but then there was little about her that Rema didn't know, and Sylvia loved this.

"Keep going," Rema ordered.

Next Sylvia pulled out a whisper-thin, ribbed, black tank top. The fabric felt deliciously slinky in her hands. "I love it." Looking up, she tried to not look doubtful. "It's the right size, but it looks really small."

"It stretches," Rema said. "I bought a red one for myself, and it's the same size and I'm larger than you. You'll need to wear a push-up. You have one, right?"

Her friend was talking bras of course. "Somewhere," Sylvia said vaguely. It belonged to the life that she had labeled *before children*. Hopefully she hadn't donated it, or worse, outgrown it. She met Rema's gaze. "I can't believe you did this. This is so nice."

"And there's one more thing." Rema's eyes twinkled. "Every outfit needs the right accessories."

There was something leather and heavy at the bottom of the bag. At first she thought it was a belt, but it was too wide. Puzzled, she lifted it out of the bag then laughed.

"A tool belt? You got me my own tool belt?"

Rema's gold earrings swung as she nodded. "Complete with a pink hammer."

"It's so cute!" Sylvia enthusiastically strapped the tool belt around her waist and stuck the hammer in a loop. "I feel so professional," she said, striking a few poses. "Thank you, Rema. You're like my fairy godmother."

Rema shrugged off her thanks. "The receipts are all there in case you want to switch something." She popped the tab to her soda and took a sip. "I'll warn you in advance the tank top is a little lower cut than you're used to wearing. Hence the push-up."

Sylvia held the shirt up against her chest. "I can't wait to try it on—I'll wear it this Saturday when Wilson's home."

Rema nodded approval. "That's exactly what I was thinking." She sipped her soda and a thoughtful expression came into her soft brown eyes. "There's one thing though, that's been bothering me about this whole plan."

Sylvia put the shirt down. "What's that?"

Rema drummed her fingernails along the side of the can then stopped when she realized what she was doing. "I know you want the kind of marriage that you read about in your romance novels, but Sylvia, I honestly don't think it's possible to have that kind of relationship."

Sylvia sighed. "I know nothing is perfect. But I don't want Wilson and I just to be roommates, I want us to be soul mates." She hesitated, wanting to say more, but afraid that doing so would only point out the shortcomings in Rema's relationship with Skiezer.

"I love Skiezer," Rema said as if she'd read Sylvia's mind. "And I complain about him all the time, but deep down inside I know he's going to be there for me. He's not going to cheat on me, or walk out on our family, or come home drunk." She paused. "So what I'm saying, Sylvia, for what it's worth—I think it's better sometimes to accept what you have and not look for more than someone's willing to give you.

"I don't expect Skiezer to meet all my needs—different people play different roles in my life. You're my best friend, and I tell you stuff, Sylvia, that I'd never tell Skiezer in a thousand years. Not because I don't love him, but because he wouldn't understand. Maybe it's a man thing. I honestly don't know. Just go into this with your eyes open, okay?"

Sylvia put her hand over Rema's. "I hear what you're saying, and I love you for saying it. But here's the thing, Rema. I believe that God hears all our prayers and He answers them. Maybe not in the way we want, but in the way it's supposed to be."

Rema sighed. "You say that now, but can you live with it if nothing changes—or things get worse? Whenever I try to make things better with Skiezer, I end up sitting in my closet feeling hopeless. But if I just accept that things are the way they are—it's better." She paused. "Sometimes, Syl, hope is a cruel thing. It makes you hungry all the time and leaves you empty when what you want doesn't happen." Her lips tightened. "This Proverbs Plan—it could backfire on you. I don't want to see you hurt."

Sylvia didn't want to think about being in a marriage where she and Wilson lived in the same house but different worlds, or imagine the loneliness she felt now amplified a thousand times, but she couldn't help it. She was scared, but also determined. "If nothing's there, nothing's there," she said, "and I'll have to figure out how to live with that. But if something's there, and I think there is, I have to go for it, Rema."

Rema sighed. "I thought you'd say that. But if you end up in the closet, Syl, bring your cell and call me. I've had a lot of experience sitting in closets."

Chapter 8

The house was dead quiet as Wilson closed the front door behind him. He strained to hear the boys talking, laughing, possibly fighting, or the sound of footsteps running along the upstairs hallway. He stepped to the foot of the staircase and listened. There wasn't even the faint murmur of Sylvia's voice as she read the boys a nighttime story.

Frowning, Wilson set his briefcase on the floor. He'd known he was cutting it close, but once again the meeting with Bruce had gone longer than he'd been able to control. He hadn't wanted to appear eager to leave, not while the branch manager's position at the new bank was up for grabs, but deep inside he'd been chomping at the bit to get home.

He started up the steps. Even though the boys were sleeping, he'd give them a nighttime kiss. However, halfway up, he met Sylvia, who was starting down. She was wearing a pair of loose-fitting sweat pants, a white T-shirt from their pre-kid vacation in Cancun, and her hair was still damp from the shower. He knew she would smell slightly fruity—like ripe peaches—and feel soft and curvy in his arms. He thought this, and then his mind jumped back to Simon and Tucker.

"Hey," he said. "Is it too late to say good-night to the boys?"

Sylvia put her finger to her lips to shush him. "Yes. I just put them down."

So technically, they weren't sleeping. Wilson hesitated, weighing his need to see his sons with the knowledge that going into their bedrooms might get them excited. While part of him really liked knowing they were happy to see him, another part knew that if the routine was disturbed it could be hours before they'd settle down, and overtired kids tended to have super-sized meltdowns.

Well, it was Friday night. The boys could sleep later tomorrow. He started to go around Sylvia but then stopped himself. Neither boy ever slept late. Tucker, in particular, was an early bird and would probably pounce on him and Sylvia before six in the morning. He promised himself that tomorrow he would make up for the time he hadn't seen them during the week. They'd work on their balsa wood racers, and he would play videogames with them.

He followed Sylvia back down the stairs and into the kitchen. Sinking wearily into a ladder-backed wooden chair, he unbuttoned his shirt as Sylvia pulled his dinner plate out of the refrigerator and stuck it in the microwave. Soon the faint smell of something delicious reached his nostrils.

"What is it?" he asked, stretching out his legs and feeling himself start to relax.

"Lasagna." Sylvia poured him a tall glass of the peach-flavored iced tea he liked. "Vegetable lasagna," she amended. "I tried a new recipe. The boys hated it of course. But it's healthier. I think it was the zucchini they didn't like."

"I'm sure it's great. The boys need to learn to eat their vegetables."

"Tucker was doing pretty well until Simon started calling it puke-chini."

Wilson laughed. He wouldn't admit it to Sylvia, but zucchini wasn't his favorite vegetable either. The microwave pinged, and a moment later Sylvia set a steaming plate in front of him. Zucchini or not, it smelled great, and it'd been hours since he'd had the ham sandwich. He took a big bite and tasted Sylvia's homemade spaghetti sauce, a recipe that had come over with Sylvia's grandmother from Italy.

"Awesome," he said, taking another bite. So far, this was one of the better modifications Sylvia had made to their diet. He knew she wanted both of them to lose some weight, and while he liked how Sylvia looked, every time he looked in the mirror it seemed like the tire around his waist was getting bigger.

"So how was your day?" Sylvia asked, slipping into the seat across from him.

"Busy," Wilson said. He thought about telling her about the conversation he'd had with Bruce Maddox about the merger— specifically about the possibility of a promotion to branch manager of the new bank—but he hesitated. It wasn't a done deal. It wasn't like he'd actually been offered the job. He knew even the suggestion of a move would be unsettling for Sylvia. Why upset her over something that might not happen?

He took another bite of vegetable lasagna and bit into a large chunk of zucchini. He chewed it slowly, realizing that he really wanted to tell Sylvia about the job, and he really wanted her to be proud of him. Maybe he would take her out to dinner, somewhere nice, and he could present it in a way that would make a relocation sound like a good thing.

He realized the room had gotten very quiet. "How about you," he said. "How was your day?"

Sylvia sighed. "Fine," she said. "Took the boys to school, dressed up as Mr. Slice, came home, did housework, went grocery shopping, picked the boys up from school, played Avatar ball in the pool, went over homework, cooked dinner, gave the boys baths, story time and bed."

The details passed at dizzying speed. "That sounds like a nice day," he said, and his thoughts drifted. There would be other candidates interviewing for the position of course, both from other branches and from other companies. He needed to make sure he stood out. But how? He had an MBA, but then so would many others, and a lot of the guys would be younger than him.

"Wilson?"

He looked up. "Huh?"

"What were you just thinking? You disappeared for a little while."

He smiled apologetically. "Work stuff. I'm sorry." He went to take another bite of the lasagna and discovered he'd eaten all of it.

"You want some more?" Sylvia offered.

He thought about his expanding stomach and shook his head. "No. But that was great." He pushed his plate forward. "Thanks." Now that he'd finished eating, he felt the fatigue of the week setting in. "I'm glad it's the weekend."

"Me, too," Sylvia replied. Standing, she took his plate to the sink and rinsed it off. "You should sleep in tomorrow. I'll get up with the boys."

"No, you should sleep," he said. "I'll get up."

"Honestly, I don't mind." Sylvia set his plate in the dishwasher, and then began wiping down what looked like spotless counters.

His thoughts drifted back to work. While he knew the financial side of the business, he wasn't as familiar with the personnel side. Being good with numbers wasn't going to be enough to guarantee him the job—he needed career-development plans for the existing personnel. Plans that could be tied into new product offerings. He felt strongly that the future of banking lay in online services, and that the key to pulling ahead of the competition lay in installing the most user-friendly software.

He frowned because his ideas would mean powerful servers and desktops with the latest applications. He had to keep the costs down or they'd laugh at him.

He was aware, suddenly, that Sylvia was looking at him. He wondered, guiltily, if she'd asked a question. He let the silence lengthen, and then she turned around and began wiping the counter again. He sensed he'd disappointed her but wasn't sure what he'd done. His mind quickly flashed through a list of possible things he might have missed, like birthdays, anniversaries, an important meeting with the school or a doctor that she might be expecting him to ask about. He couldn't come up with anything—except being late. Again.

"This work stuff. This merger," he amended. "It won't be forever." He forced a smile. "Soon you'll be seeing more of me than you want."

Sylvia tucked a dishtowel onto the bar across the oven. "No problem," she said. "I was wondering if you'd like to watch a movie with me on the couch."

Wilson sighed in relief, grateful she wasn't mad at him. "I'd love that," he said.

It was a romantic comedy, and although he would rather have seen something with more content, he had to admit that Sylvia cuddled next to him was pretty awesome. When his mind started to slip back to work, he forced himself to follow the plot unfolding on the television. Soon, it was hard to keep his eyes open. He fought for a while, but the next thing he knew, Sylvia was nudging him. The movie was over, and it was time for bed.

Chapter 9

It was still dark in the bedroom when a heavy thump hit the bed and Sylvia levitated a couple of inches off the mattress. "Tucker," she groaned, keeping her eyes closed. "That wasn't funny."

The little boy giggled then crawled over to her. Still half-asleep, Sylvia registered his warmth, his little-boy smell, and then the hardness of his skull as it smacked her chin as he made space for himself on the pillow.

She prayed he'd go back to sleep but wasn't really surprised when Tucker whispered, "Is it time to get up?"

Sylvia managed to open one eye. Both of Tucker's big eyes were millimeters from her own. They gleamed almost black in the darkness that was just beginning to lighten in the room. "No," she whispered. "Not until you see some sunlight."

She closed her eyes. Tucker jostled the bed, and then she felt something rolling up the side of her leg and begin climbing her hip. A moment later, Tucker began making a motor-like sound, and she realized he was running his Matchbox car over the side of her body.

Her first impulse was to tell him to stop it, but then she realized that if she did this, he'd only move the racetrack to Wilson's body and wake him up.

"Vroom," Tucker whispered hoarsely. "Vroom-vroom."

Sylvia shushed him as the car climbed her hip. She glanced over at her sleeping husband, wondering if he was really sleeping through this or just playing possum. It didn't matter; the Proverbs 31 woman rose before dawn and so would she.

With a sigh, she pushed back the covers. "Come on," she whispered. "I'll put on cartoons for you. But you have to be quiet," she warned.

Tucker happily let her lead him through the semi-darkness to the living room, where she set him up on the couch with a bowl of cereal. Turning on the television, she asked him to stay there while she took a shower and got changed. The little guy's gaze already was glued to the talking construction machines on the set, and he nodded eagerly.

Tiptoeing back into the bedroom, Sylvia headed for the shower. The warm water helped wake her up. Feeling more cheerful and refreshed, she pulled out the outfit Rema had bought her. She felt even better when the old push-up bra still fit. Pulling on the shorts and black tank top, she looked at herself in the mirror.

The copper-colored hair was a mess—but the outfit—it fit perfectly. The tank top was a little lower cut than she normally wore, but it wasn't obscene or anything. It simply showed her curves, which she admitted, had taken on new life in the push-up.

The cuffed denim shorts hugged her hips and ended mid-thigh. The end result was casual but sexy. She felt renewed confidence in herself as she dabbed styling gel in her hair. The final step was to buckle on her new tool belt. The width of the leather made her waist look smaller than it actually was, and the pink hammer looked adorable hanging from its strap.

Wilson sat up in bed as she passed through the room. Blinking sleepily at her, he reached for his glasses on the end table. "Syl, what are you wearing?"

She put her hands on her hips and sucked in her stomach. "Nothing special. Go back to sleep, honey."

Wilson continued to stare at her. "Are you wearing a tool belt?"

"Yes."

His gaze slid over her body and his jaw dropped slightly. With a slight growth of hair covering his chin, he looked manly and adorable. "Is that a new shirt?"

"Yes." Sylvia felt the wire from the push-up digging into her side. No wonder she'd shoved this bra to the back of her drawer. It was worth it though, to see that look in Wilson's eyes. "I thought I'd fix some things around the house today."

"Come repair me," Wilson invited, tenting the covers.

Sylvia laughed. "Wilson, Tucker is right in the next room."

Wilson looked straight into her eyes. "So what? Just lock the door."

Sylvia hesitated. She was definitely up for some fun, but unlike Wilson, she had no illusions about Tucker being preoccupied for too long. She didn't think it would be too fun being in bed with Wilson as Tucker knocked on the door and begged to be let inside.

Simon wouldn't be asleep much longer either, and if the two of them were banging on the door. . .it'd be totally embarrassing. She crossed the space between herself and Wilson and planted a kiss on his lips. "I'd love to, honey, but I think any second we're going to hear the pitter-patter of little feet."

The words were no sooner out of her mouth when Simon, with Tucker hard on his heels, burst into the room. Both boys jumped on top of Wilson and began wrestling him. As Wilson pretended to be overwhelmed by the attack, Sylvia quietly slipped out of the room.

In the kitchen, she poured herself a hot cup of coffee. After adding a generous amount of cream and sugar, she sat down at the kitchen table and pulled the honey-do list from its magnet.

So far, she'd power washed the driveway, taken the minivan to Sears and gotten the oil changed and new windshield wipers installed. She still needed to tighten the bolts on the toilet seat in the guest bathroom—it tended to swing around when you sat on it— clean the gutters, and fix the washing machine. In addition to all those chores, she still had the usual ones—a house to clean, laundry to wash, grocery shopping, and two young boys to watch.

In fact, all these chores would require a lot of energy. Since she'd be burning a lot of calories, she decided to make blueberry pancakes and bacon for breakfast.

"Watcha wearing, Mom?" Simon walked into the kitchen wearing a pair of Spiderman pajamas. His blond hair stuck straight up from the wrestling, and his thick glasses made his blue eyes look even larger and more owlish than usual. Tucker, as usual, was hard on his older brother's heels.

"It's a belt for weight lifting," Tucker replied, as if this were obvious.

"It's a tool belt," Sylvia corrected gently. "Today I'm going to fix some things around the house. It'll hold my hammer and pliers. That sort of thing."

"Great," Tucker replied. He stuck his fist through one of the smaller loops on the belt. "Can I help?"

Sylvia braced her legs as Tucker attempted to dangle his full weight from her tool belt. "Of course," she said. "But I think your dad wants to spend some time with you today."

"We're going to work on our racers," Simon confirmed. "The derby is next week. We're sanding my car to round the edges and make it more aerodynamic." He said this last word slowly, pronouncing it carefully and a little proudly.

"That sounds good," Sylvia said, cracking an egg into the batter while continuing to balance Tucker, who was proving to have good arm strength.

"Aero-dy-namic means the air moving around so my car won't slow it down as much," Simon explained. "Dad told me."

Sylvia gently extracted Tucker's fingers from her belt and immediately felt like she'd lost forty-five pounds as her son's feet touched the ground again. "When you put the wheels on, I have a can of WD-40 in the garage. Your dad uses it on the tires of my bike to make them roll easier. Maybe it'll help your car, too."

Simon's eyes studied her, unblinking. "That's illegal."

"Illegal? You sure?"

"It's in the rules, Mom. Didn't you read them?"

"Of course," Sylvia replied, and dropped a spoonful of batter on the grill to see if it was hot enough. Just where, she wondered, had she put the information package for the Pinewood Derby? Hopefully Simon wouldn't ask for it. "I just don't have them memorized."

"Well I do," Simon stated. "Want to hear?"

"Maybe later," Sylvia said gently.

"Hey Simon," Tucker exclaimed, "*Peter Possum*'s on."

Although Sylvia monitored the amount of TV the boys watched

during the week, on Saturday morning she let them have their fill. As the look of delight replaced the worry on Simon's face, she felt herself relax. "Go on," she said, "I'll call you when the pancakes are ready."

After breakfast, Sylvia went right to work. She left Wilson and the boys in front of the television and headed for the laundry room. The washing machine had been misbehaving for weeks. Whenever it reached the spin cycle it began making a thumping noise that increased exponentially as the machine picked up speed. If she didn't jump on top of it by the third or fourth *whomp, whomp, whomp* it began to inch its way across the floor.

Wilson said he thought the machine was unbalanced. Sylvia had replied that the better word was *deranged*. Wilson had laughed, promised to fix it, and then promptly forgotten all about it.

Looking at the machine, which was sitting about eight inches from the wall, she decided to give Wilson's theory a try. It took some digging, but she found a level in the garage. Placing it on top of the machine, she watched the tiny little bubble slide to the left of the center line. She needed to raise the left side a bit higher.

A block of wood would be too high, but a sheet of leftover balsa wood from the Pinewood Derby racers might do the trick. Wedging it beneath the foot of the washing machine, she then placed the level on the lid. The bubble centered perfectly. Still suspicious, Sylvia turned the dial to the spin cycle and held her breath as the machine jumped to life.

Her muscles tensed as she prepared to jump on top of the lid, but the motor purred smoothly along and the machine stayed right in place. It was still way too far from the wall, but she decided she could live with that.

Feeling pretty good about the way that went, Sylvia peeked into the living room to check on Wilson and the boys. They were camped out on the sofa in front of the television. Wild Bill Hiccup, a tonsil-like creature, was using his tongue to lasso a green creature that Sylvia guessed was some sort of germ. Wilson had his laptop balanced on his knees and was peering intently into the screen.

Sylvia sighed. She didn't want to sound like a nag, but she really wanted Wilson to spend quality time with the boys, not work on his computer. "Hey," she said, "I thought you guys were going to work on your racers."

"Dad says we'll do it after he finishes e-mail," Simon replied. "He has two hundred fifty-eight e-mails in his inbox. A lot are from Jen Douglas."

"She's my boss's administrative assistant," Wilson said. "You really shouldn't be reading my e-mails, Simon."

Sylvia thought of the pretty brunette she'd met at the Christmas party at Wilson's office. Jen was nice, outgoing, and had a killer figure. Part of Sylvia wanted to take a look at those e-mails, but then she reminded herself that she trusted Wilson. She might not always understand him, but she trusted him.

"Sorry, Dad." Simon shrugged. "They're kind of boring anyway. What's a merger?"

"It's when two companies or businesses combine into one business." Wilson shut the lid of his laptop abruptly. "Is this a transformer cartoon?"

Simon laughed. "Dad, Wild Bill Hiccup is a germ hunter. He tracks down germs and then eats them."

Sylvia left them discussing the possibility of science actually developing a soldier-like cell that could attack disease. Maybe

Simon would grow up to be a researcher and cure cancer—a disease that had claimed the lives of both her parents within months of each other. Sylvia knew she was a little biased when it came to thinking that God had blessed Simon with remarkable gifts, but still, his mind was like a sponge, and he was fascinated by science.

"I'll be outside if anyone needs me," she said, heading outside to tackle the gutters. It wasn't just that they needed cleaning; it was because Wilson really didn't like doing it. It always put him in a bad mood, and although she had encouraged him to hire someone, so far he wouldn't let her. Wilson's father had always done stuff like that around the house, so she figured Wilson felt he should, too.

It wasn't hard to drag the ladder to the front of the house. From the top rung, she could reach the gutters easily. For a moment though, she paused to enjoy the view. A bright red cardinal perched in a tree just yards from her, and a beautiful garden of wildflowers bloomed in her neighbor's backyard.

The mess in the gutter was less pleasing to her eye. It looked like the bed of pine needles could harbor something slimy and gross, like fat, finger-sucking slugs. Gingerly, she stuck her hand into the gutter.

When nothing bit her, Sylvia started to relax. You couldn't raise two boys and be squeamish. She'd cleaned more than her share of vomit and other gross stuff. *Think of this as mixing a meatloaf. You're at the part when you mix the raw egg in with the hamburger meat.*

While this helped, she suspected it would be a long time before she made meatloaf again. The worst part about the job, she decided, was moving the ladder so often. Going up and down the steps was exhausting. It was like being on an exceptionally wobbly StairMaster.

The sun had come out in full, and sweat glued her new top to her body.

She'd really rather be inside, watching Wilson and the boys build their racers or curled up in her favorite chair reading her book. She thought longingly of a glass of sweet tea and air conditioning. Despite herself, she found herself thinking about what Rema had said. What if she always wanted something that Wilson couldn't give her? What if things got even worse between them? Could she live with that?

"Sylvia," Wilson's voice suddenly boomed. "What are you doing up there?"

Startled, she turned at the sound of his voice. The motion made the ladder wobble, and for one terrible second she feared it would topple backward. She grabbed at the gutter for balance and support and felt something sharp slice her arm.

"Sylvia," Wilson shouted, sounding scared. "You come down right now."

The ladder steadied. When she glanced down, she saw Wilson gripping the steel sides of the ladder tightly. "I'm fine," she said. "You just startled me—that's all."

Her arm stung a little, and when she glanced down, a thin line of blood was trickling from a cut near her wrist. It was a small cut, but fairly deep. It hurt, but what bothered her more was getting blood on both the tank top and cute denim shorts Rema had bought her. She held her arm up and away from her body.

"Sylvia—you're bleeding."

"I'm okay."

"Can you make it down?"

"Of course. It's just a little scratch." Still holding her arm away from her body, she began to back down the ladder slowly.

The cut had started bleeding harder, and when Wilson examined it his lips tightened. "That's not a little scratch. You need stitches." Before she could protest, he whipped off his shirt—a green polo she'd bought him last year for Father's Day—and wrapped it around her arm. "Go wait in the car," he ordered. "I'll get the boys."

Chapter 10

A nd then he drove me to the emergency room and waited with me while the doctor stitched me up." Sylvia held out her bandaged arm and all four friends sitting around her kitchen table leaned forward to inspect it. "It took five stitches, and I had to get a Tetanus shot." Sylvia held her arms about a foot apart. "The needle was this long."

There was a chorus of long, sympathetic sighs, concerned looks, and voices overlapping that said, "Are you okay, Sylvia? Why didn't you call us?"

"It really wasn't a big deal," Sylvia said, "but I love knowing that if I needed you, you'd all help."

"Of course we would," Andrea said. "Remember when I had the emergency hysterectomy? You did everything for me—took care of my kids, brought me meals, cleaned my house?"

"You've picked up my kids from daycare like a hundred times," Kelly said, "when I've had to work late."

"Not to mention all the times I've called you to help with one of my ministries," Susan said. "And you never point out that I've over-committed myself again, even though that's the truth."

Sylvia held up her hand to stop everyone. "You guys are making me sound like a saint, which I'm not. All of you have been great friends to me and helped me out plenty of times. Now, who wants some applesauce cake? I know it's a little off the diet list, but I figured apples are healthy, right?"

Everyone took a piece. Sylvia topped off the coffee cups and listened hard for any noises that might indicate Wilson and the boys, who were upstairs, might be on the move. She'd only scheduled the meeting tonight because she'd thought Wilson would be on a business trip. His meetings, however, had been rescheduled.

"I'm sorry you hurt your arm, but Sylvia, I think it's really romantic the way Wilson took care of you." Susan paused to beam at Sylvia. "What better way to show that he loves you?"

"Susan's right," Andrea added with a smile. "Wilson came through for you, Sylvia. This plan is working even better than I thought it would."

Sylvia sighed. "Honestly, it wasn't that romantic. Wilson turned green at the sight of all that blood. The doctor made him sit with his head between his legs while I got stitched up. Luckily some nice nurse kept an eye on the boys."

"You should have paged me," Kelly said. "I would have come and helped you."

Sylvia looked at her whisper-thin friend. As a pediatric surgeon, Kelly already worked terrible hours. Sylvia always felt like if one more thing was added to Kelly's plate, she would break into a million pieces. "I know," she said, "and I appreciate it. But honestly, it wasn't that big of a deal." She reached for a piece of the homemade applesauce cake she'd been unable to resist baking that afternoon.

"Go on, Syl," Rema urged. Her brown eyes sparkled. "Tell the best part."

Sylvia looked over at her friend, who was already grinning in anticipation.

"Well," Sylvia began, taking a deep breath, "the whole way to the hospital we tried to minimize the accident so the boys wouldn't get scared. I thought we did a pretty good job, but when we got to the hospital, the registration lady asked what happened to me. Before Wilson or I could answer, Tucker burst into tears and said really loudly, 'Mommy cut her wrist.' I'm telling you—you could have heard a pin drop in the waiting room."

"They thought Sylvia tried to commit suicide." Rema burst into laughter. She tried to speak but couldn't get anything out. After a few tries, Rema managed to surface and get out, "Tell them, Sylvia." And then she started laughing again.

"The entire room went dead quiet, and registration lady's eyes practically popped out of her head," Sylvia said. "She picked up the telephone, and within a minute there was a doctor taking me back into the examination room."

"I'd pay anything to read the doctor's notes," Rema said, a note of glee in her voice as she wiped her eyes. " 'Note to staff. Do not leave patient unattended in room with exposed gutters.' "

Everyone around the table exploded with laughter. Sylvia tried to hush them—Wilson was, after all, upstairs in his office working.

"So all and all, week two was a success," Andrea said, after everyone had some time to calm down. "What's next?"

Sylvia cut a worried glance at the stairs. Andrea had a loud voice which worked well in the courtroom, but she hoped it wouldn't carry to Wilson. "Maybe we should just call it a night," she said. She lowered her voice. "Now that I've oiled the hinges to Wilson's office door, I can't hear him coming anymore."

"You need to tie a bell around his neck," Rema suggested unhelpfully.

"We'll keep it quick," Andrea said, "but I think we need to look at the next verse."

Susan opened her Bible. Flipping through tissue-thin pages, she looked up when she found the right passage.

" 'She is like the merchant ships, bringing her food from afar. She gets up while it is still night; she provides food for her family and portions for her female servants.' "

"We already talked about the merchant ships part," Rema protested. She dabbed the corner of her eye where her mascara had started to run. "Why are you bringing it up again?"

Andrea tapped her pencil on her legal pad. Her sharp blue eyes blinked. "Because before, we were trying to interpret it in context of the verse preceding it. We never really figured out what it meant. We can't just skip verses that are hard to understand."

"I'm probably being too literal," Kelly mused, "but if I had to paraphrase this, I'd say something like: The Proverbs 31 woman is a good cook and serves her family healthy meals." She shook her head. "I totally get that. You really can't underestimate the value of good nutrition. I see a lot of obese kids, and most of the time it's because they're eating way too much fast food."

Sylvia fervently hoped that her applesauce cake didn't fall into the unhealthy food category. However, she couldn't help but notice Kelly hadn't eaten any of it. She was sipping that herbal concoction in her metal thermos. "I try to serve good meals," Sylvia said, "but sometimes when the boys have activities after school, I really don't have time to cook."

Rema nodded in agreement. "Back when the Bible was written, I'm sure the moms were busy, but they didn't have to factor in car pools, soccer practice, cub scouts, and other activities into their schedules." She forked off another large bite of Sylvia's cake. "I know we could just say no to our kids and not let them do so much stuff—but then they'd be the only ones staying home—they'd have no friends. Not to mention that if you want your kids to play on any of the sports teams in high school, you have to start them young."

Andrea and Kelly exchanged glances. As successful, professional women, both of them worked long hours. For years they had juggled their schedules with their husbands', swapped favors with other parents, and at times hired teenagers to get their kids to music lessons, sports practices, and other stuff.

"Rema's right," Kelly said after a moment. "This verse makes it sound like you can't be a good mother if you rely on takeout."

"Not exactly," Andrea countered. "Look at the text. It says she buys imported foods, brought by ship from distant ports—it doesn't mean she has to cook them. Plus the woman in this verse has servants."

"You have a cleaning lady," Susan pointed out. "Not that I'm suggesting you aren't a great mother," she quickly added.

"In our house," Kelly ventured, "Milo does most of the shopping and cooking, so how does this verse apply to me?"

There was a moment of silence as each woman seemed to ponder the question. The passage didn't seem geared toward a household in which the woman worked and the man stayed at home.

"That's hard," Sylvia agreed. "But the main thing, I think, is that you work hard for your family. That you do the best you can." She crumpled her paper napkin and put it on the table. "That you serve them, even when you'd rather sleep late or put your needs ahead of your family's."

"Excellent," Susan said, giving Sylvia a beaming smile. "When my Bible study ladies came to this verse, we spent a lot of time focusing on how we, as wives, could make the relationships in our families stronger. I'm not just talking husband-wife. There are siblings, parents, children—not to mention the whole in-law side of things." She paused as Rema, who didn't get along well with her mother-in-law, groaned dramatically. "This is the only verse in the passage that talks about the Proverbs 31 woman in relation to her family." Her gaze came to rest on Sylvia. "Dear," she said, "maybe this week you could try to think of something that you could do as a family."

Sylvia blinked. Just what did they all enjoy? Besides going out to Mexican restaurants and watching television? There were video games, but she didn't think Susan meant playing Xbox 360 would bring them closer together as a family. What they needed, Sylvia considered, was a common goal. Something they could all work toward together.

"Whatever you do, don't do family game night," Rema warned in a gloomy tone of voice. "Or you'll end up sitting in your closet like me."

"What about a family getaway trip to somewhere fun?" Andrea suggested. "Look on the Internet for one of those last-minute getaway deals. Blake and I had a super time in Phoenix."

Sylvia brightened. Planning a spontaneous long weekend with Wilson and the boys sounded fun. But then she thought of the long hours Wilson was putting in at the bank. He'd say he was too busy. And besides, the Pinewood Derby race was the next weekend. She needed something now—not two weeks from now.

She stopped with her cup of coffee halfway to her lips. The Pinewood Derby. Both boys were entered, and Wilson already was involved in helping the boys build their racers. This week she could take a more active role in helping the boys get ready—build a practice track or make team T-shirts or something. The race had been important to Wilson when he was a boy, and he'd been talking it up for months.

Setting her mug on the kitchen table, she smiled at her friends. "I have an idea," she said.

Chapter 11

From his study upstairs, Wilson heard the muffled voices and occasional bursts of laughter coming from the kitchen. He leaned back in his computer chair and stared at the spreadsheet on the screen without really seeing it.

Who would have thought a church group could be so much fun? Usually, the thought of the friends in the Bible study group he and Sylvia attended every other week made him feel good. Yet tonight, hearing the laughter of Sylvia and her friends made his insides churn. It reminded him of the deep roots they'd developed in this town. If he got the promotion he wanted, he'd be taking Sylvia away from the church and all her friends.

Yet were her friends more important than his career?

The question haunted him. Their pastor said that the Lord liked to introduce change into people's lives in order to use them in new ways. It was possible that this promotion was part of God's plan for him. However, Wilson worried that as his responsibilities increased, so would his hours. He closed his eyes and prayed as he had a hundred times. *Please, Lord, if this promotion is Your will for me, let it happen. But if You want me stay in my current role, could You please give me the strength to turn down the job?*

He strained for some sign that God had heard him, but all he heard was another burst of laughter from downstairs.

I know You are a good God, he prayed. *Help me do what's right.*

He opened his eyes and stared again at the spreadsheet on the computer. His business plan for the new bank was getting longer by the minute, but he kept thinking of new things to add—and just that very day the federal government had changed the way banks could charge for their services, which completely threw off the numbers he'd been working with.

He downloaded the new federal government mandate and was puzzling through ways of getting around it, when the door to his study swung open. His oldest son, Simon, stood framed in the doorway. In his Spiderman pajamas and clutching a stuffed monkey so old it looked as if its fur had molted, his son looked small and infinitely vulnerable.

"Dad?"

Wilson pushed back from the computer. Simon's eyes looked glassy, and his cheeks had a reddish hue that meant he was either running a fever or about to cry.

"You okay, buddy?"

The little boy nodded he was fine, but it was clear he wasn't.

"Come here," Wilson said gently.

Still clutching his monkey, Simon slowly closed the distance between them. Leaning forward, he placed his hand on his son's forehead. It was warm, not hot, which meant no fever. He brushed Simon's short blond hair to the side. "What's going on?"

Simon looked up at him with huge blue eyes. "I can't sleep. Mom and her friends are making too much noise."

He smiled as Sylvia's voice rang out with a clear, "No!"

Simon looked at him as if willing Wilson to do something.

"I'll tell them to keep it down." Wilson started to get up, and then settled back in his chair. It was rare that he and Simon had time alone together, mostly because of Wilson's job. Even this past weekend, when he'd consciously decided to give the boys more attention, it hadn't gone as he'd planned.

He studied Simon's face. A hundred new freckles seemed to have popped up overnight against his fair skin. The boy had Sylvia's slender, straight nose and mouth, but Simon had gotten the Baxter blues. "What do you say we give your mom a little more time with her friends and you hang out here with me?"

Simon nodded.

"So," Wilson began, "how was school today?"

"Good."

"Just good?" Wilson smiled. "You do anything fun?"

Simon shook his head. "No."

He looked harder into his son's face. Simon was pretty verbal and had a really good sense of humor. Usually he had at least one funny observation to make about his day. "You're really quiet," he said. "You sure something isn't wrong?"

Simon glanced over his shoulder as the voices drifted up from below them. "Will you read me a story?"

Wilson nodded. Taking his son's hand, he led the boy back to his room and tucked him beneath his Spiderman comforter. "What story do you want?"

Simon gestured to the children's book of bedtime stories that sat atop a stack of other books. Wilson hesitated. Wasn't that a little young for him? "You sure, buddy?"

"Yes. Read *Davy and Goliath.*"

Wilson flipped open the pages to the desired story. He was about to read the first line, when he glanced at Simon, who was biting his lip.

"What is it," Wilson pressed gently. "I can see something's really bothering you." He thought hard. Simon was the consummate overachiever—something Wilson not only related to, but also privately approved. "Something wrong at school? Like a bad test?"

"No." Simon stared hard into Wilson's eyes as if trying, telepathically to tell him something.

"Did you fight with Tucker?"

"No."

Wilson raked his fingers through his hair. "What then?"

Silence, and then, to his surprise, two small tears leaked from the corners of Simon's eyes. Wilson's first thought was to run for Sylvia, but when he started to stand up, Simon shrank back into the pillow. "Dad, don't go."

Wilson sat on the edge of the bed and wiped a wet streak from his son's cheek with his thumb. "I want to help you. I love you very much—whatever you tell me won't change that."

Simon blinked hard. His throat worked, and the color grew even brighter in his face. There was a long silence, and then Simon blurted out, "It's about the race, Dad. It's this weekend and we haven't finished my race car."

Was that it? Wilson worked to arrange his features into a sympathetic expression. "You're going to do great. Don't worry."

Simon blinked up at him. "But you said we'd finish my race car over the weekend and you didn't."

Wilson felt his cell vibrate from its holster around his belt. He was unable to keep his hand from pulling the Velcro open. "Well," he began, trying to ignore the urge to check and see who the caller might be. "Your mommy got hurt. We had to take care of her."

"I know," Simon said. "But the race is this Saturday."

"And we'll finish your car this week—I promise."

"Tomorrow?"

His cell, thankfully, had stopped buzzing. "Yes, tomorrow," Wilson assured him then grimaced. He was going on a two-day business trip. "We'll do it on Friday, and if we don't finish, we'll work on it Saturday. The races aren't until the afternoon." At least he thought they started in the afternoon. Actually he had no idea. Sylvia usually kept track of these things.

Simon looked unconvinced. "What time will you be home on Friday?"

"I have to look at my calendar," Wilson replied, which was true, but it was obviously not the answer Simon wanted. He was about to provide more assurances when he heard the soft chirp from his computer. Despite himself, Wilson's thoughts turned back to the afternoon's visit with the outgoing manager of the bank they were acquiring. The board had offered him a pretty good settlement package. Maybe this was the manager, accepting the offer.

"What if we don't finish?" Simon asked, pulling him back into the present.

"We'll finish. I promise."

"You promised we would finish last weekend," Simon pointed out, "and you didn't."

"Because Mommy cut her arm." Wilson leaned forward and

kissed the boy on his forehead. "It's nightime, and you shouldn't be worrying about anything. Just go to sleep."

His computer pinged again. Something was happening. He felt a strong urge to respond and had to force himself to remain perched on the corner of his son's bed.

The Instant Message could be from Bruce. His boss took pride in his ability to gain a second wind around ten at night. Wilson reminded himself that Simon's well-being came before work. "Everything will be fine. Just go to sleep."

"Tucker's car is faster than mine."

"You're not competing with Tucker," Wilson reminded him. Above everything, he wanted the boys to cheer for each other and value the importance of family.

"I know," Simon said. "I tried loosening the nail holes, to get the wheels to roll faster, but all that's done is made the wheels wobble."

"You need to tighten those axles," Wilson said. "Not loosen them, and then make sure they're absolutely straight. I'll help you."

Simon sighed. "Cross your heart?"

Wilson drew a large X over his chest then grasped Simon's small hands in his own. "Now let's say a quick prayer and then you go to sleep."

"Okay."

Simon took a deep breath and began, "Now I lay me down to sleep. I pray to God my soul to keep. . ."

Something deep inside Wilson stirred at the sound of Simon's childish voice reciting the same prayer he had said as a boy every night of his life. At the end, Simon added a long string of people for God to bless, and then Wilson gave him a final good-night kiss and tiptoed out of the room.

Back in his office, Wilson checked his cell. The message was indeed from Bruce. CALL ME. ASAP. Wilson quickly hit speed dial. As it rang, echoes of the conversation he'd just had with Simon played in his mind. Imagine, his own son worried that he wouldn't have time to help him build his balsa racer.

Simon lay on his back and looked at the glow-in-the-dark constellation above his bed. He knew the names of all the planets and most of the facts about them. He was fascinated by the idea of a universe constantly expanding, extending to infinity. It was like God knew if He didn't keep the universe growing, He might get found, and He didn't want that to happen. God wanted to stay mysterious.

Simon liked mysteries, too, but mostly he liked solving them. He enjoyed learning how things worked and filling his mind with facts that he could call out at will, as if his brain was a microscope he could use to examine the world. He could see things but he didn't have to be in them.

Unlike this Pinewood Derby race.

His dad had won it when he was Simon's age. Simon, himself, had seen the racer in his father's office. It was in a box in the closet, and when Simon found it, his dad had let him take it out and play with it. His dad told him the story of how he and his grandfather had built it together. Simon listened, and from that moment on, he'd decided that when he was the right age, he'd enter the Pinewood Derby, too. He saw himself winning. He saw the look of pride on his dad's face.

He wanted to make his dad proud. Whenever he got a good

grade, his mother smothered him in kisses and stuck the paper on the refrigerator. His dad would call him "Rhymin' Simon" and throw him over his shoulder, spinning in circles until Simon's glasses fell off and he wobbled when his dad set him on his feet again.

Yep. The better he did in school, the more they loved him, and he was sure the same went for this upcoming race. He had to win. Had to be the best. If he did, then maybe his dad would start hanging out with him more—the way he used to before "something important" started happening at work. Simon wanted this desperately, even more than the chemistry set he wanted for Christmas. Every night, after he said prayers with his mom and brother, Simon added a silent one: *Please, Lord Jesus, let me win the Pinewood Derby 'cause I miss my dad.*

Chapter 12

Wilson's business trip complicated Sylvia's plan to pull the family together as they prepared for the upcoming Pinewood Derby race. Although she knew practically nothing about building a balsa wood racer, she researched construction tips on the Internet, gamely pulled out the tool box, and offered her services to the boys.

Tucker had been excited to have her help glue the wheels to the axles. Mostly he was interested in getting to the part where he could paint the body of the car. Simon, however, hadn't let her touch his racer. He'd said he wanted to wait for Wilson, who would tighten the axles.

Sylvia had gently suggested that Wilson might get caught up in work, but Simon remained firm in his decision.

Now, seated in the elementary school's conference room, Sylvia shifted in the plastic seat. If only Simon didn't care so much about this race, she wouldn't be so worried. If he won, great. If he didn't, so what? Simon, however, was determined to win. He was used to getting top marks. Used to winning geography and math bees.

Sylvia made a mental note to ask Wilson to tell Simon he'd be proud of him no matter if he won the race or not. Maybe she could talk to him on the phone tonight, after the boys went to bed. It was a conversation she definitely didn't want either boy hearing.

She didn't want to be the nag in the relationship, but honestly, sometimes Wilson could be blind to what was happening directly in front of him. Sometimes she even thought that Wilson encouraged Simon's over-achieving tendencies.

"Sylvia?"

Looking up, Sylvia met the gaze of Casey Armstrong, the president of the PTO. She was a striking woman with red hair, strong facial bones, and a slight southwestern accent. "We were just approving last month's meeting minutes. Since you didn't raise your hand, I assume you have an objection."

Sylvia shook her head and smiled sheepishly. Apparently Wilson wasn't the only one good at tuning out what was happening around him. "No, I approve them."

"Excellent," Casey said. "And now Mr. Allen will give his report."

"Thank you, Mrs. Armstrong." Principal Allen was a tall, thin man with a cleft chin, sparse blond hair, and a passion for ties with cartoon characters on them. "I've only got a couple of things to go over."

Sylvia braced herself. Whenever he said this, it usually meant he was good for at least forty-five minutes. God help them all if he turned on the overhead projector.

"Most everyone is doing really well about adhering to the dismissal procedures," Principal Allen said, "but I thought since you all are leaders of the parent community, we ought to go over them again."

Oh no, Sylvia thought as the principal pulled out a thick manila folder. Next to her Ella King, the head of the teacher appreciation committee, muttered something even worse.

Coming to these meetings was the worst part about being Mr. Slice, but at the same time Sylvia recognized their importance. It gave her a connection to the inner working of the school that she wouldn't have had otherwise.

Although Simon and Tucker were pretty verbal, they couldn't give her complete pictures of their day at school. They couldn't tell her that the school smelled of glue and cleaners, that the assistant vice principal never smiled with her eyes, that you could hear the sweet voices of the children singing as you passed in the hallway in front of the music room.

As the principal droned on, Sylvia mentally planned dinner. She'd make pork chops seasoned with chives and lemon pepper, brown rice, and steamed broccoli, since broccoli gave Wilson gas and he wouldn't be eating dinner with them because of his business trip.

On the other hand, since it was just her and the boys, maybe she'd do takeout. That new burrito place in town was pretty good. The boys loved it, and she'd have more time to spend with them if she didn't have to shop, cook, and clean up.

Amid these thoughts, some small part of her brain registered that the principal was looking directly at her. She quickly arranged her features into an alert, interested look, as if she were paying close attention, even as she continued to mull over what toppings she wanted on her burrito.

The expression, she realized guiltily, was one she used frequently whenever Wilson started talking about investing money. *I can do better,* she promised herself. *I will do better when I listen to him.*

Twenty minutes later, Principal Allen placed the last transparency on the projector. "Are there any questions?" he asked.

There was dead silence. The lights came on, illuminating a room full of silent, semi-comatose women. Someone had to nudge the PTO president, who, although sitting bolt upright, hadn't seemed to have realized the principal had stopped talking. Finally Casey managed to thank Dr. Allen for his presentation and ask for committee reports.

Deanna Williams, who chaired the school beautification committee, stood. "I'm sorry to report that we're having a *serious* drainage program near the playground entrance."

A heated argument ensued over whether PTO funds should be spent on the necessary repairs or budgeted toward more books for the library.

Both projects seemed worthy, and it soon became apparent that the room was evenly split. As the debate raged, Sylvia slowly raised her hand.

"I could run pizza nights every week instead of every other week. By the end of the year we might have enough with the money left in the budget to put in the drainage ditch *and* buy some new books for the library."

As all gazes turned to her, Sylvia blushed. Being Mr. Slice wasn't exactly a prestigious role in the PTO. In fact, she'd gotten the job because no one else was willing to wear the tights and foam costume. Up until today, she hadn't spoken up much. Mostly she'd been happy to have the vice president of fundraising speak for her. Now, she felt the other women staring at her as if they had never seen her before.

"Great idea," the PTO president declared.

Even as Sylvia reconsidered—volunteering herself for extra work meant that she'd have less time to put into her relationship with Wilson—everyone agreed that the number of pizza nights would be doubled.

"Ladies, we're adjourned," the president declared, and banged the gavel with a flourish.

Glancing at her watch, Sylvia realized it was already lunchtime. If she hurried she might be able to say hello to Tucker in the cafeteria.

The dull roar of voices and the smell of french fries filled her senses as she walked down the hallway to the cafeteria. It also served as the gym, and each day, the cafeteria workers rolled out long tables that spanned the length of the room.

Hundreds of kids sat side by side eating with their classmates. The room was so packed that it was hard to spot Tucker, and for a moment she worried that his class had already finished. But then a small dynamo launched itself into her, and she felt arms wrapping around her waist. "Mommy!" Tucker cried happily.

"Hey sweetie," she said, hugging him back. His enthusiastic greeting thrilled her, but she glanced over the top of his head a little nervously, searching for the lunch monitors. Tucker, in theory, wasn't supposed to get up from his place at the table unless he raised his hand and got permission. If someone spotted him hugging her, he could get in trouble.

Sure enough, his teacher, Linda Chin, was walking toward them with her lips set in a thin, straight line. She was an older woman with small bones; short, straight black hair; and intelligent brown eyes. Sylvia released Tucker. "Quick, go sit down," she whispered.

Tucker didn't need to be told twice. He scurried off as the

kindergarten teacher approached. Sylvia braced herself. Mrs. Chin had a reputation not only for being a really good teacher, but also for being on the strict side.

"Hello, Mrs. Baxter," Mrs. Chin said, smiling. Today the teacher was wearing a pair of black slacks and an attractive tunic top in shades of brown and green. "How is your wrist doing? Tucker said you cut it."

Sylvia winced at the choice of words and made a mental note to talk to Tucker again about how he described her injury. She tried to read the expression in the older woman's sharp brown eyes. "Yes," she said. "I cut my arm on the side of a gutter this weekend, but it's doing much better now."

The dark head bobbed. "Tucker told us about it during our story time this morning." Her voice lowered slightly. "He said you had to go to the hospital to get help."

Sylvia smiled and prayed Tucker hadn't made it sound like she needed psychiatric help. "For the stitches," she said.

Again, the head nodded. "I'm glad you're okay." She paused. "I can tell this accident has had an impact on him, so I'm encouraging him to write a short story about it. He's going to draw the pictures, and I'm going to help him write down the words. Isn't that a great idea?"

Sylvia wasn't completely sure if she was smiling or looking horrified. Tucker couldn't draw well and would probably create a stick figure with a bloody arm. Being a boy, Tucker would happily color in as much blood and gore as possible. She imagined the entire family being summoned to the school psychologist's office where they'd probably be handed a pamphlet entitled, "When Mommy Hurts Herself."

"That is a great idea," Sylvia managed. What else could she say? If she protested, it'd only make it look like she had something to hide. "Maybe you could send it home when it's finished? I'd like to see it."

"Of course." Mrs. Chin smiled. "One more thing—I was thinking that Tucker could take Bluebonnet home over the Easter holiday. Would that be all right with you?"

Bluebonnet, a blue parakeet, was the class pet. Getting asked to take her home for the three-day weekend was like winning the kindergarten lottery. Only the students who were high on Mrs. Chin's list of approval were even considered. For the past eight months Tucker had not been asked once to care for the bird, although Sylvia knew for a fact that some kids had gotten Bluebonnet for more than one weekend.

"That'd be great," Sylvia replied. "Tucker will be thrilled."

Mrs. Chin's gaze strayed to Sylvia's bandage before returning to her eyes. "I'd let you have him sooner, but I've already promised several other children."

"That's okay," Sylvia said. "Easter weekend would be perfect."

"Excellent. Pets can be very therapeutic." Mrs. Chin patted Sylvia's arm in a sympathetic gesture. "Take care, Mrs. Baxter."

Chapter 13

Sunlight streamed through the big glass windows as Wilson pushed open the glass doors and stepped into the cavernous room. He stood for a moment, taking in the hushed voices, the almost reverent quiet of a business that played such an important role in people's lives. Where would the world be without banks?

He straightened his shoulders and inhaled the scent of clean, cool air, made even sweeter with the possibility of what could happen here. He knew the blood and guts of this bank, every loan, every investment, every profit, every loss. It had been his life's work for nearly a year. Now, being here and knowing that the acquisition had happened gave him an even deeper connection to the bank. *You could be mine,* he thought.

His gaze strayed to the kiosk in the center of the room. It blocked the tellers' views of who might be standing in the front of the bank. It was a potential security issue, and he'd recommended the bank remove it. He wanted an open sitting area, with the glass-walled offices visible. He wanted to minimize any chance of robbery.

"Hey Wilson," Jen said. Today her long brunette hair was tied in a messy knot and she wore a navy skirt suit that ended just about her knees. She held out a Styrofoam cup. "They've given us an office in the back," she said. "Want some coffee?"

"Sure." Wilson couldn't stop looking around the area, mentally updating the old Burroughs mini-computer system with a client-server, GUI-based system. He felt the furtive stares of the bank employees who tried to pretend that his arrival was business as usual.

Following Jen, he stepped into one of the offices in the back. It held a laminate wood desk, a matching credenza, and a painting of a man standing thigh-deep in water, fishing. The last time he'd gone fishing, Wilson recalled, both boys had refused to let him hook the worms because they couldn't stand to see them hurt. Instead of fishing, he and the boys had hiked an hour until they found the perfect spot for the worms' new home. They'd dug a hole, released the worms, and stopped for ice cream on the way home.

Wilson set his computer bag down and took a sip of coffee. Jen had added just the right amount of cream and sugar, and when he complimented her, she blushed.

"The accountants are in the conference room down the hall," Jen explained. "You need to take a look at these." She set a thick manila envelope on the counter.

Wilson immediately began to thumb through the stack of papers that made up the purchase agreement. Although the basic agreement had been well-established, the implementation schedule constantly changed. He paused at a section Jen had highlighted. His stomach tightened as he recognized the human resources information.

"Bruce wants you to focus on employment contracts. According to our work redundancy analysis, we're looking at a 30 percent overlap between the two banks."

Wilson frowned. "That's a bit higher than we thought."

Jen nodded. "It's mostly middle management that's affected." She leaned close enough to him that he could smell her perfume, a thick scent of roses that tickled his nose. "Bruce wants you to make recommendations for the cuts."

"Oh." Wilson remembered the furtive looks that'd been directed at him when he'd walked into the bank. He'd never fired anyone before and didn't like the idea at all. He pretended to study the documents in front of him, but mostly he was trying to think of a way out of firing anyone. He'd take a hard look at attrition. Maybe he could come up with a very competitive voluntary retirement plan.

"Wilson," Jen said, her voice lowering but nonetheless sounding excited, "I probably shouldn't tell you this, but when I was in Bruce's office, I saw a draft of a new organizational chart. Your name was in the box for the new branch manager!"

The news, although not a complete surprise, hit him like a jolt of electricity. He looked up at her in delight, thinking that Bruce must already have spoken with the other board members. Although he had yet to officially interview for the position, unofficially, it seemed he'd already gotten the promotion.

"You're going to love it here," Jen continued. "I grew up in the next town over."

"*If* I get the job," Wilson pointed out. "I mean, it's not official, so please don't say anything to anyone."

"Of course I wouldn't." Jen walked to the doorway and paused in the frame. "You can't say anything either, but I'm penciled in as the new assistant branch manager." She paused to let this sink in.

"*Your* new assistant branch manager."

Wilson blinked. "Congratulations," he said, but inside he was wondering when Bruce had intended to give him the news. He'd thought, as branch manager, he'd have all the control in staffing. Obviously he'd been misled.

Not that Jen wouldn't be great for the job—he had huge respect for her as a professional. But did he want her as his second-in-command? They'd be spending a lot of time together. She was single and undeniably attractive. *"So what,"* a small voice inside him said, *"it's not like you'd let anything happen."* Jen knew he was happily married, and they'd never discussed anything more personal than her cat, Henry, who left hairballs the size of golf balls on her bed whenever Jen went out of town. Still, how was Sylvia going to feel about that? She trusted him, he assured himself. It wasn't going to be a problem. The real issue was saving as many jobs as he could.

"We'll make a great team." Jen flashed him a smile and headed down the hallway.

Shaking his head to clear his thoughts, Wilson opened his computer bag and pulled out his laptop. By the end of the day, his spirits had improved considerably. The audit was going well, the new disclosures weren't as bad as he feared, and best of all, he'd figured out a way to reduce the number of people who would be let go.

Jen poked her head into his office. "Hey," she said, "it's after five. The auditors have left for the day. How about you and me grab a bite to eat?"

Wilson drew his hand through his hair, brushing over the smooth, small bald spot. He'd planned to work a few more hours and then grab something on his way to the hotel. But the thought of food made his stomach growl, reminding him that he'd only had a small sandwich and chips for lunch.

"I know this great little Tex-Mex place," Jen continued. "It's just a hole-in-the-wall kind of restaurant, but the food is authentic. If you like Mexican food, that is."

Wilson hesitated. "I have a couple of e-mails to send."

Jen took a step closer and lowered her voice. "People are waiting for you to leave before they go home. They don't want you to think they're not hard workers."

Wilson released his breath. He'd been an idiot not to think of that. Of course people were worried about holding on to their jobs. In this economy, who wouldn't be? Still, he hesitated. Jen was a single, attractive woman, and he didn't want rumors to start. "Is there somewhere within walking distance? I'm afraid I still have a lot of work to do tonight."

Jen smiled. "I know the perfect place."

After a day inside, the cool air felt great. He felt himself enjoying the walk as they crossed the street and strolled deeper into the downtown area. He kept the pace slow in deference to Jen's high heels, and she seemed delighted to point out various landmarks.

As they passed the library, he pictured Sylvia, who loved books, spending many happy afternoons taking the boys there.

There was an attractive town center with a green. Every Christmas Eve, Jen explained, people gathered in the town green to sing carols or ride in the horse-drawn carriages. Increasingly, he felt like he, Sylvia, and the boys could be happy here. It was a larger town than the one they were used to, but they would enjoy having more dining and shopping options. It would be a good move for them. The *right* move for them.

At Comida Buena he wolfed down a plate of beef enchiladas. Jen talked about Henry, her cat; he described the Pinewood racers that the boys were building. In the far back of his mind, he realized it felt awkward, dining alone with Jen, but he dismissed the uneasy feeling. He wasn't interested in her as anything but a friend and co-worker. The fact that she was a woman was insignificant. Or at least it should be. In the future it would be easier. There would be other dinners, but team dinners. He'd make sure of that.

Although they ate fairly quickly, when they paid the bill Wilson was dismayed to see it was after eight o'clock. The boys had gone to bed, and once again he'd missed the opportunity to call and say good-night to them. He was angry at himself and didn't talk much on the walk back to the bank to drop Jen at her car.

He dialed Sylvia on his cell on his way to the hotel. The machine picked up, which meant Sylvia probably was still putting the boys to bed. He left a short message explaining that he'd had to work late again, but even to his own ears it sounded lame. Why couldn't he have remembered to call them earlier? It wasn't like he didn't love them—that they weren't more important than work.

God came first in his life, but otherwise, he valued Sylvia and the boys more than anything. He'd always believed that it had been no coincidence the day he'd stepped into First National and seen a beautiful brunette with big brown eyes and the smile of an angel standing behind the teller's counter. He'd been new to the bank, so she hadn't recognized him as anything but a customer.

"Can I help you, sir?" she'd asked, and he'd been surprised to find that his feet had carried him right up to her.

He'd stood there, awestruck, wanting to extend the moment, and wondering what to say that wouldn't reveal himself as the geek that he was. He silently recognized the irony of having an undergraduate degree in computer science and an MBA in finance and yet he had nothing to say.

In the end, he'd finally held out his hand. "I'm Wilson Baxter," he'd said. "The new guy."

She'd gripped it warmly. "Sylvia Gardano. Welcome."

Wilson had known right away that Sylvia was the one for him. He'd taken it slowly, however, not just because they worked for the same bank, but because he'd never had a serious relationship. It wasn't that he didn't like girls—he did. And it wasn't like he didn't date, because he had. He just didn't let things get serious, never told a girl he loved her. He'd drifted along, letting school and work define his days and waiting for God to send the right girl into his life.

Looking into Sylvia's warm brown eyes, he'd thought the moment had come. It'd taken him a month to ask her out, and even then it was only for lunch. He hadn't wanted to risk coming on too strong, making a mistake or scaring her away.

Things changed one night when, somehow, they'd been talking about college. Hoping to impress her, Wilson rattled off some of his credentials, National Merit Scholar, summa cum laude from Cornell, and a MBA in finance.

Sylvia put her hand on his arm and looked deeply into his eyes. "I like that you're smart," she said, "but you're more than that, Wilson. You're kind. I like how you treat people. You always look pleased to help somebody—like they're the ones who've done you a favor."

Nobody, not even his parents, had ever told him something like that. Oh he knew his mom and dad loved him, but he knew they also liked to brag about his accomplishments. He liked the way Sylvia saw him. It was almost as if she didn't care if he ever got another award or promotion in his life. He looked into her eyes and said, "I'm falling in love with you, you know."

Which was precisely why, Wilson thought as he walked into his hotel room, he was so determined to give Sylvia the best life possible. With this promotion, he could even give her a membership in the local country club.

He dropped his wallet and keys on the dresser and plopped down wearily on the edge of his bed. He glanced at the floral print on the tan wall, the flat screen television, the blackout shades framed by curtains that had no warmth or charm. He could have been in any hotel anywhere. And where he wanted most to be, he realized, was home.

Chapter 14

Relief washed through Sylvia at the sight of Wilson's Beemer pulling into the driveway. He'd kept his word and come back from his business trip early. A quick glance at the kitchen clock confirmed that it was almost exactly five o'clock. She watched him unload his suitcase and computer bag from the trunk and sling his garment bag over one shoulder.

Meeting him at the front door, she greeted him with a smile and stretched up to kiss him on the lips. "Hey," she said, taking the garment bag off his shoulder, "you made it."

Wilson set his bags inside the front door. "Yeah," he said. "I just beat the Friday rush hour." The words were barely out of his mouth when the boys ran toward him. Launching themselves like small missiles, they jumped the last few feet into Wilson's arms, pushing him back a step. Catching them, Wilson laughed and swung them around in his arms. "I missed you guys," he said.

"We missed you, too," Sylvia said.

Tucker settled himself on Wilson's hip. "A kid in the cafeteria threw up today."

Sylvia met Wilson's gaze and smiled. "There's a stomach virus going around school."

"Uh-oh," Wilson said. He set Simon on the ground. "How about you, Simon? How was your day?"

"It was cool. We're making planets out of paper-mache. Did you know, Dad, that most of the textbooks are wrong? There're more than nine planets."

Sylvia, who had been hearing about Simon's desire to become an astrophysicist since he came home from school, steered them all toward the kitchen. "Come on," she said, "the tacos are ready."

"I love tacos," Tucker, still riding his dad's hip, called out happily. "I bet I can eat more than you can, Simon."

"It isn't a competition," Sylvia warned, even as inside she acknowledged that Tucker was probably right—he would out-eat his older brother. Tucker, although shorter, outweighed Simon. And, at the rate Tucker was growing, he might even be taller than Simon by next year. Already, strangers sometimes mistook the boys for fraternal twins. She knew it had to bother Simon, but whenever she tried to talk to him about how some kids were faster growers than others, she'd see something in his eyes shut down.

Instead of rising to Tucker's challenge, however, Simon looked up at his father. "After dinner, are you going to help me build my racer?"

Wilson ruffled Simon's short blond hair. "Of course," he said. "I'm looking forward to it." Over the boy's shoulder he met Sylvia's gaze. There were dark shadows under his eyes and a tired strain etched around the corners of his mouth. Wilson never slept well in hotels. "Are you tired, honey?"

"A little," Wilson admitted. He loosened his tie. "Mostly I'm just glad to be home."

Sylvia smiled. "Was it productive?"

"Yes." He leaned back against the kitchen counter as she stirred the meat in the skillet. "Jen and I worked on a revised implementation schedule. You wouldn't believe how the new federal regulations are going to complicate things." He took a deep breath. "Those tacos smell great."

"They're turkey meat. Less fat. You eat okay on your trip?"

She looked up in time to see the expression of guilt in Wilson's blue eyes and shook her head. "Admit it. What'd you have for dinner?"

"Beef enchiladas."

He'd always had a fondness for those. She pictured a group going out, Wilson throwing all her attempts at healthy eating to the wind. "Who'd you go with?"

"Just Jen and me."

She lifted her brows. "The two of you?" She didn't want to jump to conclusions, but Jen was single, attractive, and flirty. Was this the reason Wilson had been so distracted lately?

Wilson sighed. "It wasn't like that. Trust me. The restaurant was walking distance to the bank and the most personal thing we talked about was the size of the hairballs her cat hacks up every time she goes out of town." He stepped closer, facing her from across the other side of the island cooktop. "She's a nice lady, but, you are the one I love." He leaned across the distance to plant a kiss on her lips. "Boys, did you know you have the most beautiful mommy in the whole wide world?"

There was a chorus of yeses, and then Tucker launched himself at Wilson, grabbing hold of his lower legs and clinging to him like a monkey. Sylvia shook her head ruefully. Watching her husband interact with her son, she couldn't imagine that the dinner was anything more than Wilson described. While she didn't like it, she'd let it drop. "Daddy! Me and Mom finished my racer. She used her empty board to make the sides smooth."

"Emery board," Simon corrected.

"Fingernail file," she automatically translated. When she'd met Wilson, he hadn't known the difference between eyeliner and mascara. A long time ago he'd sat in the bathroom watching her and talking as she put on her makeup. She'd had a lot of fun teaching him the terminology of beauty products. That was when she was working at the bank and seemed like a lifetime ago. She pulled the tortilla shells out of the oven and filled a bowl with taco meat. "Tucker, get the bowl of lettuce out of the fridge, and Simon would you please put out the cheese and tomatoes?"

"What can I do?" Wilson asked.

Sylvia smiled. "Get yourself something to drink, honey, and have a seat."

When everyone was at the table, she turned to Simon. "Would you give the blessing?"

Simon nodded. Bowing his head, he folded his hands together. "God is great. God is good. God we thank You for this food. Amen."

And thank You, Father, for a meal we are all eating together, Sylvia silently added. *And please bless our marriage and keep Wilson from temptation.*

After dinner, they cleared the table. Sylvia filled the pots and pans in the sink with water to soak while the boys ran to get their racers.

Wilson covered the kitchen table with newspaper and retrieved his drill and toolbox from the garage.

Tucker, whose racer already was finished, arrived back at the table first. He wheeled the white-and-black racer, which had been shaped to look like a whale, across the center of the table. "Look, Daddy! Mommy and I painted my car to look like Shamu!"

"Whoa!" Wilson said, giving Sylvia an impressed look. "You did whale—I mean well."

Sylvia laughed. "Thanks but we weren't *fishing* for compliments."

"Are you *fin*-ished?" Wilson asked.

"Yes, that's the end of the *tail*." She grinned as Wilson shook his head.

"No more *spouting* out bad puns," Wilson countered.

Laughing, Sylvia sat down in the kitchen chair and felt herself relax for the first time since Wilson had stepped through the door. This was the old Wilson, participating in conversations and coming up with terrible puns.

"Careful, Tucker," she warned as Tucker nearly smashed his racer into Wilson's toolbox. "I wouldn't push Shamu around too much. I'm not sure how well his wheels are going to hold up."

"Can we attach my wheels now?" Simon asked, holding up the carcass of his racer for Wilson's inspection.

Sylvia's heart caught at the look of vulnerability stamped across Simon's delicate features as he waited for Wilson's answer. Her son's skin was so pale it was nearly translucent. She could see a thin, blue vein on the side of his face near his eye. She found herself holding her breath as Wilson took the car out of Simon's hands and held it up for inspection.

"Well," he said, "before we set the wheels, we need to fill the cuts we made with epoxy glue and let that set."

"Why can't we just glue the axles in now?" Sylvia asked, thinking that was exactly what she'd done with Tucker's car.

Wilson pushed his glasses higher on his face. "You could," he admitted, "but drilling through the epoxy instead of the balsa wood will give us a straighter, more consistent hole."

Sylvia worked to keep her expression neutral. Didn't Wilson realize it was the day before the race and there was still a ton of work that needed to be done? "That sounds great, honey, but won't it take a long time for the glue to dry?"

Wilson was already extracting the bottle of epoxy from his toolbox. "Of course not," he said heartily. "It'll be dry in an hour and a half."

"We still have to attach the wheels, and paint it—"

"Don't worry. We have plenty of time." He gave Simon a reassuring smile. "Your car is going to be the fastest, coolest car out there."

"What about mine?" Tucker demanded. "Will Simon's be faster than mine?"

Wilson took Tucker's car and tested each wheel. "Both your cars will be equally fast."

"Mommy built a track upstairs. We tested it, and my car goes really fast," Tucker said. "Only sometimes it doesn't go completely straight. Once it fell off the track."

Wilson flipped the car over. "I'll have to look at it," he said. "Could be the bolts are tighter on one wheel than another."

He set the car on the table and gave it a small push. The racer rolled easily, but not completely straight. Wilson frowned and repeated the test. "I think we can fix this," he said, "by adding a little more weight to the front of the car and adjusting the screws on the axles."

He pulled out his pliers and set to work on Tucker's car. Wilson didn't notice, but Sylvia did, the slightly, almost haunted look of disappointment in Simon's eyes. "I can do that," she offered, "while you work on Simon's racer."

Wilson was already lost in the task at hand. "We'll do both," he promised.

But by the time Wilson was satisfied with the wheels on Tucker's racer, and the epoxy set, it was past ten o'clock. Restless and whiney, Tucker, who was getting overtired, had started a game of poking Simon in the ribs, although Sylvia had specifically asked him to stop.

Although Simon was usually pretty patient with Tucker, he also was tired, and each time Simon poked him, he yelled more loudly. Once, he had even gone so far as to push Tucker. The happy-little-family moment Sylvia had envisioned was disintegrating by the moment.

"I think Tucker's car is good to go," Wilson said, setting the black-and-white racer on the kitchen table. "Now let's check and see if the epoxy is dry on Simon's."

The words were no sooner out of his mouth when Tucker began running around the kitchen table. Each time he passed Simon, he jabbed him with his finger and laughed.

"You cut that out," Sylvia warned as Tucker streaked past, his blue eyes nearly demonic with mischief. "This is your last warning."

Tucker managed to evade her, circle past Wilson, and come in for a lightning-quick jab at his brother, who howled as if he'd been fatally stabbed.

"Tucker James Baxter! We told you to stop that!" Wilson thundered. He started after Tucker, who laughed and darted into the living room. A moment later, Sylvia heard something crash. She ran into the room in time to see the shattered lamp on the floor. Wilson scooped Tucker under his arm and marched toward the stairs. When Tucker saw her, he began to cry. "Mommy! I'm sorry!"

Sylvia started after them. "Wilson," she said, "he's just overtired."

Wilson didn't pause. "That doesn't excuse him," he said. "I'm putting him to bed, and then I'm coming right back."

She caught one last glimpse of Tucker's red face twisted in misery, and then the two of them disappeared up the stairs. Part of her wanted to go after them, but she knew Wilson would see it as undermining his authority and not trusting him to be a good parent.

She sighed. The lamp lay in pieces on the floor. It had been her parents', and was one of the few pieces she'd kept when she and Wilson had had to close up her parents' house a few years ago.

Kneeling, she picked up the larger pieces, wondering if they could be glued together, and knowing that she should probably just throw the whole thing out. *It's just a lamp,* she told herself, *and not even a particularly valuable one.* Not monetarily. But it was a piece of her past.

She studied the shards, picturing her mother sitting in her overstuffed club chair, reading by the light of this lamp or knitting a pair of socks for someone. Socks—for Pete's sake. Who even knitted anymore?

She shook her head. Her mother would have told her not to worry about one silly little lamp. What was important, she'd have said, was that no one had gotten hurt. But someone had gotten hurt, Sylvia realized. She had.

"Mom?"

Sylvia turned. Simon was standing right behind her, peering over her shoulder.

"Yeah?"

"Will Dad come back downstairs?"

Sylvia didn't answer for a moment. She was still thinking about the lamp, but then she saw the worry in her son's eyes. It was getting late and little progress had been made on Simon's racer. She straightened slowly. "He said he would. Now please stand back so you don't get cut, and let me clean up this mess."

It took awhile before Sylvia was satisfied that there weren't any slivers of porcelain on the floor. She'd given Simon some milk and cookies to eat while she worked, and when she finished cleaning, she was relieved to see that he'd eaten them all.

Together they went upstairs to see what was taking Wilson so long. Sylvia wasn't really surprised to find him asleep next to Tucker in the twin-size bed. Gesturing for Simon to be silent, she slowly backed out of the room and closed the door quietly.

"He'll be up early," she promised Simon as they walked to the adjoining bedroom. "Don't worry. Your racer will be ready." And it would be—even if she had to do it herself.

"The race is at three o'clock," Simon said. "And I have to be there even earlier for inspection."

Sylvia put her hand on the narrow wing of his shoulder blade. It felt so fragile, and at the back of her mind she found herself worrying that he was too thin, that she should make him eat more. "Setting the wheels won't take long." She felt her worry switch to irritation. Wilson could have been less of a perfectionist and spent the evening working on Simon's racer instead of focusing on Tucker's. Tucker honestly didn't care if he won or not. But Simon. Simon was different. He felt things to the bone. He hadn't missed that Tucker was the one who had gotten all Wilson's attention.

"You know," she said carefully, "we love you no matter what, right?"

Simon glanced up at her. The expression in his eyes made him look much older than he was. "I know you do."

"So does Dad," Sylvia said firmly.

It was after eleven-thirty before Sylvia finally got Simon off to bed. In the silence of her bathroom, she washed her face, brushed her teeth, and then slipped on a cotton nightgown worn thin with use.

Padding back into the master bedroom, she glanced around the room at the queen-size bed with its green comforter, pale yellow sheets, and stacks of pillows of every size and shape. A floral, wing-back chair with an ottoman sat near the windows, and atop the dark wood dresser sat an abundance of family pictures.

It was a room more comfortably than expensively furnished. Wilson had let her pick out everything, and she'd tried hard to make it feminine enough to be romantic, and at the same time masculine enough for Wilson to be comfortable.

Unfortunately, right now it was an empty room. Something she acknowledged was beginning to feel more like the norm than the exception. All too often she went to bed while Wilson worked upstairs in his office. Too many nights she read her romance novels until she was too tired to keep her eyes open. She missed the comfort of his presence as sleep slowly came to her—the last minute, sleepy whispers of something he'd forgotten to tell her, or him simply telling her he loved her.

But it wasn't like that anymore. Wilson said it was because he had work, but deep inside Sylvia wondered if he'd simply gotten tired of her. If she couldn't compete with the challenges, excitement, and yes—rewards, of his job. And now maybe even with Jen.

Smoothing back the comforter, she slipped beneath the cool sheets. *Dear God,* she prayed, *I miss my husband. I miss talking to him, and I miss the way things used to be. I know we couldn't live the way we do if Wilson didn't have such a good job, but I don't think You mean for things to be like this. I don't mean to be complaining, Lord— or ungrateful—but sometimes I wonder if this is what You want for me.*

And Simon. I'm scared for him about tomorrow. Please help him understand that he's loved whether he wins or loses. And keep Tucker safe, and help him with the impulse control. Please bless our family and friends with good health. Thank You for always loving us. Amen.

Chapter 15

Wilson cracked open one eye. In the semi-darkness, Tucker's face loomed over him as pale as the moon and so close it looked gigantic. "Go back to sleep, Tuck," he moaned. He attempted to turn onto his side and found himself pressed tightly against a wall, which surprised him because there wasn't any wall next to his side of the bed.

"Dad." Tucker's breath was hot in his ear. "Can I get up now?"

Ask your mom, Wilson started to say and then realized he wasn't in his own bedroom. The evening before slowly came back to him—building the racers in the kitchen and then chasing after Tucker, who'd knocked over the lamp in the living room. After Wilson had given him a lecture about controlling his impulsive behavior, he'd lain down next to Tucker who'd clung to him like a small monkey. In the process of soothing him, Wilson had fallen asleep.

Without his glasses, Wilson had to squint at the bedside clock. "You can get up," he agreed. "But you have to be quiet when we go downstairs so you won't wake your mother." He held up two fingers. "Scout's honor."

Tucker gravely mirrored the gesture. "Scout's honor," he echoed.

In the kitchen, Wilson put on a pot of coffee and cleared a spot on the kitchen table. He set out the Cap'n Crunch and poured Tucker a small glass of orange juice. Tucker immediately attempted to fill his bowl to the point of overflowing with the cereal, and Wilson had to grab the box from him. "Take it easy, buddy," he said.

Sometimes it felt like he was always telling Tucker what to do, correcting his behavior, or arguing with him in a way that he never had to do with Simon. Part of it was the age of course. Tucker was two years younger. But that was only part of it. Where Simon was thoughtful, Tucker tended to be impulsive; where Simon was gentle, Tucker was rough. Simon followed the rules; Tucker was constantly testing the limits.

He loved both boys equally, but he worried more about his relationship with Tucker. Which was why, last night, he'd been sure to give Tucker a lot of attention. He might have missed helping Tucker put together his car, but he'd been sure to make sure that car was as good as he could make it.

The coffee gurgled from the machine; Tucker slurped his cereal. Wilson saw the backyard slowly become illuminated in the morning light. Today he'd focus on Simon.

"Can I watch a cartoon, Dad?" Tucker asked.

Wilson glanced over at the empty bowl. "After you put away your dishes."

"But what if I want some more later? When Simon wakes up?"

Wilson sipped his coffee and reconsidered. "Okay," he said, "as long as you don't leave your bowl for someone else to put away."

"Okay," Tucker agreed, and then ran into the living room.

Wilson, following more slowly, was in time to watch him vault over the back of the couch. A moment later, Tucker found the two remote controls that operated their television and punched in the correct sequence to get the set working. "It's like we're mission control and trying to launch a rocket out of Cape Canaveral," Sylvia liked to say whenever they settled down to watch the news or a movie.

Sylvia. He glanced at the empty spot on the end table and felt badly for her. He wondered what had happened to the lamp, and if it were repairable or she'd put it in the garbage. It'd belonged to Sylvia's mother, and he remembered how she'd chosen to put it out when they had probably more valuable items stored in the attic. He resolved to ask her about it.

While Tucker watched his cartoon—a show about talking, rainbow-colored ponies—Wilson retrieved his laptop from the hallway. He figured he had just enough time to check his e-mail before Simon woke up and they started work on his son's racer.

He used his remote access code to get into the bank's Intranet and a moment later was pulling down thirty-five new messages. The one marked "urgent" caught his eye immediately. It was from his boss and had been sent at six o'clock that morning. *Just when did Bruce sleep?* he wondered.

Opening the message, he scanned the contents and groaned. The net of it was that Robert Hovers, one of the members on the board of trustees for the bank, was in town for a couple of hours and Bruce had set up a breakfast meeting. Bruce wanted Wilson to take Robert through the latest numbers and the remaining action items in the merger. He also wanted Wilson to bring his résumé.

Wilson shifted on the couch. The last part of the message was only a sentence, but he didn't need Bruce to spell it out. Although technically this was a meeting about the merger, it was really about Wilson—about establishing his credibility and advancing his career. This was his opportunity to gain face time with one of the board members and thereby gain his approval when Bruce nominated him for the branch manager's position.

Wilson hit REPLY then hesitated. Frowning at the screen, he considered telling Bruce that he had a family commitment and declining the meeting. It wasn't like he'd had any advance notice, and Bruce had to respect that if Wilson had to choose between work and family, he'd choose family every time.

At the same time, the meeting was at nine o'clock in the restaurant of a hotel about a half hour away. Wilson would have just enough time to modify the résumé and get to the meeting. He ran his fingers through his hair. He felt the polished skin of a bald spot no larger than a penny—but a bald spot all the same. Time was running out for him, the spot said. If he blew this promotion, there might not ever be another one.

He glanced at his watch with its big face and multiple silver gears showing the different times around the world. Sylvia had given it to him as an anniversary gift, and looking at the time reminded him of her, which usually was a good thing, except for now. But she didn't understand the whole situation—she didn't know about the big promotion. If she did, she'd tell him to go to the meeting.

And, the meeting was at nine o'clock. It wouldn't go more than an hour, which meant he'd be home by 10:30 to help Simon. There'd be plenty of time to finish Simon's racer. He typed Bruce a quick note, and then headed to the guest room where he sometimes changed when he got up earlier than Sylvia. In less than ten minutes he was shaved, dressed, and ready to go. He left Tucker with instructions to let Sylvia sleep a little longer, and then wrote her a quick note which he left on the kitchen table. Ignoring the carcass of Simon's racer that looked at him reproachfully, he grabbed his car keys off the kitchen counter and headed out the door.

"I'm going to kill him," Sylvia announced when she walked into the kitchen and saw Wilson's note scrawled on the back of an envelope.

How could he do this? Go to a meeting on the morning of the Pinewood Derby? How could he not realize how hurtful it would be to Simon to wake up and find that his father had left him with a half-finished race car and the derby only hours away?

"I'll kill him and put him in a hole in the backyard," she stated firmly.

"Kill who?" Simon asked, walking into the room. He was still dressed in his Batman pajamas and his short hair was sticking up in every direction.

"Ah, nobody," Sylvia said and turned the envelope upside-down. "Let's make pancakes." Her mind whirled. Anger at Wilson warred with the need to protect Simon from learning that Wilson had broken his promise to him. Could she delay the breakfast long enough for Wilson to get home? "We'll make chocolate chip ones," she said brightly, and reached into the cabinet for a mixing bowl. "With happy faces. We'll have bacon, too."

Simon's face brightened as she'd hoped it would. "Bacon?"

She nodded. "As many pieces as you like."

Although she'd hoped to keep Simon distracted, the first strips of bacon weren't even out of the package when Simon picked his racer up off the table. "When do you think Dad's going to get up?"

Sylvia froze. It was like the music had stopped and she was the one left holding the hot potato. She didn't want to lie, and yet she didn't want to upset Simon with the truth.

"He's up already," Tucker announced, running into the room with a towel attached to his pajamas like a cape. "I'm hungry," he said, eyeing the strips of bacon dangling from her fingers.

"Dad's awake?" Simon looked around as if he expected his father to pop out of the pantry or from behind the kitchen curtains.

"He went to work," Tucker announced, climbing up on one of the kitchen stools.

Sylvia watched Simon go very still as he digested the news. Very deliberately, he turned so that she couldn't see his face. "It's going to be okay, Simon," she said. "He's coming back in less than an hour."

But he wasn't back at 10:30 as promised, and although Tucker had eaten ten pancakes, Simon had long stopped. He was sitting on the couch, reading a book about the planets, but every few minutes he would glance up at the clock on the mantel and then at the front door.

He was suppressing his anxiety, which was something Wilson tended to do. She studied the top of her son's head and thought how alike he and Wilson were. Tucker tended to be more like Sylvia. She wondered if Wilson saw that, and if it was why he paid more attention to Tucker.

At 11:00, Sylvia suggested that she and Simon, together, drill the axle holes and set the wheels on the racer. Simon shook his head. "I'll wait for Dad," he said. "He promised."

"I'm sure he'll be here soon," Sylvia said, but inside she wasn't sure at all, which said a lot about her confidence in her husband's word. For the first time she had a true inkling of the frustration and unhappiness Rema dealt with on a regular basis with Skiezer. For the first time she looked out the kitchen window at the kidney-shaped pool and wondered if she was strong enough to make the marriage work. When had this double-parent role become the norm?

Dear Lord, she prayed, *help me hold it together.*

She decided to wait until 11:15 and then insist that she and Simon work on the racer. She'd assembled Tucker's, and although his car had pulled to the left before Wilson adjusted the screws, it had been raceable.

At 11:12, however, Wilson breezed through the door, all smiles and apology and eager to get started. He opened his arms, and after the briefest hesitation, Simon walked into them. Over the top of Simon's head their eyes met and he mouthed, "I'm sorry."

Something inside wouldn't let Sylvia accept or even acknowledge his apology. Her lips tightened, and she turned away, swallowing the fury, bitter as a pill in her mouth.

For the next two hours they worked steadily on the racer. Wilson drilled the holes then supervised Simon, who carefully threaded the axle rods through the body of the car. They lubricated the axels and screwed on the wheels.

"You can test it now," Wilson said.

Sylvia held her breath as Simon pushed the car down the center of the table. Something inside relaxed when the car pulled neither to the right or left, and Simon smiled. They weighed the car on her meat scale, and when they saw it was well below the allowed amount, Wilson drilled some more holes in the bottom of the car and they added a few metal washers. Finally, Wilson was satisfied, and Simon pulled out the oil paints.

Sylvia made grilled cheese sandwiches as Simon painstakingly painted the body of his racer black. She tried not to glance at the clock, or urge him not to be so meticulous, but it seemed like time was flying by. The car had to dry before Simon could apply the decals and then there still was that final coat of gloss.

The truth was they never should have left everything to the last minute. She glanced at Wilson, biting back a scathing comment about him going to work instead of starting work on the car earlier. It would only upset Simon, who was happily absorbed in painting.

They used her blow dryer on the cool setting to get the paint to dry faster, and then Simon added the red stripes and the silver decals for the headlights, windows, and windshield. He pasted a large number seven on the car's hood then held the car up for his father's inspection.

"Perfect," Wilson declared. "All we need is the top coat."

While Simon carefully painted the car with the clear polish, Sylvia hauled Tucker upstairs to put on his cub scout uniform. After she finished getting him dressed, she grabbed Simon's uniform out of his closet and hurried downstairs. Both Baxter men were still obsessing over the way the car rolled. She glanced at the clock. "Come on," she said, "we have to get going. Put these on," she ordered, handing Simon the clothing.

The trip to the elementary school wasn't far, but parking was a nightmare. They ended up pulling off to the side of the road at the front of a long line of cars that also hadn't been able to fit into the school's lot.

A quick glance at her watch told Sylvia they didn't have a lot of time to make the two o'clock inspection time. She grabbed Tucker's hand, Wilson took Simon's, and they hurried down the street.

By the time they reached the elementary school, Sylvia was sweating, panting, and completely stressed out. The derby was being held in the gym, but the crowd had already overflowed into the hallways. Sylvia's heart sank at the thought of the long line that would be at the inspection station. The information sheet had been very specific about the 2:00 p.m. deadline. The kids could be disqualified if they were late.

She turned to Wilson. "We have to hurry," she said over the dull roar of voices around them.

Wilson nodded and began leading them through the packed crowd. He was the blocker, his large body creating enough space for Sylvia and then the boys to pass through quickly before it closed again.

As they moved deeper into the gym, Sylvia glimpsed the long yellow plywood race tracks, obscured by the parents and kids already standing close by.

When Wilson stopped short, she nearly bumped into his back as they took their place in the inspection line. Peering around his back, Sylvia saw about ten sets of parents and children ahead of them. She looked at her watch and mentally calculated. It was going to be close. Turning to the boys, she gave them a reassuring smile. "Don't worry. We're going to make it."

Tucker nodded. His yellow neckerchief had already slipped out of the metal slide. Hiking her purse higher on her shoulder, Sylvia bent to fix it. More eye level with the kids, she caught Simon's gaze and saw he was clutching his racer protectively to his chest. She reached out to give his shoulder a reassuring squeeze and earned herself a fierce look. Too late she remembered that as a second grader, she wasn't supposed to do anything motherly to Simon in public.

If what Rema said was true, soon Simon wouldn't even want to be seen with her in public.

The line shuffled forward slowly but steadily. Sylvia became even more stressed as the minutes passed. Nobody else got into line behind them. Finally at 1:53 Tucker stepped up and handed the man seated at the inspection station his racer.

Sylvia held her breath as "Shamu" was held close to the inspector's eye, examined from every direction, and then placed on a scale. It passed the weight limitation of five ounces, and Tucker was given an entry number and directed to track one.

"I'll take him," Wilson volunteered when they saw Tucker was in the first heat. "You stay with Simon then meet us at the track."

Sylvia nodded and stepped closer to Simon, who was still clutching his racer protectively.

"Let's take a look," a middle-aged man with dark hair, a broad forehead, and a white goatee smiled encouragingly.

Simon nodded. He started to hand over his racer, but it soon became apparent the car was stuck to his shirt. He looked at Sylvia with an expression of confusion. "Mom?"

Sylvia blinked at the Pinewood Derby racer glued to Simon's uniform. The clear coat they'd applied to the car must not have been completely dry when they'd left the house. Because of the way Simon had been clutching the car, it had bonded to his shirt. She held down the blue fabric. "Pull," she ordered.

Simon set his small jaw, there was a small ripping sound, and then the racer peeled off his shirt. He handed it over to the inspector, who laughed and told Simon that there was no rule that the paint had to be completely dry before the race.

He asked Simon a few questions about the construction, complimented the glue job in the axle holes, and then placed the car on the scale. Sylvia held her breath as the needle swung past the five-ounce limit but then steadied within the accepted weight.

"You pass," the inspector said, "track two, heat nine." He handed back Simon his car and then made some notes in a fat binder. Checking his watch one final time, he closed the binder. "Inspections are closed!" he yelled. "Let the races begin!"

Chapter 16

Sylvia and Simon wiggled their way through the packed gym to track one. The three-lane yellow tracks were about thirty feet long and already surrounded by parents and kids, who pressed around it like passengers awaiting their luggage at an airline's baggage claim area.

Sylvia stood on her tiptoes, craning her neck for a glimpse of Tucker and Wilson. Fortunately Wilson was tall and his light brown hair caught her eye near the front of the track. With Simon in tow, she managed to squeeze her way up to them.

"Everything go okay?" Wilson shifted, allowing Sylvia and Simon a better view of the track. Before Sylvia could answer his question, the crowd roared as the first cars sped down the incline.

"Yeah," she said, struggling to be heard over the cheering. "Simon's car wasn't quite dry and stuck to his shirt, but. . ."

"What?"

She shook her head and raised her voice. "I'll tell you later."

Wilson nodded. "Tucker goes third." His voice, deeper than

hers, carried over the dull roar of voices around them. "When's Simon's?"

"Ninth heat," Sylvia shouted, just as the first racers swept under the finish line and the crowd erupted in even louder cheers.

"Good," Wilson said. "Look, Tucker's on deck."

Sylvia followed the direction of Wilson's gaze, and her heartbeat accelerated when she saw her youngest son near the base of a wooden block. Soon it would be his turn, and she couldn't help wanting him to win. Her stomach tightened as the next round of race cars sped down the track.

Tucker wasn't watching though. He was talking to a boy with dark skin and curly black hair standing behind him. Both of them were laughing about something.

Tucker didn't look the least bit nervous, which seemed impossible because Sylvia suddenly felt like jumping out of her skin. She started to whip off a quick prayer and felt Wilson's warm hand wrap around her fingers. She glanced at him and felt the shared love of their son bonding them together. And then Tucker's heat was announced and she was screaming at the top of her lungs as Tucker's car flashed past, head-to-head with two very sleek-looking racers.

Tucker had the middle lane, and as the cars reached the long, flat part of the track, his black-and-white car appeared to be slightly ahead. She jumped up and down—as if that would make it go faster—but she couldn't help herself. But then seconds later, to her joy and disbelief, Tucker's car streaked under the finish line a fraction ahead of both cars.

Sylvia gave a happy jump. "Whoo-hoo! Go Tucker!" She turned to Wilson. "Can you believe that? He won!"

Wilson grinned. "He sure did." He gave Simon a high five then kissed Sylvia on the lips. "Come on," he said, "let's go congratulate the winner."

Sylvia felt the warmth of success shoot through her. All the anxiety about getting to the race on time seemed to leave her, and as they moved toward the finish line, she realized it all was happening just as it said in the Proverbs—they were coming together as a family. She mentally chided herself for having any doubts.

They found Tucker off to the side, talking with an adult volunteer who was recording the race results. It was a best-of-three heat, with winners racing winners.

Sylvia embraced Tucker. "I'm so proud of you," she said, and planted a big kiss on his cheek. (Tucker was younger and thereby less embarrassed by her.)

"Good man," Wilson said, ruffling Tucker's light brown hair and grinning proudly. "I think we might even have a division champion!"

Simon stepped forward. Smiling, he gave his brother a hug. "Congratulations," he said, and the rest of his words were drowned out by the crowd as another set of racers started down the track.

Tucker went off to get back in line for his next heat. Wilson, Sylvia, and Simon squeezed into a small gap near the track to watch. Turning to her, Wilson slipped his arm around her waist and smiled. "It just doesn't get better than this, does it?"

But it did get better, because about fifteen minutes later Tucker won the next heat, and then the finals of his division. After the announcement, Wilson hefted the little boy up on his shoulders and, to Tucker's delight, did a small victory dance.

Sylvia took pictures with her cell phone—she'd forgotten her good camera in the mad dash to the elementary school. "Get in the picture," she urged Simon, who obediently stood beside his dad and Tucker, and if his smile was a little strained, it was understandable. He still had his races to worry about.

Sylvia couldn't help feeling proud of herself as well as of Tucker. They'd built that car together, sanded down the sides with her emery board, and painted it to look like Shamu. And now it had won the kindergarten division. Imagine that!

The races moved along quickly. Soon the first-grade troops were finished and it was the second graders' turn. Sylvia felt herself getting nervous all over again—and it didn't help when she saw Simon's small, pale face peering out from the top of the start of the track.

He was in the lane farthest from them, and she leaned forward as far as she could for a better view. *Dear God,* she prayed as the announcer began the countdown, *please let him win.*

The crowd yelled as the announcer boomed, "Go." All three cars rolled forward at the same time. Sylvia yelled encouragement to Simon's black racer, but almost immediately it seemed to slip behind the other cars. *Maybe when it hits the flat part of the track it'll catch up,* Sylvia told herself. But her hopes were in vain. When the three cars passed under the finish line, Simon's was clearly in third place.

Sylvia shot Wilson a look of distress, and then they all hurried to the finish line. They got there just as Simon retrieved his racer from the track official. Although outwardly, Simon seemed fine, when Sylvia looked into his eyes, she saw a look of dazed disbelief.

"Good job," she said, bending to give him a quick hug and kiss. "I'm proud of you."

Simon shrugged and mumbled something that sounded like, "For what?"

"For participating," Sylvia said, struggling for the right words. "For doing your best."

"My best wasn't good enough," Simon said so softly that if Sylvia hadn't been leaning toward him she wouldn't have heard.

"Yes it was," she said.

"You'll get them in the next heat," Wilson promised. "You just had a fast group."

"Your car was the coolest looking," Tucker added, and Sylvia shot him a grateful smile.

"No it wasn't," Simon said flatly. "The decals on one side came off when my car stuck to my shirt." He looked at Sylvia, as if somehow she could fix everything, and her heart ached because she couldn't. "I want to go home."

"The Baxters never give up," Wilson stated firmly. "There are still two races left."

Simon looked at her again, and this time Sylvia read fear in them. She'd seen this look in his eyes when Wilson had taken them all to the amusement park and asked who wanted to ride "The Thunderbird." Tucker had shouted a mighty "yes" and Simon had gamely agreed. He'd paled as they'd neared the kiddy rollercoaster. The whole ride he'd kept his eyes closed and a death grip on the railing. As soon as he got off the ride, he'd thrown up.

This time, however, it wasn't a scary rollercoaster. Sylvia suspected it was the fear of failing—of losing the race and letting down Wilson. Poor Simon—this race was the main reason he'd joined the Cub Scouts. At the same time, Wilson was essentially right. You didn't give up just because you didn't win.

"It doesn't matter if you win or lose," Sylvia said, hoping to ease some of the pressure. "This is just supposed to be for fun." She nudged Wilson with the tip of her sneaker.

"Your mother is right," Wilson said. "But let me look at the car. Maybe one of the axles needs more lubricant."

More lubricant, however, didn't help Simon's car, which lost all of its remaining races, although coming in a close second in one of them. Simon, looking almost physically ill from the loss, managed to hold it together and shake hands with the boys who had beaten him.

The ride home was mercifully short but unnaturally quiet. In the backseat, Tucker, clutching a foot-high gold trophy, sat next to a silent and visibly morose Simon. Sylvia wasn't sure what to do. On the one hand, she wanted Tucker to enjoy his victory—take him out for ice cream and shower him with praise. On the other hand, making a big deal out of Tucker's win would only make Simon's loss more painful.

This stunk, Sylvia decided, trying to balance one child's needs over another's. No matter what she did, it would be wrong.

Wilson pulled the minivan into their garage. As soon as he parked, the boys jumped out of the car and ran into the house. Sylvia and Wilson followed more slowly. Before they got into the house, she grabbed Wilson's arm. "You need to talk to him," she said, "make sure he understands that you don't care if he lost."

Pausing, Wilson looked at her. "Of course I don't care if he lost," he said, "but we're not going to baby him. What bothers me is that he's sulking about it. He needs to be more supportive of his brother."

"Wilson, he's seven."

"He's old enough to be a more graceful loser."

In the family room, Simon jumped onto the couch and pulled a plaid throw blanket over his head. Tucker squatted on the rug beside him.

"We can share it," Tucker said, lifting the blanket and attempting to push the trophy into his brother's hands.

"I don't want to!" Simon shoved the trophy away.

"Hey," Wilson said. "Your brother was just trying to be nice." He put his arm around Tucker. "I'm really proud of you." Taking the gold trophy from the little boy's hands, he studied it, smiling. "So where are we going to put that?" Wilson asked. "The mantelpiece maybe?"

"Yes," Tucker agreed, eyes shining.

"The mantelpiece it is then." Wilson shifted an ornate mantel clock and several framed silver photographs to make room. "How's that?"

"We should put both cars on the mantelpiece," Sylvia suggested, "because we're proud of both of you."

"Great idea," Wilson agreed, setting Shamu next to the trophy then looking around for Simon's racer. "Simon—where's your car?"

Simon pulled the crocheted throw blanket up to his chin. "I don't want my car on the mantelpiece. I want to throw it out. It isn't good enough."

"Of course it's good enough," Wilson said. Crossing the room, he crouched, eye level to Simon. "Winning is nice, but it's not everything. In fact losing is sometimes a good thing. It makes you try harder. Next year, we'll redesign your car—try a different shape. We'll sand the axles more carefully." He squeezed Simon's shoulder. "I'll help you. We'll kick some Cub Scout butt."

Sylvia watched tears pool in Simon's eyes and the way he widened his eyes to keep them from spilling out. "You say that, Dad," Simon said, "but you're always working." His voice was thick, filled with tears. He was clenching his fists, and his face was combination of sheet-white and blotchy red.

"Simon," Sylvia said, but gently, "be respectful of your father."

"It's okay." Wilson pulled Simon into his arms and hugged him hard even as the little boy resisted. "Next year will be different," he said. "I promise."

"You promised to help me this year," Simon mumbled. "And you didn't." His breathing became more rapid, and he buried his face into Wilson's shoulder. "You love Tucker more than me."

"Of course I don't," Wilson said, not releasing Simon, who was struggling to get out of his arms and crying. "I love both of you equally. You are my sons."

"No," Simon cried. "No you don't love me."

"Yes I do," Wilson said. "Next year I'm going to help you build another race car. Not because I care if you win or not, but because I like spending time with you."

Simon pulled back. He'd stopped crying and his face looked all at once old and young, wise and slightly jaded. He seemed to search his father's eyes and crumpled, unspeaking into his father's shoulder.

Later, Sylvia sat in the green wing chair in their bedroom trying to read her novel—a romance as usual. It was late—getting the boys to bed had been even more exhausting than usual. Wilson had helped, but then he said he had to check his e-mail and would be right there—but that was a half hour ago. She was determined to stay awake until Wilson came to bed.

She set the book aside when she realized she'd read the same page four times. Crossing her arms, she stared at their bedroom door and wondered how much longer Wilson was going to be. Simon had been disrespectful to Wilson, but essentially he'd been right, and this was what she needed to discuss with Wilson.

He seemed to be taking forever, and she felt fatigue mixing with the anxiety over the day's events. She got up, splashed some water on her face, and was drying it with a towel when Wilson walked through the bedroom door.

He rubbed the skin on his face and said, "What a day."

Sylvia walked into the room. "I know."

"I'm pooped. All I want is to go to sleep."

"Wilson, we need to talk."

This was her cue to him that she had something serious to say. He looked up, surprise and maybe even dread was reflected in his blue eyes. "We do?"

As if he didn't know! "Yes. You broke your promise to Simon—you told him that today would be about building his racer, but then you snuck out to work before we got up. He was looking forward to spending time with you, Wilson, and building that car together. Don't think he's forgotten that you won your Pinewood Derby when you were his age."

Wilson's face tightened. He took a long time answering, which Sylvia viewed as a sign that she was right. "I didn't have a choice," he said at last. "And I didn't break my promise—I did help him put together the race car. Maybe it was rushed, but there's stuff going on at work. . ."

"There's always stuff going on at work," Sylvia said, fatigue making her sharper than she'd normally be. "I don't see what could possibly be more important than your kids."

Wilson took a step toward her, but she moved backward, out of his range and crossed her arms.

"Nothing is more important than you, Simon, and Tucker," Wilson said. "But there are things about the merger that are happening fast now."

She didn't want to hear anything about the merger or the bank. "There are things happening in your family," she said. "Our boys are growing up really fast." She couldn't tell if she was getting through to him or not and shook her head. "I'm beginning to feel like I don't even know you anymore—like we're ships passing in the night."

Something about the word *ship* teased her brain, and she knew in a vague sort of way it had to do with Proverbs 31, but she didn't feel like even trying to be an excellent wife. It was much easier being an angry, righteous wife.

Wilson ran his fingers through his sandy-colored hair, met her gaze, then sighed heavily. "I'm up for a big promotion," he said. "That's why I've been working so hard lately. Bruce has me penciled in for the new branch manager's position, but I have to get approval from the board. I had coffee with one of the members this morning. It ran kind of late."

Sylvia blinked at him. "You what?"

"I'm interviewing for a new job." A proud-looking smile lifted the corners of his mouth. "I've been dying to tell you, but I wasn't sure if it would happen or not."

Sylvia studied his eyes, saw the excitement glowing softly in them. "Branch manager?"

"Yeah," Wilson said. "Of course there'll be other candidates. But I have Bruce's full support, and I think today went well."

"I still can't believe you went on an interview without us even talking about it."

Wilson nodded. "I'm sorry. I should have told you sooner."

"The new job," Sylvia murmured, "would you be taking Bruce's place?"

He shook his head. "No. The new bank."

"The new bank?" Sylvia found the next words hard to get out. "We'd have to relocate?"

Wilson nodded. "Only five hours from here. You'll like it there, Sylvia. With the promotion I'll get a healthy increase and some major perks. We'll be able to afford a bigger house. The schools are great, too—they're rated even higher than the ones here."

Sylvia sank down on the edge of the bed. Dear God, was she hearing this correctly? Wilson had practically accepted a job that required relocation, and he hadn't even discussed it with her before he interviewed for it?

"I know it's a lot to take in," Wilson said, reaching for her hand. "And if you don't want me to take this job, I won't."

Sylvia searched his eyes. She saw the truth in them and knew he really would turn down this job if she said no. But he really wanted it, so how could she ask him to turn it down?

Her heart ached at the thought of leaving Rema and her other friends. The local elementary school was perfect—both boys were thriving there. She loved their church and the friends she'd made there. She and Wilson had a great life here—didn't he see that?

"Couldn't you get a promotion here?"

Wilson shook his head. "Bruce still has years before he retires."

"Oh." Sylvia still couldn't bring herself to tell Wilson she was open to relocating.

"So what do you think, Syl? Are you up for a new town and a new adventure?"

She opened her mouth. Nothing came out. She swallowed and tried again. "I don't know." The habit of supporting him, of supporting his career, made her add, "Maybe."

"Why don't you think about it?" Wilson smiled encouragingly. "We could even drive out there—look at some houses, see the town. Nothing is definite though. All of this is confidential."

"Can I at least tell Rema?"

Wilson hesitated. "Can she keep this private? Just for a little while longer?"

"Yes."

"And you'll keep an open mind?"

Sylvia managed to nod, but she sensed that as far as Wilson was concerned, the decision was already made.

Chapter 17

Sylvia was sitting by the edge of the pool when the latch to the back gate clicked open. Two small boys wearing baggy, knee-length bathing suits with bright Hawaiian prints charged barefoot across the grass. Following at a slower pace, and with the black-and-white Border collie straining at the leash, was Rema.

A cheer went up from Tucker and Simon at the sight of their friends. Sylvia laughed as the small brown bodies launched themselves into the air and cannonballed into the water.

Unclipping the dog, Rema settled on the ledge of the pool beside Sylvia. "Okay. I'm dying to hear it—how did the derby go?"

Sylvia trailed her foot through the water. Although the race had only been yesterday, it already seemed like ages ago. "Depends on whether you ask Simon or Tucker."

The black-and-white dog, Cookie, circled the pool with its feathery tail wagging hard. It barked excitedly as the boys tried to coax it into the water.

Rema followed the direction of Sylvia's gaze. "I didn't have the heart to put him in the crate. I hope it's okay to bring him."

Sylvia nodded. Judging from the way the dog was looking at the boys, she could tell it was dying to get to them. "Can Cookie swim?"

"All dogs can swim," Rema stated confidently. She fell silent though as the dog crouched with its butt high in the air and looked down into the water as if it was trying to judge its depth. As the boys urged him, Cookie slowly slid face-first into the pool. The dog immediately sank below the water.

Rema rose, but before she jumped into the pool, the dog's black-and-white head appeared at the surface line. A moment later, Cookie began paddling furiously toward the boys. It was an odd, almost vertical motion, as if the dog were trying to climb out of the water.

"I told you all dogs could swim," Rema commented. Her eyes, however, never left the dog. "Liam," she shouted, "make sure Cookie knows where the steps are so when he gets tired he can rest."

"Okay, Mom." Liam, Rema's oldest son, two years older than Simon, was one of Simon's best friends. He was a tall, dark-haired kid with Rema's eyes and Skiezer's height and build. He liked the games Simon invented, like Avatar Ball, which was a modified kind of volleyball, but played in the pool with a rubber ball.

"So tell me about the derby," Rema prompted. "What's so big you couldn't tell me on the phone?"

Sylvia sighed and moved her legs in the water. "Basically Tucker won everything and Simon lost everything." She glanced at her sons to make sure they weren't listening. "Simon had a nuclear meltdown, and Wilson and I had an argument."

"Ah, family time," Rema said. Her brown eyes were full of sympathy. "It gets you every time. Family vacation is the worst. Takes me weeks to recover." She peered a little anxiously at Sylvia.

"That was supposed to be funny, honey."

"It was. I'm sorry." The stitches in Sylvia's arm where she had cut herself on the gutter itched. She absently scratched at the bandage. She dreaded telling her about Wilson's promotion/move, but she also desperately needed Rema's opinion on what she should do.

"So what happened?" Rema swept back her hair and tied it without any kind of hair tie into a complicated knot.

"First, Wilson went out of town, and then. . ." Sylvia shrugged. "Oh, I don't know. It's a long story."

"I like long stories," Rema said. "And I don't have to be anywhere until six o'clock soccer practice. So spill it."

As the boys and the dog splashed around the pool, Sylvia told Rema about Wilson slipping out to a business meeting instead of helping with Simon's racer, the stress of getting to the derby on time, Simon's loss and subsequent meltdown when they got home.

"But that's not the worst thing." Sylvia felt herself start to get upset and took a deep breath. "Wilson's up for a big promotion and we might have to move."

"No way," Rema announced firmly. "You're not moving."

"Hopefully not. But it explains why he's been so obsessed with work lately. Rema, he really wants this new job."

Although Rema's eyes were hidden behind a pair of oversize dark glasses, the tightness around her mouth reflected her dismay. "Couldn't he just long-distance commute?"

Sylvia shook her head. "It's like five hours."

"Oh." Rema shook her head as if she still couldn't believe Sylvia's news. "Do the boys know?"

"No. It's still iffy. I promised Wilson you wouldn't tell anyone either."

"Not even Kelly, Andrea, or Susan?"

Sylvia sighed. "Not yet."

"I won't tell a soul," Rema promised. She looked at Sylvia. "Oh my goodness," she said. "You can't move. What would I do without you?"

Both women jerked back as one of the boys threw the rubber Avatar ball and it splashed right in front of them. Cookie, paddling fast, retrieved it, and with his long tail acting like a rudder swam back to the boys.

"What would I do without *you*?" Sylvia looked unhappily at her friend.

"So don't go," Rema stated firmly. "Tell him that you don't want to relocate."

"He did say that if I didn't want to move, he wouldn't make me," Sylvia admitted. "I just feel like since he's the one working, I should support what he wants, and if that means move, I should move."

"Connor," Rema shouted at her youngest son. "Get *off* your brother's back. Do you want to *drown* him?" She turned back to Sylvia. "That's silly. Just because you don't get a paycheck doesn't mean you don't work. Being a stay-at-home mom isn't easy. I've told Skiezer if he had to pay for someone to do the stuff I do every day, he'd be bankrupt."

Sylvia looked away from Rema at the boys playing ball with the dog. They made a picture that seemed to imprint itself all the more in her brain because there might not be many more afternoons like this. "He really wants this job."

Rema shook her head. "*Connor*, I'm *warning* you for the last time. The next time you jump on top of anyone, you're out of the pool for the rest of the day!" She patted Sylvia's leg. "What about you? What do you want?"

Sylvia's ears rang from Rema's shouting. "I want to stay here, but I want Wilson to be happy. If he isn't happy at work, he isn't going to be happy at home. If relocating is what Wilson feels is best for our family, then we should do it."

"What makes you think *he* knows better than you what's good for your family?"

Sylvia blinked. "I don't know," she admitted. "But what if I make him give up the promotion and he ends up resenting me? I don't want something like this getting between us." She paused, watched the dog swim another lap after the ball, then shrugged. "I think it would be easier to deal with the move than deal with the guilt of not moving."

Rema lifted her dark glasses and studied Sylvia's eyes. "That's just hogwash. You need to tell him how you really feel."

"If I tell him how I really feel, he'll turn down the job. I'm kind of hoping that he'll figure out that I wasn't exactly jumping up and down with joy when he told me last night." Sylvia smiled as the boys tried to pull Cookie onto an inflatable raft with them and the whole thing capsized. "And I'm kind of hoping that something will fall through and he won't get the job."

"Wilson's a genius," Rema said flatly. "He'll get the job." She fussed with a strap on her bikini top. "If you want to stay, you're going to have to do something fast."

"Yeah, but what? Pray that he doesn't get the promotion?" Sylvia shook her head. "That doesn't seem right, not when I know Wilson is praying that he gets it." She paused as the boys managed to haul the Border collie onto the raft. Sopping wet, the dog struggled to find its balance and then shook wildly, spraying the boys, who whooped with laughter. Even Simon seemed to have put the whole

Pinewood Derby thing behind him and was having fun.

How many afternoons would they have left like this?

Rema's brow furrowed. "Maybe," she said, "what Wilson needs is a wake-up call. Something to remind him of all the good stuff about your life here."

Cocking her head, Sylvia studied her friend's tanned face. "That sounds great, but what?"

Rema thought for a moment. "How about an intervention? We'll call everyone and have them give Wilson reasons why moving is a bad idea. And if he doesn't agree"—she drew a line across her throat—"we'll kill him."

Sylvia shook her head. "The only kind of intervention that would help is Divine intervention." In the back part of her mind, the mom part of her remembered that she needed to defrost hamburger meat for dinner. It would just be her and the boys again—Wilson was working late and planning on grabbing something in the office.

"Well, maybe our group will have an idea. We're still on for Tuesday night at Andrea's house, right?"

Sylvia nodded. She probably would need to get a babysitter though. No way could she count on Wilson getting home at a reasonable hour. "Yeah, although between you and me, I'm beginning to wonder if we should just put the Proverbs Plan on hold. Honestly, I don't think it's working very well."

"We don't know that." Rema's lips straightened into a serious line. "Everything that's happened could be exactly part of God's plan for you."

"I know." Sylvia sighed. "It's just kind of discouraging so far."

"You need a pick-me-up," Rema said. "A new outfit, with shoes, and jewelry—and nothing on sale. It'll help."

Sylvia leaned back on her arms. Shopping was Rema's antidote to just about anything, but Sylvia knew it wasn't the solution for her. She looked up at the fluffy white clouds and watched them morph into different shapes. Just what kind of plan did God have in mind for her? Why did He always have to be so mysterious? And above all, why would He ask her to give up this town, this house—these friends—when it felt like they were the only things holding her together?

Wilson was determined to get home early. He knew Sylvia was upset with him over the way he'd handled the Pinewood Derby thing, and he wanted to make it up to her. Although he had a meeting scheduled, he decided to blow it off. He'd call her from the road to let her know. He'd also stop and buy her a dozen roses. No, he'd get sunflowers. Sylvia loved them.

And Simon—imagine him thinking that Wilson didn't love him as much as Tucker. He had been tired and disappointed when he'd said that. Wilson was sure he didn't mean it, but he would spend more time with him. Tonight he'd suggest he, Simon, and Tuck play hoops in the driveway.

He was powering down his PC when Bruce stepped into his office. For the next thirty minutes he quizzed Wilson on his plans for an advanced online banking system and the proposed reallocation of personnel.

"Excellent work," Bruce concluded. "You're thinking just like a branch manager. Now all we need to do is increase your visibility with the executive board. You play golf, Wilson?"

Did miniature golf count? Wilson didn't think so. Sports weren't his forte, never had been. "No sir," he said.

"Tennis, then? I used to play three sets twice a week before the hip replacement. Justin Eddelman is looking for a doubles partner."

Wilson could hardly keep a ping-pong rally going. He shook his head. "Sorry, sir."

The older man sighed. "You might want to take some golf or tennis lessons. The higher you go in business, the more you need personal contacts as well as business ones. As many deals are made at the country club as in the boardroom."

When was he going to take golf lessons when he worked more than seventy hours a week? Wilson rubbed his temples. "I'll look into it."

"Sylvia, too," Bruce suggested. "Sunday mornings the wives like to get out. Golf and then brunch afterward. Margie and I used to be practically unbeatable—unless we wanted to be." A sly look formed on his face. "If you know what I mean. Sometimes it's just as important to lose as it is to win."

Wilson thought of Simon, who was far from understanding this lesson.

"You and Sylvia should consider taking golf lessons."

Wilson nodded but doubted this would happen. Judging from her reaction to the prospect of moving, he'd be lucky if she swung at the ball and not his head. *She'll come around,* he assured himself. But the idea of a sport was not entirely a bad one. He saw himself throwing a softball with the boys, maybe shooting hoops with them. They had a basketball net in the driveway, and now both boys were old enough to start playing.

"You can borrow my clubs," Bruce offered. "With my hip, I

can't get out there anymore."

"Thank you, sir." He glanced at his watch and struggled to curb his impatience. Bruce didn't seem to realize just how late it was. "Is there anything else you want?"

"No," Bruce replied. "I wanted to tell you that Ron McKensy from the Dallas branch is campaigning hard for that branch manager's job. You have my support, but McKensy is teeing off with Justin Eddelman on Sunday morning."

After Bruce left, Wilson continued to think about Bruce's news. He knew McKensy by reputation, and he would be a tough competitor.

He turned on his PC and settled back into his seat. He needed to present a business plan so dazzling, so profitable, so creative that the board couldn't help but pick him. (Even if he couldn't swing a golf club to save his life.)

Okay, he'd already presented a plan to Bruce, but that plan was outdated now. Today, he'd created a voluntary retirement plan that would significantly reduce the number of layoffs. His mind whirled with ideas, even as his eyes burned with fatigue. He realized there was no way he'd be having dinner with Sylvia tonight, or pretty much any night until things were settled.

It occurred to him suddenly that the more hours he worked at the bank, the more hours Sylvia had to work at home without him. She'd looked tired and certainly hadn't been acting like herself lately at all. Now, with his promotion, there'd be extra work for her as well. She'd have to get their house ready for the market. Plus he'd want her help, too, in picking out the new house.

No doubt about it, Sylvia needed someone to lend a hand cooking, chasing after the boys, and catching up on all the household repairs. Unfortunately, it couldn't be him.

And it couldn't be just anybody, Wilson realized. It had to be someone who loved the boys, a male figure who the boys would respect, and someone Sylvia could trust wholeheartedly.

In short, Wilson realized, she needed his father to visit for a few weeks until everything settled down at work. Although it was late, his dad would be awake. He picked up the telephone and made the necessary plans.

Chapter 18

Andrea Burns lived in one of the newer, more upscale neighborhoods. The houses were big, mostly contemporary brick-and-glass colonials, but there were a few stucco Mediterranean-style homes that sprawled across their large, immaculately landscaped lots.

Whenever Sylvia drove down Andrea's cul-de-sac, she always enjoyed the irony of knowing that while Andrea lived in a 4,000-square-foot mansion, it had been a little wooden cabin that had brought the two of them together.

About four years ago, Sylvia and Rema had gone on a retreat for mothers sponsored by their church. It had been hard leaving the boys with Wilson, but she'd been excited about the prospect of getting away, of meeting other mothers, and studying God's Word in a beautiful lakeside setting.

She hadn't counted on the water being the color of chocolate milk, the cabin smelling of mold, or the family of mice living in the cabinet beneath the sink in the bathroom. But then neither had her four new roommates—Rema, Susan, Kelly, and Andrea.

Their toilet had run continuously, the mattresses felt like they'd been stuffed with rocks, and there was a scary, strange stain in the bathtub, but somehow these things hadn't mattered at all.

Over the weekend something almost magical happened. In that little cabin, everyone had opened up to each other, prayed with and for each other, and talked long into the night.

The bond they'd formed had endured over the years, even though their schedules hadn't always allowed them to get together as frequently as Sylvia would have liked.

Pulling up behind Rema's Suburban, Sylvia parked the minivan. Wilson had asked her not to tell everyone about his possible promotion, but it was going to be really hard. She squared her shoulders and rang the bell.

Andrea opened the massive, solid-wood double doors. As usual, she was wearing one of her fabulous power suits. This one was charcoal gray with a faint navy-and-black weave. Her heels were high, and her gold jewelry impeccable. She took the plate of cookies out of Sylvia's hands and kissed her on the cheek. "Come on in," she said, ushering her into the cool, dark interior of her house.

Sylvia took a seat on a plush, chenille sofa and sipped peach iced tea from a long, tall glass. Rema and Susan were already there. As they waited for Kelly, Sylvia got caught up a little on what had been happening over the past week in her friends' lives.

They were discussing Susan's latest volunteering project— running a youth mission trip—when Kelly called to say that she'd been held up at the hospital and they should start without her.

Settling into a coffee-brown recliner, Andrea turned to Susan. "How about you lead us in prayer?"

Sylvia set her glass down on the glass-topped coffee table. Joining hands with Rema and Andrea, she bowed her head as Susan began.

"Heavenly Father, we thank You so much for the opportunity to get together and study Your word. Father, we ask that You be with us tonight and that we put aside our wants and our desires in order that we will know Yours more clearly. In Jesus' name. Amen."

Sylvia looked up. "That was beautiful, Susan."

"So," Andrea said, pulling out her leather notebook and opening to a blank page. "Last time you were working on the verse that focused on family. How did the Pinewood Derby go?"

Sylvia wrinkled her nose. "Not exactly as I envisioned," she admitted. "Wilson had to go on a business trip, so there really wasn't much family bonding time." She went on to tell them about Tucker's big win, and Simon's equally big loss.

"But then Tucker shocked me," Sylvia continued, "instead of rubbing it in that he won, he was really kind to Simon and even offered to share the trophy." She felt her eyes tear at the memory. "It was like seeing a glimpse of the man he's going to grow up to be."

"I think that's really awesome," Susan said and reached for one of Sylvia's homemade oatmeal chocolate chip cookies. "Maybe your family didn't come together the way you thought, but it sounds like your boys learned some important life lessons."

"That's what Wilson said. I hope so." Sylvia studied the sprig of mint in her iced tea. Unfortunately Simon had also learned some tough life lessons, namely that his father would sometimes let him down, and that promises could be stretched and bent until they didn't resemble their original shape at all.

"I know it's hard to see your child lose," Andrea offered, "but sometimes it's the best thing that can happen to them. Personally,

I've always learned more from the cases I've lost in court than the ones I've won."

Sylvia eased back on the couch as the women offered examples of how their failures actually made them stronger or opened doors to better opportunities. She knew they were right, but they hadn't had to fish Simon's race car out of the trash, or wipe the tears from his face, or try to explain that he wasn't a disappointment to them.

Sipping her tea, Sylvia found her thoughts slipping to her mother. Sylvia's dad had worked long hours, but it hadn't been an issue. Why?

Maybe it was just a different time. Yet when she thought about her mom, the word *content* came to mind. Throughout disappointments and dramas Sylvia's mom had somehow stayed above it all, loving her even when Sylvia felt completely unlovable. Like when that boy Courte Hodges had asked her to the prom—and then unasked her. Sylvia still remembered her mother's arms around her, holding her, telling her that God had something even better planned for her.

But did He? The whole prom thing hadn't worked out. She'd ended up staying home, unhappily playing album after album and trying not to listen to the inner voice that said that her hips were too big and her hair too bushy.

After she'd graduated high school, she'd made it through college and then gone to work, still waiting for that something better to come along. There had been many long, lonely years. When she'd met Wilson, she thought her real life, the one she was supposed to be living, had finally begun.

But now it all felt like the ground beneath her feet was disintegrating. Wilson wasn't in love with her anymore, and she was about to lose her home and her friends. It was prom night all over again.

Sylvia set her glass down. Did it have to be prom night all over again? Did she really have to lose everything? Maybe God wanted her to stop waiting around for Him to fix things and fight for what she wanted.

"Sylvia?"

Sylvia turned toward Susan's voice. Her friend had her Bible open.

"We thought we'd get started on the next verse," Susan said and began to read: " 'She considers a field and buys it; out of her earnings she plants a vineyard.' " Susan paused, but when no one commented, she continued. " 'She sets about her work vigorously; her arms are strong for her tasks. She sees that her trading is profitable, and her lamp does not go out at night.' "

"That's probably enough," Susan said. Her gaze swept around the circle. "Did any of the verses speak to anyone?"

There was a long silence, which didn't surprise Sylvia. She knew she wasn't supposed to think literally—but it was hard to translate buying and planting a vineyard into a suburban Texas town.

"Maybe you'd better read it again," Andrea suggested. "I have an idea, but I'm not sure."

Susan read slowly. Sylvia closed her eyes and tried to concentrate, but she found herself thinking about Wilson and their potential relocation. Maybe the part about buying a field wasn't for growing grapes—maybe it was about building a house and starting a new life somewhere else. She felt her stomach knot.

"The part about the fields," Andrea said, tapping her yellow pad with a polished red fingernail. "It's a metaphor. It's about making good investments and managing them."

"I don't think this verse is just about money," Rema countered. "I think that it's about attitude—of being strong and independent and having the confidence to make decisions without relying on anyone else." She sat up a little straighter on the couch. "I think the Proverbs 31 woman is independent. When she knows a field is the right one for her family, she buys it and develops the land. She doesn't turn it over to her husband and ask what he wants her to do with it." Rema looked straight at Sylvia. "The Proverbs 31 wife is empowered, not submissive."

The look in Rema's dark eyes said Sylvia should tell Wilson to turn down the promotion and not think twice about it. Sylvia pleated the fabric at the hem of her cotton skirt. The decision wasn't that simple. Marriage was about compromise and sometimes sacrifice. "The Proverbs 31 wife would probably sell the field if her husband asked her to."

Rema rolled her eyes. "Then the Proverbs 31 wife would be making a very big mistake. She could be sitting on top of an oil field, especially if she lived in Texas. She should be smart enough to know when her husband is about to make a terrible mistake."

"Even if the house were sitting on an oilfield, the Proverbs 31 wife would have to move anyway," Sylvia pointed out. "You can't grow a vineyard and have an oil well in the same field."

"But then she'd have enough money to buy a new field, right next door to the old one," Rema said firmly. "Because when you find a good field, you should stick with it."

There was a moment of silence. Sylvia studied the confused looks on Susan's and Andrea's faces. She wished she could tell them what she and Rema were really talking about.

"I really don't think this is about fields or grapes," Andrea said.

"You both are being too literal." She turned to Susan as if Susan were the referee about to make the call on a play. "What do your notes say the verse about the fields really means?"

Susan adjusted her glasses and consulted her notes. "Well, it says that Andrea was on the right track. The Proverbs 31 wife is enterprising, prudent with money, and energetic." She lifted her gaze to Sylvia. "How do you feel about that?"

Sylvia thought for a moment. "Wilson handles all of our investments. He's really good at that stuff, so I don't worry too much about it."

Translation—the principal's PTO presentations were exciting compared to discussions on stock portfolios, bonds, and mutual funds. Wilson happily spent hours on his computer making sure they invested their money, wisely. Since Sylvia tended to be financially conservative, it wasn't an issue between them. But maybe, she considered, this attitude was part of the reason it felt like they each lived in their own world.

"I guess I could take a more active role," Sylvia said slowly. "Wilson would be thrilled if I showed an interest in managing our money."

"I don't think having a discussion about money is very romantic," Rema said flatly. "In fact, it sounds like a terrible idea to me. The last time Skiezer and I talked about our finances, he tried to put me on a budget and we didn't speak for a week."

The three of them laughed.

"I know talking about money doesn't sound very romantic," Susan said, sipping her iced tea, "but I don't think we should skip this verse, especially considering that Wilson is a banker. He has a passion for finances."

Sylvia picked up another cookie. "He really does," she confirmed. "Give the man a spreadsheet and he's a happy camper."

"This could be a really good thing," Andrea mused, fingering the long strand of pearls that lay on her peach-colored silk blouse. Her blue eyes were bright and intense. Sylvia could almost see her brain spinning.

"I'm thinking that you should ask Wilson to go over your financial situation with you," Andrea began. "Just the two of you, together—no kids. Let him explain the areas he feels best about, your goals for the future, and stuff like that."

"I don't see what good could come from going over their financial portfolio." Rema met Sylvia's gaze. "I think Sylvia needs to be more direct with Wilson, and simply tell him what she wants." Her raised eyebrows implied that what Sylvia wanted was for Wilson to turn down the promotion.

Andrea silenced her with a glare she probably had perfected when she needed to stare down the prosecuting attorney. "The point is that when Wilson starts talking about something he enjoys, he'll open up. He'll get excited about sharing his knowledge with Sylvia, and his defenses will drop. Before you know it, you could be having a really deep, intense conversation that has nothing to do with money." She gestured excitedly. "Passion could lead to passion! Don't you see how amazing this verse is—talking about finances when Wilson's a banker?"

Sylvia tried to look appropriately awed at the connection. Inside she was struggling with the idea of trying so hard to meet Wilson's needs when she was mad at him for dumping this whole promotion thing on her.

Sylvia forced a smile. "You're right. But with Easter around the corner, I'll probably have to wait a little while to plan this." By then she could tell everyone about Wilson's promotion and stop trying to be the Proverbs wife.

Andrea pulled out her Blackberry and punched a few buttons. "You should aim for a Friday or Saturday night—so you can sleep late in the morning. And schedule it for after the boys are in bed. How about the second week in May?"

How about never? Sylvia thought glumly, but forced herself to pull her appointment book out of her purse. She blinked when she saw the date. "But that's our anniversary," she said.

Every year they celebrated it at the same restaurant and each of them ordered the same meal. They'd debate, but skip dessert, and then Wilson would give her a nice card and a charm for her bracelet. It was all very nice, but Sylvia felt a little discouraged thinking about it.

"Sylvia can't talk finances on their anniversary," Rema protested.

"You're forgetting," Andrea said sternly. The silver bracelets on her arm jingled as she gestured. "It could lead to talking about budgeting for a romantic getaway to Hawaii or something." She gave Sylvia an encouraging nod. "You have that pretty little bistro table by the pool. I suggest you invite Wilson to a romantic dinner on your deck." She glanced at Susan. "We'll help. You won't even have to cook."

Once Sylvia had dreamed of going to Italy and looking up her ancestors' homes, but that was a long, long time ago. Everything was different now. She had to bite her lip to keep from blurting out that the conversation might consist of Wilson extolling the joys of his new job until she couldn't take it any longer and pushed him into the pool. However, since Wilson had sworn her to silence about the promotion, she found herself agreeing to Andrea's idea. Secretly, she figured she'd cancel the plans once Wilson's job change became public knowledge.

Chapter 19

Sylvia was hoping Wilson would be awake when she got back from her meeting. She had a lot of questions about where Wilson stood in the interview process. If he got the job, how soon would they have to leave? Would the boys be able to finish out the school year? When would they start looking for a new house?

Wilson was asleep, however—snoring to be exact. Slipping beneath the comforter next to him, she realized that she was still too wired from the evening to sleep. She fumbled for her novel on the bedside table and switched on the tiny reading light. On impulse she picked up her Bible.

"Her lamp does not go out at night," Sylvia recalled as she found her place in the book. Maybe, like her, the Proverbs 31 wife had things on her mind and a husband who snored. She pondered the verse a little longer, and then opened her romance and read until she realized she no longer comprehended any of the words.

There was a cup of coffee and a note sitting on the kitchen table for her the next morning. Taking a sip, Sylvia picked up the scrap of paper with Wilson's handwriting scrawled on it. *I love you, Sylvia,* it stated. *We'll talk more tonight.* He doodled some hearts along the margins. She took a sip of coffee, warm and sweet with just the right amount of milk. She reread the note then slipped it into the pocket of her robe.

For the next hour, Sylvia dashed around making lunches for the boys and finding lost items. Finally they were out the door. After she dropped the boys off at school, she stopped at the grocery store, picked up more cold cuts and the makings for a spaghetti dinner, then drove home.

In the silent house, she put away the groceries then headed upstairs to gather the laundry. As always, she marveled at the amount of clothing two small children could go through—and then found herself getting sentimental as she stuffed a pair of jeans that had been Simon's and were now Tucker's into the machine.

They weren't babies anymore, and it made her sad to think that part of her life was over. She thought of the ivory-colored crib in the attic. She really should donate it—it wasn't doing anyone good just sitting there. It wasn't like she and Wilson were going to have another child. She evened out the load in the machine. Was this true? Deep down, Sylvia knew she would be thrilled to have another son, or a daughter.

She twisted the dial to the machine and listened to the powerful gush of water filling the drum. When she was pregnant with Tucker, she'd been certain she'd have a girl. The due date was right on her mother's birthday, and she'd seen this as God filling the hole that had opened up inside her at her mother's death. She'd never tell Tucker, but before he was born she'd thought of him as Melanie April.

"Melanie April," Sylvia whispered to herself. She pictured a little girl with plump, rosy cheeks, her auburn, curly hair and Wilson's blue eyes. She could almost feel the chubby weight of her in her arms. Sylvia drew herself up short. She was forty years old. Forty. She was too old for another child. God had blessed her with two healthy, beautiful boys. She couldn't love them more.

Besides, a little girl would grow up, just like a little boy, and soon Sylvia would be at the same point in her life as she was now—the kids in school, a husband who worked long hours, and a house that suddenly felt very empty.

Stepping back from the machine, she told herself to get busy. It would be years before the kids went to college, and only hours before they got back from school. Besides, Easter was a week from Sunday and she had a lot to do before then. Returning to the kitchen, she called Honey-Bee-Ham. When the machine answered, she left her name and number. Hanging up, Sylvia worked the menu. Along with the ham, she'd make honey apples, new potatoes with herbs, sautéed green beans, and a salad with crumbled blue cheese and spicy pecans.

Rema would bring dessert—she always brought banana cream pie and everyone loved it.

Reheating her coffee in the microwave, she sipped it slowly. Wilson had made it for her. She thought of his large hands stirring in the right amount of milk and sugar. It was a small gesture—his making it for her—knowing how she liked it—but it meant something to her.

She touched the note in her pocket. Wilson should have discussed the potential promotion with her before he interviewed for the job, but she knew his heart, and it was good. He wouldn't ask her to relocate lightly. She thought of Rema, who loved Skiezer, but had a difficult marriage. Outwardly they seemed fine—an attractive, successful couple—but Sylvia knew differently. All Rema's jokes aside, bottom line, their arguments had opened up a rift between them. Skiezer and Rema weren't best friends, and at times they weren't friends at all. Sometimes Sylvia wondered if Rema and Skiezer were going to make it. She didn't want that kind of marriage.

Finishing her coffee, Sylvia rinsed her mug and put it in the rack to dry. She didn't want to be at odds with Wilson, and it was clear to her now how badly communication between them had broken down. They needed more time together, which reminded her of the next step in the Proverbs Plan she had promised to take.

She reached for the phone but then had a better idea. For ages Wilson had been asking her to send him an electronic calendar request when she wanted to schedule something with him. She'd never done it before, but today seemed a good day to start. She headed upstairs for the home PC in Wilson's office.

The phone rang just as she was viewing Wilson's calendar on the computer. It was a man from Honey-Bee-Ham. As she confirmed the details of her order, Sylvia blocked off a portion of Wilson's schedule, typed in "Anniversary Dinner" and put the location as "poolside, semi-formal." As a final flourish, she attached an RSVP and tagged the calendar request with an exclamation mark to flag it "high priority" in his inbox.

She hit SEND as she agreed to pick up a 15-pound ham on the Saturday before Easter. Sitting back in the chair, she smiled, pleased with her multi-tasking abilities and imagining the surprise on Wilson's face when he got her meeting request.

She was moving the wet laundry to the dryer when the doorbell rang. Straightening, Sylvia hoped it was Rema. Eager to share the details of her morning, she ran downstairs.

Throwing open the door, Sylvia started to say, "Well I hope you brought your bathing suit," when the words died on her lips. There, standing on her front doorstep wearing a checkered short-sleeve shirt, green shorts, and a pair of calf-high black socks was her father-in-law.

Sylvia's mind raced. Joe wasn't due until a week from Friday. Today was only Wednesday. Had he gotten the dates wrong? She searched his weathered face for a clue, even as she gave him a welcoming smile.

"Joe! This is a lovely surprise!" Never in nine years of marriage had he shown up unannounced on her doorstep. "Is everything okay?"

"Oh yes," he said cheerfully. His blue eyes, the exact shade as Wilson's, peered at her kindly. "Wilson told me about everything that's happening. I thought you could use some extra help."

Three oversize suitcases sat on the porch next to Joe. She stared at their bulging sides and swallowed. It looked more like Joe was moving in with them than spending a few days. "Extra help?" she repeated a little faintly.

Joe beamed. "With the house and the boys. Wilson told me all about the big promotion."

"He did?"

"He said he might have to do some traveling between the banks until things get settled. He sounded so unhappy about leaving you alone, Sylvia, that I knew he needed me to come."

"So Wilson knows you're here?"

"Oh no. It's a surprise. If either of you knew I was coming, you might start fussing—doing extra cleaning or shopping." He straightened his narrow shoulders. "I'm here to work. My tool kit and power tools are in the car." He gestured to an older-model blue Buick parked in front of their house. "Of course, if I'm in the way, I'll just drive home."

Home was a long drive away—fourteen hours to be exact—in the small town in Oklahoma where he had retired from the oil company where he had been working for twenty years. "Of course I want your help," Sylvia said, stepping back and opening the door wider. "Don't just stand there. Come on in."

She reached for one of the suitcases. It was heavy and required both hands to drag it over the threshold. He must have packed a lot of clothes. She pushed back a sense of foreboding. Joe's last visit had been extended several times because every time he was supposed to leave he pretended to be sick.

"You sure I'm not barging in on you in the middle of something?" Joe asked, following her into the cool air-conditioning.

"Absolutely nothing," Sylvia assured him. "Let's get your bags settled in the guest room then have a glass of iced tea."

"Iced tea sounds great," Joe said. "We can put together a list of things you want me to do while I'm here. If you're going to put the house on the market, we should plant some flowers. Petunias or impatiens would be nice in the front. People like flowers. It makes a house look happy."

Sylvia's brow furrowed as she dragged the suitcase up the first step. "Wilson told you we're selling the house?" What else had her husband shared with her father-in-law that he hadn't told her? Maybe she was going to have to reconsider killing him.

"Not exactly," Joe admitted. "But spring is the perfect time to sell. We're already late, but don't worry, there's still time. You sure that suitcase isn't too heavy for you?"

"It's fine," Sylvia assured him. Family photos on the wall tracked her progress up the steps. "What else did Wilson say about the move?"

"Just that he was a little worried about you and the boys because he said it was going to be pretty busy for the next couple of months." Joe paused. "Two young boys can be a handful. Fortunately I'm available for as long as you need me." He chuckled. "I work cheap. All you have to do is feed me. And I like everything."

"But your medical appointments—"

"Any medical care I need, I can get right here, Sylvia. More of my prescriptions are mail order now. And I have a list of referrals from my doctors."

Sylvia reached the landing. "That's great," she managed. "We're glad to have you—and the boys will be so excited when they get home from school and see you."

"I can't wait," Joe replied. "I brought them basketballs. I figure we can put that hoop in your driveway to good use."

The hoop had come with the house. To date, neither boy had been able to throw the ball high enough to play basketball, but Sylvia didn't point this out. "They'll love it," she assured him.

As they passed Wilson's office on their way down the hall they heard a pinging noise. "What's that?" Joe asked.

"It's from the computer," Sylvia replied. "That's the noise it makes when someone sends an e-mail."

The words were barely out of her mouth when the computer chirped again. It made noise several more times on the way to the guestroom. It was still making noise after Sylvia brought up the third suitcase and set out fresh towels for Joe.

Concerned that the machine was malfunctioning, she walked into the office. As she downloaded her e-mail, she was amazed to find she had eighteen new messages. This wasn't normal. She hardly ever got e-mail. But she was more puzzled than concerned when her gaze skimmed the messages and she saw they were all from people at Wilson's bank.

She hesitated. Was this spam or some new computer virus that would infect their PC if she opened up one of the messages? She peered more closely. None of the e-mails had attachments. All of them looked like replies to the calendar request she had sent Wilson.

Saying a quick prayer, Sylvia opened the most recent message. It was from Jen Douglas.

Skimming the content, she realized that Jen was asking her what Sylvia wanted her to bring to the anniversary party, which was surprising, because Sylvia hadn't invited her. She fought the panic building up inside. Had she somehow invited everyone in Wilson's office? And were all these other e-mails acceptances?

"Is everything okay?" Joe asked, walking over to her.

Sylvia had a terrible feeling as she gazed into his steady blue eyes. "I think I goofed," she admitted. "I was trying to schedule something on Wilson's calendar, but it looks like it went to everyone in his office." Sylvia cringed as she saw a reply from Wilson's boss. "What do I do?"

Joe peered over Sylvia's shoulder and studied the list of e-mails. He was a quiet for a few minutes and then straightened slowly. Placing his gnarled hand on her shoulder, he squeezed gently. "There's only one thing you can do," he said gruffly. "Start planning a party. A big party."

Chapter 20

They were hanging plastic eggs in the maple tree in the front yard when Wilson pulled the Beemer into the driveway. Cutting the engine, he sat for a moment taking in the sight of Sylvia in a pair of cutoffs, standing on a ladder straining into the branches of the tree. And then his gaze went to his father. Wilson hadn't expected him to arrive this early, but he was relieved to have his help.

On the lawn, Simon and Tucker were running around and scattering plastic eggs. Not scattering, he realized, but throwing eggs at each other. The eggs were so light, however, they were having trouble reaching each other, which both boys seemed to find hilarious.

Wilson was relieved to see Simon having fun. The boy had been so upset over the Pinewood Derby, but watching him now, it looked like everything was okay.

Stepping out of the car, Wilson walked onto the lawn. The boys spotted him and ran up to him. Crouching, Wilson braced himself as their combined weight slammed into him. If Simon hesitated a second longer than Tucker, it was only because Tucker was rougher and Simon probably didn't want to get in his way.

Holding the boys in a strong hug, Wilson straightened. Growling, he spun them around. They howled with laughter, and Wilson turned even faster.

"Do it again, Daddy," Tucker shouted as he set the boys on the ground.

"First I want to say hi to your Poppy." Wilson still couldn't get over that his father had taken it upon himself to show up so early—but then the day had been full of surprises.

Wilson had been in a meeting when Dale, a rangy, dark-haired kid from accounting, had poked his head into the conference room and asked Wilson if he should bring his swimsuit.

"What are you talking about?" Wilson had asked.

"Your anniversary pool party." Dale, only a couple of years out of college and as smart as they came, had grinned. "Your wife just invited everyone in the bank."

"Ha ha," Wilson had said. "Very funny." But when he'd returned to his office, he'd seen the calendar request Sylvia had sent out. He'd called her immediately, and although she had apologized and tried to explain everything, it still didn't change the fact that now they were entertaining everyone in his office and at a very critical point in the interview process.

"It's great to see you, Dad." Wilson hugged his father then drew back to study him. Shorter than himself, and with a neck fused into a persistent forward tilt, Joe nonetheless looked tan and healthy. His bald head was as freckled and glossy as ever. "You're looking well."

"Thanks, sonny boy," his dad said. "You look pretty good, too."

"Hi, honey." Sylvia stepped from behind his father. "You're just in time to put out Peter Rabbit."

Peter Rabbit was the giant Easter inflatable they stored in the attic. Last year it had consistently blown the fuse, and they had learned to limit the appliances they turned on when Peter was inflated.

"Just let me get changed," he said. "Wait until you see it, Dad, it's the most tacky thing you've ever seen."

"I saw it last year, remember?" Joe smiled at Sylvia. "It's fun, not tacky."

It didn't take long to retrieve the inflatable rabbit from the attic and then to stake it to the ground in the front yard. Everyone cheered when Wilson turned on the power and Peter slowly inflated until it towered above them all. Wilson glanced at Sylvia and felt something solid and strong and happy pass between them. It was Easter, a time of celebration and of rebirth. Some of the anxiety Wilson had been carrying around seemed to leave him. More than ever, anything, especially a new start, in a new town, seemed possible.

It was with this in mind that after dinner—a delicious meal of homemade lasagna, hot, buttery garlic bread, and a crisp salad—that Wilson asked Sylvia if she wanted to go for a short walk around the block. "I'm sure Dad won't mind watching the kids for a little while."

"Go for a long walk," Joe said and winked at the boys. "I'm thinking that it's time Poppy showed you how to build a proper tent in the game room."

The boys cheered.

"Just don't use the flat screen to anchor it," Wilson warned, and then he and Sylvia stepped out the door into the balmy April evening.

It was just getting dark, and lights had come on inside the neighboring houses. As they walked to the end of their cul-de-sac, Wilson reached for Sylvia's hand. "Are you upset about my dad showing up early?"

"No—not really. Not anymore." She paused. "I was at first because it sounded like you'd discussed the promotion with him and it was all settled that we were moving." She glanced sideways at him. "Are you mad about me inviting everyone at the bank to our anniversary?"

He laughed. "No. Actually, everyone's pretty excited about it."

"I know. Just about everyone is coming." They walked a few steps in silence. "I'm really sorry, Wilson. I meant for the invitation to be just for you and me. I hope this doesn't mess up anything about your promotion."

"It won't," Wilson assured her. "In fact, Bruce said he thought business entertaining was good for my image."

"Your image?"

"As a candidate for branch manager."

"Oh." Sylvia walked for a moment in silence. "So this promotion, it's going to happen, isn't it?"

"Maybe." He glanced at her sideways. "Hopefully. Jen saw my name on some organization charts."

"That's great."

Did she really mean it? They walked a moment in silence. Wilson debated telling her what else Jen said. It wasn't going to help his case if he told her Jen had been penciled in as assistant branch manager. On the other hand, he'd already made a mistake in waiting so long to tell her about his possible promotion.

"Jen's been slated for assistant branch manager," he said.

Sylvia didn't speak for a long moment. "At the new bank?"

"It's all still being worked out, but yes, that's the way it's looking."

"You really think it's a good idea for her to be your assistant?"

Although it was something Wilson had wondered himself, he found himself getting defensive. "What do you mean, Sylvia?"

"What do you mean, Sylvia?" She imitated the arguably pompous note in his voice perfectly. "I mean she's a single, attractive woman."

"You have nothing to worry about. I told you. You're the one I love. Besides," he added, "it isn't like this is set in stone. Now there's a guy competing with me from the Dallas office. He's got good credentials and is pushing hard." Wilson shook his head. "It's going to come down to who has the most support from the board of trustees."

"Well," Sylvia said, "they'd be idiots not to give you the job."

He waited, suspecting she had something else to say and wasn't wrong.

"But I still don't like the thought of you and Jen working together every day."

He sighed. "It isn't my choice. But so many things still can change. But you're right and I will suggest that she be given another position."

They'd come to the small park in their neighborhood. Although it was empty now, the swing set, jungle gym, and balance beam gave mute testimony to the presence of children in their neighborhood. Just behind a covered pavilion was a lake stocked with fish and turtles. Wilson himself had brought the boys here to fish, but when Simon had seen the hook, he'd flatly refused. They'd ended up feeding bread to the ducks.

"Don't you think we have a great life here?"

"Absolutely," Wilson agreed. "But we could have a great life somewhere else, too." He hesitated then plunged forward. "I've had the same job for years. And to be honest, I'm ready for a change. The boys are young. This is the time to do it."

Sylvia didn't say anything.

"It could be an adventure," Wilson added. "We could explore a new part of Texas, meet new people. . ." His voice trailed off as Sylvia continued to keep her gaze firmly fixed on the concrete pathway. "The economy is bad," he stated. "When we condense the two banks, there will be job cuts. I want to make sure I stay in a good position to provide for you and the boys."

"So you're saying your job might go away if you don't take this promotion?"

"I don't think I would get laid off," Wilson said, "but it wouldn't be a good career move to turn down this opportunity—if I get it."

"This new job," Sylvia said slowly, "would you have more time to spend with me and the boys?"

"Initially? Probably not," Wilson admitted. "This bank needs a total rehaul. I'm talking physical renovations, personnel changes, new technology—the operating systems are real antiques. The magnitude of the merger is enormous, Syl."

But so was the opportunity. It began to pour out of him then, all the information he'd been storing up, all the plans he'd spent hours forming. He wanted her to understand being a branch manager wasn't an ego booster, it was a chance for him to make a positive impact on a community. To turn something that was failing into something successful. Affect people's lives in a positive way. Build a legacy he could be proud of.

He talked for a long time, and when he finally finished, they had come full circle and were standing at the start to their street. He stopped walking, not wanting their time together to end without hearing he had her full support for the new job.

Turning, he tried to read her face. It was dark, but he thought she looked sad, as if she were digesting bad news. Maybe he was wrong, and it was just the way the shadows played across her face. He'd just given her a lot of information, and they had both been up since six that morning. He ran his fingers through his hair. "So what do you think?"

She shifted her weight, opened her mouth, and then closed it.

"What?" he pressed.

"It's great to see you so excited about something," Sylvia said. "But. . ."

"But what?"

"But I'm scared if you take this job, you're going to get sucked into work, and the boys and I are never going to see you."

"That's crazy. You and the boys mean everything to me."

Sylvia pinned a gaze on him that even through the semidarkness reached deep inside him. "When you talked about work, Wilson, your voice got really animated, and you went on for like twenty minutes straight."

"Because I wanted you to understand what the job means."

"I get that," Sylvia said. "I just wish you had the same enthusiasm for me and the boys." Her voice lowered. "You never talk about us like that."

"Of course I do," Wilson stated firmly. "You're just not around when I talk about you and the boys."

Sylvia shifted her weight and seemed to consider her words very carefully before speaking. "We're drifting apart, Wilson. Don't you feel it? There's your world and there's mine."

Drifting apart? Wilson leaned forward. What was she talking about? They had a great marriage. He shook his head. "No," he said. "We're not drifting apart. I love you."

"I love you, too, but the most excited you've been about spending time with me is when we were running for our lives from that wild pig."

Wilson almost laughed, but the sheen of tears in her eyes stopped him. "Sylvia, you mean everything to me. You are my total world."

"You say it, but it doesn't *feel* like it." She waved his hands away when he tried to reach for her. "It feels like I'm trying to talk to you, but you don't hear me."

Wilson pulled back as an unexpected rush of defensive anger swept through him. He had just shared his heart with her, and now she was mad at him because he wasn't listening to her? What about her listening to him? He heard the stiffness in his voice as he said, "What are you talking about?"

"Our family. Us. Have you really thought through what moving us will do?"

Wilson frowned. "Of course I have. I've checked out the schools and looked at some possible neighborhoods. I wouldn't ask you to go someplace where I didn't think you or the boys would be happy." He ran his hand through his hair and his fingers went unerringly to the small bald spot. "This promotion will mean more money, Sylvia. We could have a bigger house and take some great vacations. Plus there's college to think about. I know the boys are young, but we need to be saving now."

"I appreciate that," Sylvia said, "But maybe what we really want is to see more of you." She twisted her hands together. "I know you're working really hard. But. . .I miss you. I don't want to lose you—lose us."

He looked into her eyes and felt the anger drain away. She loved him, and this was all he'd ever wanted. The rest could be worked out. "You'll never lose me," Wilson promised. "You're stuck with me for life, and if I get this job, it'll be a better life." He paused to let this sink in. "This stuff we're going through right now—it's temporary. I won't always work these hours. They'll have to make a decision soon, and after they do, we'll talk and decide together what the best thing is for our family."

"And if it's staying here?"

"Then we stay," Wilson said, but then he couldn't stop himself from adding, "But promise me you'll see the town and look at a few houses before you decide. I think you'll really like it. There're parks for the boys and lots of restaurants and stores."

Sylvia put her hand on his arm and shook her head. "Let's just get through Easter, okay?"

"Okay, but how about a road trip the weekend after?"

"We're going to be busy getting ready for our anniversary party, which reminds me, now that it's a work party, I'm going to need help. I want to tell Andrea, Susan, and Kelly what's going on."

He thought for a moment. Sylvia did need help. Word was already leaking out at work. Although he preferred to wait before they let their friends know, he didn't see any harm. "That'd be fine as long as they know nothing is definite. Now what about house hunting? How about the week after our anniversary? We could bring the boys."

"And that's supposed to talk me into going?"

He laughed. "Okay. The boys can stay home with Dad. But will you at least look?"

"Yes," Sylvia said.

He heard the lack of conviction in her voice but decided it was something that would change once she realized how exciting this opportunity could be for them. Leaning forward, he kissed her lightly on the lips. "You won't regret it," he promised.

Chapter 21

The elementary school let out for a long weekend on Thursday afternoon. Anticipating an even longer car line than usual because of the holiday, Sylvia and Joe drove to the elementary school a half hour earlier than usual. Even so, the car line already backed onto the main road.

It took Sylvia ten minutes after school dismissed before they entered the school's parking lot. As they inched forward, Joe noticed the muddy ditch between the field and the building.

"The playground needs to be releveled," he commented. "Unless you've got a good drainage pipe, after it rains you're going to get a lot of standing water, which means mosquitoes, Sylvia. Mosquitoes carry West Nile."

"I know," Sylvia said. "We're fundraising for it. Wait until you see me in my Mr. Slice outfit."

Joe laughed. "I'm sure you look great." He kept his gaze fixed on the playground. "If I'm still here, I could help with the project. I'm not so old that I've forgotten how to be a good civil engineer."

Sylvia studied the back of his bald head. She wondered if she and Wilson would still live in this town long enough to see it happen. "That'd be great," she said.

They picked up Simon from the line of second graders, and then Sylvia pulled the minivan forward a few more feet and waited as Tucker disentangled himself from a group of boys. When she saw the birdcage, covered with a white cloth, she remembered they were getting another guest for Easter—Bluebonnet, the class pet.

"What you got there?" Joe asked as the doors to the minivan slid shut behind Tucker.

"Bluebonnet," Tucker said proudly. "I get to have him for Easter and write a story and take pictures about what he does at our house."

"Mrs. Chin is very big about reading and writing," Sylvia confirmed as she kept a slow pace with the car moving in front of them. "All the students get a turn taking Bluebonnet home. They keep a journal, and at the end of the year Mrs. Chin combines all the stories into one book with pictures."

"It's so cool," Tucker said. "Can I take a picture of Bluebonnet next to Peter Rabbit?"

He meant, of course, the giant inflatable Easter bunny on their front lawn. "I don't see why not," Sylvia said.

"Simon!" Tucker suddenly yelled. "Stop!"

Sylvia very nearly slammed on the brakes.

"I just want to see what he looks like," Simon said loudly.

"You can't lift his cover! Mrs. Chin said so!"

"I wasn't lifting the cover! I was looking underneath it."

"You'll scare Bluebonnet!"

"Maybe he's scared now and you just can't see it," Simon pointed out. "We should look and see if he's okay."

"Mom!" Tucker shouted. "Make him stop!"

"I'm just trying to help!"

"Simon," Sylvia said sharply. "Leave the bird alone. You can see him later, after he gets settled when we get home. Tucker, stop yelling." They picked up speed as they passed out of the school zone. "And don't forget," she added, because distraction was an essential part of resolving conflicts, "we have three dozen Easter eggs to dye."

"That means we get eighteen each," Simon calculated with impressive speed. There was a pause, and then he added, "Unless you or Poppy want to dye some. In that case it would be—"

"Plenty for everyone," Sylvia said.

"I'm going to dye one blue so that it looks like Bluebonnet," Tucker announced. "It'll look like he's laid an egg."

"He's a boy, Tucker," Simon pointed out. "Boy parakeets can't lay eggs." He hesitated a beat. "Can they mom?"

The way Simon's mind worked, Sylvia could almost predict her son's next question would be how baby parakeets were conceived. Out of the corner of her eye, Sylvia saw Joe grinning widely and guessed he thought the same.

"No they can't," she agreed, and put on her turn signal. "But boy parakeets can help take care of the eggs." She didn't want to raise boys who later in life wouldn't do their part in child raising.

"You mean sit on them and keep them warm?" Tucker exclaimed. "I wonder if Bluebonnet would do that if we put an egg in his cage."

"It'd be way too giant for him to climb onto," Simon said as they turned into the driveway. "It'd be like a chicken trying to sit on a dinosaur's egg."

"Then we could put a blanket over it," Tucker said. "That would keep it warm, wouldn't it, Mom?"

"Honey, there are no baby chickens alive in the eggs we buy from the store."

This silenced both boys from the topic of hatching chickens. Inside the house, Sylvia gave the kids a quick snack of sliced oranges and rice crispy treats. Afterwards, she cleared the kitchen table and Joe spread newspapers over the surface. With Bluebonnet unveiled from the cage cover, watching from his spot on the kitchen counter, Sylvia brought out two boxes of Easter egg dye and then placed two sets of bowls on the table.

Last year, the Easter egg dying session had ended with Tucker having a meltdown when Simon had mixed all the colors together and turned all the dye a muddy brown.

As the boys nearly climbed onto the table watching with interest, she poured water into the bowls, added vinegar, and the small, colored tablets, which immediate began to dissolve.

"Cool!" Tucker shouted as the dye began to dissolve and the bowls filled with an assortment of rainbow colors. "Can I get started?"

Simon already was stirring up the dyes with the thin metal loop for holding the eggs. The loop had always made Sylvia think of a magnifying glass without the glass, and as a child, she had held it up numerous times to look at the world through it.

"Can I have some extra bowls? I want to make some other colors," Simon asked.

Sylvia retrieved the cartons of eggs which she'd hard-boiled earlier and handed Simon four extra mixing bowls. She met Joe's eyes and smiled as the boys eagerly added their eggs to the dye.

Sylvia remembered dying Easter eggs in the cheerful red-and-white kitchen of her childhood. She and Tyler had spent hours bent over the kitchen table, dunking their eggs the darkest shade they could get them. By the time they'd finished, their fingertips had been stained a dark purple color.

She made a mental note to call her brother and wish him a happy Easter. It'd been ages since they'd spoken. Maybe this summer they could all get together—rent a house on the beach or choose a spot halfway between Washington and Texas. She didn't let herself dwell on the fact that they had been talking about this for years and it'd never happened. It'd been that way growing up, too, she reflected. Even then he'd seemed to have his own life that was separate from hers.

Joe nudged her. She followed the direction of his gaze and she watched as Simon pulled his egg out of a bowl of yellow dye. He had created an interesting, marbled effect by covering parts of the egg with his fingers.

"Hold on," Sylvia ordered. "I want to get my camera." She raced off to her bedroom for the Nikon. By the time she got back, all the bowls had eggs in them. Simon was furiously mixing colors like a mad scientist, and Tucker was proudly holding up a robin's-egg blue egg. He'd also gotten blue dye on his fingers, shirt, and eyebrows.

The kitchen table had taken several hits of spilled dye. Joe sat between the boys, happily coloring an egg. He had a smear of red dye on his cheek. Sylvia quickly snapped the picture. She kept taking shots until the boys started to protest and Joe proclaimed he was seeing spots from the flash.

"Come and sit down," he urged her. "Stop taking pictures of everyone having fun and have some fun. Life is too short not to take the time to dye an Easter egg."

Like Mary and Martha, Sylvia thought. A time to work and a time to sit and learn, appreciate the moment. She put down the camera and picked up an egg.

Sylvia decided to celebrate Good Friday with a nice dinner on the back deck. She knew Wilson was working and wouldn't be home until late. Joe, however, volunteered to grill the salmon, which was the only kind of fish the boys would eat. Sylvia made butter noodles and steamed asparagus. By the time Wilson got home, they were ready to eat.

Wilson gave the blessing, which Tucker interrupted with a mighty belch. Although he quickly apologized, Sylvia suspected Tucker had done it on purpose and pinned a look on him that said *"don't do that again."* He shrugged and tried to look innocent, but a smile hovered about his mouth.

The boys ate quickly—Simon loading up on noodles and picking at his fish, and Tucker eating a lion's share of everything. After they'd cleaned up, Wilson turned on the pool lights and the boys jumped into the water.

Sylvia, Wilson, and Joe settled back to watch. The air had cooled, but the pool was heated to eighty-two degrees. Neither boy seemed to feel the slight chill in the air as they splashed around, their skin glossy in the blue lights of the water.

"They're good kids," Joe said, settling deeper into the cushions of the padded chair.

"Most of the time," Sylvia agreed, watching Tucker spit water right into Simon's face through a long, Styrofoam pool noodle. "Tucker needs to learn more self-control."

Simon grabbed the pool noodle and turned it so that the water sprayed back at Tucker. Both boys laughed.

"Maybe we should be a little tougher with Tuck," Wilson said. "Give him more time-outs, or take away his television time."

"Oh he's fine." Joe waved his bony hand dismissively. "He'll grow up in time." He paused. "And he's very funny. I almost laughed when he burped when you were blessing our meal."

"Dad," Wilson said. "That's terrible. I'm glad you didn't encourage him."

Joe shrugged his thin shoulders. "When you get to be my age, you learn that laughter is a wonderful thing. It heals what hurts and makes you feel young."

"I'm glad it makes you feel that way," Wilson said, "but there's a line between funny and disrespectful."

This was true, and while Sylvia agreed with Wilson, she also appreciated Tucker's free spirit. She looked at Joe. It was dark now and he seemed very old and wise. "Was Wilson ever like Tucker when he was growing up?"

"He was a rule follower and a people-pleaser." Joe smiled at Sylvia. "When he was really young, he was a crybaby."

"Gee thanks, Dad, for making me sound so appealing."

"I'm only telling the truth," Joe said, sounding unfazed. "You were very sensitive, but also bright and loving. Alice always said you would make someone a great husband."

"And he does," Sylvia said, and winked at Wilson. "Most of the time."

"You can see," Wilson remarked dryly, "who Tucker takes after."

"I don't burp during the blessing," Sylvia pointed out. "But once I got a terrible case of the hiccups in church." She'd been in her

twenties, sitting next to her mother in the pew, and in the middle
of the reverend's sermon, she'd started to hiccup. Sylvia's timing had
been terrible—every time Reverend Thomas had paused, Sylvia had
filled the silence with an uncontrollable hiccup. This had given her
mother the giggles, which had given Sylvia the giggles and made her
hiccups even worse. Sylvia remembered her mother's face, flooded
with color, alive with laughter.

Sylvia had loved this about her mother—her ability to enjoy her
life and her faith. She took God seriously without ever taking life
too seriously. *I really miss you, Mom,* she thought. *I miss talking to
you—and I wish that you were here to see the boys grow up.*

"Oh for goodness sakes! You'll see me in heaven." Sylvia could
almost hear her mom's voice—half-assuring, half-scolding—as if
she couldn't believe Sylvia had any doubt at all. *"And until then,"*
this same voice said, *"you love those boys for me."*

Those boys meant Wilson, too. Her mother had adored him.
Sylvia looked at her husband, his eyes crinkling and his teeth bright
and even as he laughed at something Joe had said. He seemed more
relaxed than he had in ages, maybe because for once he wasn't sucked
into work.

"Have you given much thought about house hunting?" Joe
asked.

"Not really," Wilson said, exchanging a quick look with Sylvia.
"I'm still in the interview stage, Dad."

"It wouldn't hurt to take a look around," Joe said. "Springtime
is when most people put their houses on the market. You'd get the
best selection if you look now."

"Anyone want coffee?" Sylvia suggested, hoping to change the
topic, or at the very least remove herself from the conversation.

She started to rise to her feet but stopped when Joe said, "Please sit, Sylvia, there's something I've been wanting to talk to you both about. Something I've been thinking about ever since Wilson called me."

The serious look on Joe's face gave Sylvia a very bad feeling. Her mind flashed to her father-in-law's health. Last year when he'd visited them, he'd thought he was having a heart attack and Sylvia had taken him to the emergency room. Fortunately it had turned out to be indigestion. She hoped he didn't have cancer, just thinking the word sent a small shiver through her.

"I'm getting older and what time I have, I want to spend with you and my grandkids," Joe said calmly. "When Wilson talked about moving, I thought, why not move, too?" Joe looked from her face to Wilson's. "At first I thought about buying a house close to you, but then I wondered if you would be interested in looking for a house with an in-law apartment. I would be happy to help with the down payment and mortgage."

After a long pause Wilson said, "You want to buy a house with us?"

"I'm just throwing it out there," Joe said. A very slight defensive note crept into his voice. "As you're making your plans, it's something to think about." He patted Sylvia's hand. "I wouldn't be extra work for you, honey. I can cook, clean, and I'm pretty handy around the house." He smiled. "And you'd have a built-in babysitter."

"But Dad, what about Sugar Hill? You've lived there for thirty years—all your doctors are there." Wilson's voice sounded slightly strained, and he cast a definitely anxious look at Sylvia.

"I've gotten great reports from my cardiologist, my internist, my urologist, and my dermatologist. . .*and* my dentist. I'm sure they'll be glad to give me some referrals."

The gazes of both men turned to Sylvia. Joe, living with them full time? She hadn't seen that coming, and although she wasn't completely sure how she felt, she couldn't just squash the hopeful look in his eyes. Ignoring the way Wilson was trying to signal her with his eyes, she smiled at her father-in-law. "I think it's a great idea," she said.

"You do?" Joe beamed.

"Sylvia and I will need to talk more about this, Dad," Wilson said, and cast another look at Sylvia that clearly asked *"What in the world are you thinking?"*

Joe steepled his fingers. "Take all the time you want," he said gravely. He couldn't, however, seem to stop the grin that tugged and tugged then finally stretched into a wide smile. "I think this is going to be the best Easter ever."

Chapter 22

On Easter morning Rema, Skiezer, and their boys arrived a little after eleven. Rema was wearing a cream silk dress with a pale pastel pattern, and her dark hair was swept up in an elegant chignon. Leaning forward to hug her, Sylvia smelled the floral scent of expensive perfume. "You look gorgeous."

"So do you," Rema exclaimed. "That purple is great on you."

"Thanks," Sylvia said. It was one of her favorite dresses—sleeveless with a very slimming A-line shape. She'd paired it with the strand of pearls that Wilson had given her as a wedding gift and a pair of pearl stud earrings. Although the outfit wasn't new, just that morning she'd gotten several compliments at the early service.

She moved forward to hug Skiezer, which proved difficult, not just because he was six foot six and built like a linebacker, but because he was balancing a pie tin and a crystal bowl filled with fruit.

"Happy Easter," she said, and then she saw Connor and Liam behind him. Cookie, the Border collie, danced with excitement on the end of his leash.

"I couldn't leave Cookie in the cage on Easter," Rema said apologetically, pushing the dog down as it jumped on Sylvia to greet her. "I didn't think you'd mind if I brought him."

"Of course not," Sylvia said. "Cookie is part of the family. Aren't you, Cookie?"

The Border collie all but turned itself inside out wagging his tail and squirming all over as Sylvia rubbed behind his ears. Then the dog spotted Simon and Tucker and nearly exploded with joy. The dog loved kids and dragged Connor and Liam toward them. There was a chorus of excited voices and chaos as the dog managed to wrap the leash around them.

"Skiezer, Rema," Sylvia said as the kids untangled themselves and then raced up the stairs with the dog. "You remember Joe Baxter, Wilson's father?"

"Of course," Skiezer said. He was a tall man with a dark complexion, coarse features, and short, curly black hair. "I'd shake your hand, Joe, but you might end up wearing banana cream pie."

"That's no deterrent," Joe said, patting Skiezer's broad shoulder. "Banana cream pie is my favorite." He reached to take the tin from Skiezer. "Can I help you with that?"

"I don't know," Rema teased. "Can we trust you?"

Joe laughed and gave her a kiss. "Happy Easter, sweetheart."

"Happy Easter to you," Rema said. "Sylvia, where's Wilson?"

"Oh, he's in the backyard, finishing hiding the eggs. Joe and I stuffed about two hundred. Come on back—let's put those in the kitchen."

"And I ate as much candy as I stuffed," Joe said, shuffling along with her into the kitchen. "Sylvia got the good stuff—M&M's, Kit Kats, Three Musketeers—you name it. When I was a kid, we hunted hard-boiled eggs. My dad was so good at hiding them that come summer we'd be finding eggs all over the backyard—under bushes, in the garden, everywhere. Not even the raccoons would eat them. Nothing smells as bad as a rotten egg."

"You should try smelling Cookie's breath," Rema said, high heels clicking on the tile floor. "One whiff will knock your socks off. I don't know what that dog eats." Opening the fridge door, she shifted around a few items then gestured for Joe to place the pie inside.

"He eats the same food as us," Skiezer deadpanned.

Rema shot him a death look, and he laughed loudly.

Sylvia laughed and checked the food in the oven. The yam casserole needed about thirty more minutes, and the Honey-Bee ham, delivered yesterday, was warming nicely under its tent of foil. The beans were prepped, and the salads were ready except for the dressing.

Wilson came through the back door, kissed Rema's cheek, and exchanged hey man's and thumps on the back with Skiezer.

"Are we ready?" Sylvia asked.

"Yes." Wilson grinned. "I even put some eggs out on floats in the pool and hid the skimmer."

"It won't stop the kids," Rema predicted. "They'll find a way. Even if they have to swim out to get them." She turned to Skiezer. "Do you have the video camera ready?"

"What video camera?" Skiezer said, and then pretended it hurt when Rema hit him lightly on the shoulder.

Sylvia called up the stairs, "We're ready for the Easter egg hunt." The four boys, with Cookie in the middle, thundered down the stairs. Handing out baskets, Sylvia lined everyone up at the back door by age. Tucker, who was the youngest, went first, followed by Connor and then Simon. Liam went last.

The adults, in unison, gave the countdown, and then Sylvia opened the door. The boys and Cookie charged outside. For the next five minutes, it was like watching a family video in fast-forward. The boys zigzagged around the backyard—grabbing eggs from the flower beds, the crook of the palm trees, the deck chairs, and grass. Cookie ran around barking incessantly and trying unsuccessfully to herd the boys into one group.

The eggs on the floats were the hardest to reach, but Simon used the hose to create a current which brought the float close enough to the side of the pool for the other kids to grab. Wilson had placed a large nest of eggs on top, and the boys quickly divided them.

Afterward, the boys came inside and ran to the game room to count their eggs. Sylvia quickly parboiled the green beans and poured the lemon chive dressing over them. Wilson began carving the ham. Rema, Skiezer, and Joe set out the salads and filled the water goblets.

Finally Sylvia lit the candles and stood back in admiration. The mahogany dining table, which had been her grandmother's, and then her mother's, and now hers, had been expanded with the help of a card table so that it could seat everyone. One tablecloth hadn't been big enough, so Sylvia had bought two matching white linen ones at Target and then overlapped them. The gold-and-white Lenox china was from her wedding, as was the Waterford glassware. The centerpiece was a crystal bowl filled with the colorful eggs she and the boys had dyed. The table had looked like this when Sylvia was a girl, and her gaze lingered, remembering her mother bustling about, her father, handsome in his dark suit, asking everyone to join hands so he could give the blessing.

"Okay, everyone," she called, "come and eat."

Soon everyone was crowded around the table, on which every inch of space was covered with dishes of food. Voices overlapped in excitement, and then Wilson said, "Before we start, would anyone like to give the blessing?"

"I would," Joe said.

They all joined hands and bowed their heads. Sylvia gave Tucker a look of warning before she closed her eyes. And then Joe's gravelly voice began.

"Father, we thank You for this Easter Sunday—for the opportunity to be together to celebrate Jesus, who died for us, and then rose again, and taught us so much about love. Because when it comes down to it, the love of You, of friends and family—of all people, really—is all that matters. Please bless this food to our use, and us to Your purpose, and help us be ever mindful of the needs of others. In Jesus' name, amen.

"Okay, everyone," Joe announced, looking up and beaming, "dig in!"

Dishes were passed around and soon everyone's plate was piled high with slices of sweet ham, tangy green beans, honey apples, and herb-flavored new potatoes. The conversation ranged from the morning's sermon, to the unlikely chance of the Astros having a better season, to Skiezer telling funny stories about golfing.

Wilson caught Sylvia's eye. "I've been thinking that Sylvia and I should take some golf lessons."

She smiled back at him. "I don't know if that's such a great idea. Remember when we visited your brother in California and we played miniature golf? We were terrible."

"That was a long time ago," Wilson said. "And we weren't that bad."

"We had to cheat, remember? Hitting it out of the barriers and doing like a zillion do-overs."

"Only on a couple holes, Sylvia," Wilson said. "Technically we didn't cheat, we just took the maximum score and moved on. And the windmill one doesn't count."

"That one was the worst," Sylvia agreed, cutting off a small piece of her ham and enjoying herself tremendously. "It was like playing pinball. Every shot came right back at us. We had the whole course backed up."

There was twittering and laughter from the kids' end of the table.

"It was only ten people or so," Wilson said, "and we asked them if they wanted to play around us."

"Miniature golf is very different from real golf," Skiezer said. He began to explain but was interrupted by the sound of Cookie barking.

"That dog," Rema said. Standing, she folded her napkin on the table. "I'd better make sure he hasn't gotten at the ham bone. He's a genius at opening garbage cans."

"I'll go with you," Sylvia said. "It's just about time for dessert anyway. Anyone want some pie and coffee?"

There was a chorus of yeses. Sylvia followed Rema into the kitchen. She was calculating how many cups of coffee to make but stopped short as she saw Cookie. The dog was standing on his hind legs with his feet on the kitchen counter peering intently into Bluebonnet's cage. His nose was only inches away from the bars of the cage. Cookie woofed, and, as if shot by a gun, Bluebonnet dropped off his perch.

"No!" Rema yelled and jerked Cookie back by the collar. Sylvia raced over to the cage. Bluebonnet lay on his back with his stick-like legs clenched. He twitched once and then didn't move.

"Oh no!" Sylvia said. "I think he's dead."

"Hold on." Rema shoved Cookie out the back door and then rejoined Sylvia. Bending over Sylvia's shoulder, she studied the fallen bird. "Maybe he just fainted, and he'll come around in a few minutes."

Sylvia shook her head. "He's not moving. What are we going to do?"

"Don't panic," Rema said, but her eyes were wide. "Maybe we should poke him with something. See if he moves."

Looking around for something to prod the bird, Sylvia tried not to think about what would happen if Bluebonnet were actually dead. Tucker would be devastated—not to mention twenty-four other kindergartners.

She found a wooden spoon with a long handle and opened the wire cage door. She gently touched the prone parakeet. When Bluebonnet didn't move, she pressed the spoon against its chest in light, gentle pulses.

"What are you doing?"

"CPR," Sylvia said. "But it's not working, and it feels really gross." She definitely was throwing out this spoon afterward. "Rema, what are we going to do?"

"Press harder," Rema stated, leaning over Sylvia's shoulder. "That bird can't be dead. All Cookie did was bark at it."

Sylvia grimly kept doing the compressions with the wooden spoon. *Please, Bluebonnet, don't be dead,* she prayed. *Breathe.*

"Sylvia," Joe's voice startled her. Turning, she saw his bent frame standing in the doorway. "Is everything alright?"

Sylvia continued the CPR. "We don't know—Bluebonnet isn't moving."

Joe crossed the room to peer into the cage. "Holy smoke," he said. "That's one dead bird. What happened?"

"Cookie barked at him," Rema explained. "I think it gave the bird a heart attack." Her face creased with apology. "I'm so sorry, Syl."

"Sylvia, you can stop now," Joe said gently. "He's gone."

"He can't be gone," Sylvia said. "Mrs. Chin is going to kill me."

Joe pulled her arm. "Come on," he said gently. "Let him go."

Sylvia pressed the bird's chest one final time, and then stepped back. Sighing, she wiped her forehead with the sleeve of her shirt. She looked at the kitchen clock and thought, *Time of death: 2:11 p.m.*

"I'm so sorry," Rema repeated.

"It's okay. It wasn't your fault. We'll figure this out."

She was reaching for the cover to the bird's cage when the four boys ran into the kitchen. "Mom," Tucker said, "what's taking so long? We want pie!"

Joe stepped in front of the cage, blocking the view of the dead bird. "We'll be out in a minute, Tuck. All of you can go back to the dining room."

Immediately suspicious, Simon stepped forward and tried to see around Joe. "Why are you putting Bluebonnet's cover on his cage?"

"Because he's taking a nap," Rema answered for Sylvia. She was wearing a wide, and what Sylvia thought was an obviously fake, smile. "And we don't want to wake him."

Liam exchanged looks with his brother. "Can we look at him? I want to see if birds really sleep with their eyes open."

Sylvia couldn't bear the thought of the boys peeking into the cage and seeing the dead bird. "Later," she said. "Right now, we need to cut some big pieces of Aunt Rema's pie. Who wants to add whipped cream to the top?"

The distraction worked. The boys immediately went to the refrigerator and retrieved the can of whipped cream. As Rema cut the pie into generous pieces, the boys took turns shooting the whipped cream into their mouths and then onto the slices of pie. They didn't ask about the bird, and for this, Sylvia was grateful.

Returning to the dining room, Sylvia picked at her pie as the kids wolfed theirs down. She dreaded telling the boys about Bluebonnet. Neither of the boys had been old enough to understand when their grandparents had passed away, so this would be the first time they'd have to deal with death. She wondered how to tell them—and when. She didn't want to ruin their Easter. At the same time, she wasn't sure how long she could hold them off from peering into the cage.

She was still puzzling this when the boys finished dessert and asked to be excused. They ran upstairs, leaving the adults alone at the table. Pushing aside her unfinished dessert, Sylvia leaned forward. "Listen," she said quietly, although the boys were nowhere near enough to hear. "We have a situation."

Chapter 23

The men listened intently as Sylvia explained about the dead parakeet. When she was finished, Skiezer sighed in disgust. "I told Rema not to bring the dog today."

Although nothing changed in Rema's face, Sylvia sensed something inside her friend shrink. "Well it couldn't have been a very healthy bird if all it took was one little woof to kill it," Sylvia stated firmly. "It probably already had a bad heart. Maybe it was about to have a heart attack and Cookie was trying to warn us." She exchanged looks with Rema. "I've heard animals can do that. Sense death."

"We'll pay for another bird of course," Skiezer said. "But unfortunately you're still going to have to deal with telling the kids." He gave Rema a long, hard look. "I'm sure they're going to be very sad."

Rema squirmed visibly. "I'll go with you, Syl, and explain to Mrs. Chin what happened."

"And you should take that dog to obedience school. I've been asking you to do that for weeks." Skiezer turned to Wilson. "You wouldn't believe the hole he chewed in the Oriental rug my mother gave us."

"Maybe he wouldn't have chewed it," Rema said, "if it didn't smell so bad."

"What a minute," Joe said, leaning forward, his wrinkled face earnest. "Do you really have to tell anyone? Why not simply get another blue parakeet—one that looks like Bluebonnet?"

Sylvia sat up a little straighter. The idea had potential. But then Wilson said, "That's lying, Dad. We can't lie to the kids in Tucker's class."

"Are you kidding? We lie to kids all the time. We lie about Santa Claus, the Easter Bunny, the Tooth Fairy, and a lot of other things."

"This isn't the same," Wilson stated with firm conviction.

"Of course it is," Joe said. "The world is scary enough without having to deal with death so young." He kept his gaze level with Wilson's. "Do you really think Sam the Goldfish lived all those years?"

Wilson blinked slowly. "You lied about Sam?"

"You were a little kid. We didn't want you to be sad."

"Just how many Sams were there?"

"I don't remember."

Wilson shook his head. "I always wondered why Sam's color kept changing, but you said it was the drops you added to the water. I can't believe you lied to me, Dad."

"I protected you. Kids will have to deal with death eventually, but why traumatize them if you don't have to?"

"Because it's the right thing to do. What happened was an accident. Kids are tough. They'll deal with the truth a lot better than a cover-up."

"Not if it's a good cover-up," Joe argued. "But we need to move fast."

Wilson raked his hands through his hair and stared at his father as if he couldn't believe what he was hearing. "Dad," he said, "this isn't a goldfish. You're not going to find a bird that looks exactly like Bluebonnet. Even if you could, it wouldn't be right." He glanced at her. "Sylvia?"

She hesitated. "I don't know. Maybe Joe's right."

"You're siding with my father?"

"We need to think about Tucker. He's supposed to keep a journal. What's he supposed to do, write how Bluebonnet dropped like a rock when Cookie barked at him? You think that's going to go over well in story time?"

"I think you and Tucker should ask to speak privately with Mrs. Chin on Monday morning and explain what happened. She'll tell you how she thinks the situation should be handled."

There was a long pause at the table. Wilson's suggestion made sense, but Sylvia dreaded telling Tucker, and she especially dreaded telling his teacher. The last time Mrs. Chin had seen her, she saw her wrist bandaged, and Mrs. Chin had inferred that Sylvia needed therapy. Now she was going to have to admit they'd killed Bluebonnet over the Easter holiday.

Skiezer put his coffee cup down on the table and laced his large hands together. "What Joe says makes sense. One of the guys I golf with is an assistant manager at PetSmart. I say we give him a call, explain the situation, and see if he can help us."

"Excellent," Joe said. "If he has a match, we'll drive over and get it."

"Dad," Wilson said patiently, "I know you're trying to help, but you need to stay out of this."

"We're just finding out if it's an option," Joe said and gave Wilson a determined look. "So relax."

"If you feel strongly, I won't call," Skiezer said, steepling his large hands together. "But since we're replacing the bird anyway, we might as well find out if we can do it today."

"I think we should let him see if we can find another Bluebonnet," Sylvia said. "I'm kind of siding with Joe—I don't think it would be terrible if we swapped out the bird."

Wilson looked at her in disbelief. "Sylvia, we need to talk. In private."

Rema shot her a sympathetic look as Sylvia stood up. Joe squeezed her arm supportively as she moved past him. "Just whistle, honey, if you need me."

In the kitchen, he leaned against the counter and folded his arms. "Is this really how you want to handle this—lie to our children, the kindergarten glass, and Tucker's teacher?"

Sylvia shrugged. "Would it really be so bad to save a lot of kids some grief? And besides, what if everyone blames Tucker?"

"They won't," Wilson said firmly.

"You don't know that," Sylvia argued. "You have no idea what Tucker's world is like. You make these statements blindly. You go to the bank every morning. You don't understand how complicated the problem is or how hard it is to be a kindergartner these days. Kids can be mean, Wilson, and Tuck could get ostracized. This could affect his whole self-esteem."

"His self-esteem will be just fine."

She shifted her weight under his skeptical gaze. "Not everything is black and white, right or wrong."

Wilson folded his arms, and his face took on that awful blankness that it did whenever they argued and he was trying to hide that he was mad at her. "Trying to pass off another parakeet as Bluebonnet is just crazy," he said.

"Is it? How many years did you happily believe you owned the same goldfish?"

There was a long moment of silence. "A long time," Wilson admitted. The corner of his mouth softened. "And to be honest, it was a little traumatic finding out the way I did." He gave her a small smile. "Come on, Sylvia. You know Tucker is going to find out anyway. How will we look as parents then?"

Sylvia rested her hip against the side of the counter. "How about we compromise? We'll tell Tucker and Simon that we took Bluebonnet outdoors to clean his cage and the bird escaped. We'll say we saw him flying south—toward South America. The class could have fun making up stories about his adventures in Rio de Janeiro."

Wilson frowned. "Syl, I appreciate that you're trying to protect Simon and Tucker. But I can't get past the lying part. We need to deal with this head-on." He stepped closer to her and his face was kind and earnest. "They'll be better people because of this."

Sylvia still wasn't convinced. "If it were just our pet, I would agree. But Tucker has to face the whole class. Twenty-four faces are going to look at him like he's a murderer. Do you know how hard that's going to be?"

"They won't be looking at him," Wilson said. "They'll be looking at me because tomorrow morning, I'm going to school with you, and we'll talk to the teacher together."

Sylvia searched his eyes. "Seriously?"

"I have an eight o'clock meeting, but I'll go in a little late."

"And if Mrs. Chin says we can just tell the kids that Bluebonnet flew away, you'll do it?"

"We'll handle it however she wants. But we're telling our kids the truth."

She thought about it then nodded slowly. "Okay—but this might not be as easy as you think it's going to be."

He held her gaze. "Or as bad as you think."

Chapter 24

The next morning Wilson walked into the kindergarten classroom carrying the new parakeet in the cage. His head pounded from lack of sleep, and there was a snot stain on the lapel of his jacket where Tucker's nose had run during his last crying spell.

He hadn't gotten more than a few feet inside the classroom when a skinny, dark-haired boy with baggy shorts and T-shirt with a dinosaur on it spotted him and yelled with the enthusiasm of someone spotting a rock star, "Bluebonnet's here!"

Immediately Wilson was swarmed with kids who tried to lift the canvas cover and peer at the bird inside. He glanced at Sylvia, standing behind him and holding Tucker's hand. She motioned for him to keep going, but just before he did, he caught a glimpse of Tucker, whose face was as white as chalk. His son's blue eyes had the glassy expression of someone walking to his own execution, and he didn't return the smile of reassurance Wilson gave him.

Feeling like a giant, Wilson stepped around the kids and the miniature desks pushed into small clusters with their tiny chairs tucked beneath. The small sink in the corner looked as if he'd have to kneel if he wanted to wash his hands. He spotted Mrs. Chin at her desk in the back of the room and plowed forward with determination.

Their plan had been to get to school early and talk with Mrs. Chin before the other kids arrived, but then he'd seen Sylvia pull the minivan to the side of the road. He'd done the same with his Beemer, and then Tucker had had a long crying session.

It seemed like his younger son had been crying ever since he and Sylvia had broken the news about the bird. Tucker had cried through the funeral service—presided over by Wilson's father, who had read excerpts from Bluebonnet's journal.

That Tucker would spend the night in their bed hadn't surprised him, but Wilson hadn't expected Simon to walk into their room in the middle of the night, pale and shaken, because he'd thought he heard Bluebonnet pecking at his window to get inside. No amount of reassurance could convince him that it was only the wind and a branch.

Behind him, he heard Sylvia say, "Go hang your backpack up, Tuck. It'll be okay."

He turned in time to catch the stricken and slightly panicked look in Tuck's eyes. In that moment, Wilson fully forgave his father for lying all those years about Sam the Goldfish.

Mrs. Chin rose to her feet. "Good morning, Mr. Baxter," she said, and reached for the cage. "I see you brought back our little friend." Her gaze traveled past him. "And Mrs. Baxter—I'm so glad to see your wrist is all healed now."

About five feet tall, small boned, with bright brown eyes, Mrs. Chin seemed a little bird-like herself, and the comparison made

Wilson dread his mission even more. "Could we please talk to you privately? Maybe in the hallway?"

"Of course," she said. "Why don't we put Bluebonnet's cage on the counter so you don't have to keep holding it? Besides," she added, smiling, "I know the kids are eager to see him again."

Wilson returned the teacher's smile although he felt himself start to sweat. "I think the bird needs to come with us," he said.

Mrs. Chin pursed her lips and cocked her head. "Oh. Well, we can talk in the hallway."

Once again, Wilson had to thread his way around the cluster of kids who blocked his path and reached for the cage. It crossed Wilson's mind that there was still time to try to pass off the bird without telling anyone, but he squared his shoulders and reminded himself that if he lied now, Tucker would know it.

He waited for a quiet moment in the hallway, and then said, "I'm very sorry to tell you that there was an unfortunate accident at our house on Easter and Bluebonnet is gone."

"Gone?" Mrs. Chin repeated. "What do you mean, gone?"

Wilson glanced at Sylvia for support. "Gone," he repeated. "As in no longer with us."

There was a moment of silence. Mrs. Chin's silver eyebrows bunched together. "What are you talking about?"

"There was an unfortunate accident," Wilson repeated. "And Bluebonnet didn't make it."

"Didn't make it?"

"He's dead," Wilson said.

"What do you mean he's dead?"

"We think he had a heart attack," Sylvia said. She touched the teacher's thin arm. "We're so sorry."

"Oh." Mrs. Chin's mouth turned down. A look of reproach came into her brown eyes. "What happened?"

Wilson shifted his weight. Out of the corner of his eye, he could feel Sylvia looking at him. He quickly explained about the accident and finished by saying, "Of course we can't replace Bluebonnet, but we thought the kids would handle it better if they had a new friend to meet."

Mrs. Chin drew back the cover and looked at the bird inside. "Well," she said, letting the cover drop, "these things happen."

"We're very sorry," Sylvia said. "Tucker knows what happened, but we've asked him not to tell anyone until we talked to you—to see how you wanted to handle it."

Mrs. Chin took off her glasses, cleaned them on the side of her denim jumper, then replaced them. She looked very disappointed in him. "The class will have to be told of course."

"Yes," Wilson agreed. "But what?"

"That Bluebonnet flew away?" Sylvia suggested in a hopeful tone of voice.

Mrs. Chin shook her head. "I'd rather handle this head-on. It's a tragedy, but it's also a learning opportunity." She was silent a moment then said, "We'll have story time first thing this morning. I'll help you, but you need to answer their questions."

"I'll be glad to answer them," Wilson said, both relieved and impatient. He already was late to an important strategy session with Bruce.

Moments later, he stood with the leaves of a plastic palm tree tickling the back of his neck. Mrs. Chin sat next to him in a rocking chair with the class clustered at her feet. On the other side of the teacher, Sylvia's mouth had a tight, pinched look. Tucker looked like he might throw up.

"Class. . ." Mrs. Chin began.

Wilson found himself thinking of Sam and how much he'd loved that fish. Whenever he walked over to the glass bowl, the fish had recognized him and swam as close to him as the space would allow. Based on all the entries in Bluebonnet's journal, he knew the kids in this class had felt just as strongly about their class pet. He felt himself tearing up a little as Mrs. Chin told the class that Bluebonnet was dead.

He swallowed hard and braced himself as twenty-five sad faces stared at him. A few girls and one of the boys began to cry and were quickly whisked away by Sylvia and Mrs. Chin, leaving him with the rest of the class.

Wilson tugged at his necktie. He wasn't sure what to say, and the silence felt awkward, yet he was afraid of what would happen next. He especially avoided Tucker's eyes.

"Do you have any questions?" he managed. In the back of the room, Sylvia was hugging a girl who was sobbing.

"Did his eyes bleed?" a boy asked, and a roar of outrage rose from the rest of the class. Before Wilson could begin to think about answering it, another boy asked if Bluebonnet might have broken his neck in the fall off his perch. Another asked how he knew Bluebonnet really was dead, and not just in a coma, like a person he'd seen in an episode of *House*.

Another wanted to know if Bluebonnet's body was in the cage Wilson had brought with him—and if he could see it. This made another girl cry. The girl sitting cross-legged next to her began to stroke the crying girl's hair.

Had Cookie been punished for killing Bluebonnet? Why hadn't

anyone in class been invited to the funeral; would there be another? Did Wilson believe in bird heaven? The questions came fast and furious, on top of each other. In a matter of moments he'd lost control. He looked for help, but Sylvia and Mrs. Chin were busy comforting other children.

Wilson's armpits grew damp. He'd faced difficult customers, gone head-to-head with peers, and even won some arguments with upper management, but in his entire career he'd never had an audience like this. Waving his arms, he tried to get everyone quiet long enough to answer their questions. "Raise your hands," he said calmly. "If you want me to answer your questions, you have to be quiet."

It wasn't easy, but he finally managed to get their attention. Quickly he explained how Grandpa Joe had read from Bluebonnet's journal at the funeral service and how it would be up to Mrs. Chin if there would be another. No, the dog hadn't been punished. And yes, Wilson believed that God took care of all the creatures He created in life as well as in death.

He was mentally and physically exhausted by the time they left the classroom. Walking back to their cars, he turned to Sylvia. "Dealing with kids is hard—whatever they pay Mrs. Chin, it isn't enough."

"Morning, Wilson," Jen said, looking up from her cubicle as he walked past. "Mr. Maddox said to send you right in."

Wilson had hoped to grab a cup of coffee and take an Advil before he faced his boss, but the look in Jen's eyes told him that

Bruce was in one of his moods, and the sooner he met with him, the better.

He tightened his grip on his computer bag, squared his shoulders, and told himself whatever Bruce wanted couldn't be as bad as what he'd just faced at the elementary school.

Inside Bruce Maddox's spacious corner office, his boss was standing in front of a dry-erase board, scribbling notes.

"Good morning," Wilson said.

Bruce kept writing. For a long moment he didn't even acknowledge his presence. Wilson remained standing. He wasn't often late, and he'd had good reason.

"Nice of you to join us," Bruce said, turning slowly. "We had an eight o'clock mandatory strategy meeting with the legal team. I needed you there."

"I'm sorry," Wilson said. "I hope you got my message that I had a family emergency."

Bruce leaned heavily on his cane as he crossed the space to his desk then eased himself into the leather chair. "Sit," he ordered, and when Wilson did, Bruce gave him an expression that was known to make junior employees spill their guts, and more senior ones squirm.

"Family emergency," Bruce prompted as Wilson neither blinked nor spoke. "Are Sylvia and the boys okay?"

"They're fine. The problem is under control now."

Wilson sensed the older man's curiosity, but his boss wasn't the kind of person who was going to be very sympathetic when Wilson explained that he'd skipped an important meeting because of a dead parakeet.

"What happened to your finger?" Bruce asked.

Wilson glanced at the gauze wrapped around his index finger and wondered how his boss would react if he told him that it'd happened when he'd introduced "Bluebell" to the class. Attempting to show how friendly the new bird was, he'd opened the cage door and offered it a treat. The bird had bitten him so hard on the finger that it'd bled. He'd had to use every ounce of self-control not to scream.

"It's nothing," he said. "Tell me about the meeting."

Bruce pushed a paper toward Wilson. "Why are you suggesting that we shut down our main server during business hours?"

For the next hour, Wilson explained about the upgrades to their existing system, which would improve their security as well as enable more functionality, especially online banking applications.

With the need to shut down the server also came an increased need for additional software funds, and although Wilson had already had this discussion with Bruce, he had to go over again the cost of the additional software licenses that would be needed.

It was almost noon by the time they'd gone over everything, and there was still one more thing on Wilson's agenda. "I met with Hovers almost two weeks ago. I thought our meeting went well, but I haven't heard anything. Have you gotten any feedback?"

"Yes," Bruce replied. "He had a few concerns."

Wilson's heart dropped to his shoes, but he managed to keep a straight face. "About what?"

"Your lack of management experience." Bruce laced his fingers together. "He's actually contemplating giving Ken Drivers another chance."

Ken Drivers? Wilson couldn't believe the board would even consider keeping the current branch manager.

"Hovers thinks it would promote stability and keep morale high if they keep him on." Bruce paused. "Plus there wouldn't be any moving expenses."

That was the bottom line—the cost of relocating Wilson and his family. Wilson thought for a moment. He wasn't about to argue anything that would threaten his ability to provide financially for Sylvia and the boys. "Drivers has also nearly driven that bank into the ground. What the board needs, Bruce, is someone new— someone with fresh ideas and an ability to drive profit."

"I totally agree," Bruce said. "However, McKensy's plan for turning around that bank is significantly less expensive than yours."

"Maybe short term," Wilson said, "but I guarantee my long-term outlook has more potential."

Bruce took a sip of coffee and shrugged. "Bottom line, you need more face time with these guys. You need to show them that you have people management as well as technical skills." He held his hand up as Wilson started to argue. "You don't need to convince me—but you need to convince them. And the more they get to know you—both socially and professionally—the better. I think you should invite them to your party next Saturday."

Invite the board? "With all respect," Wilson replied, "wouldn't it seem strange to invite a group of people to my anniversary party when I've never met most of them?"

Bruce waved his bony hand. "This is how it's done at this level, Wilson, and everyone understands. Frankly, they're looking for someone willing to make bold moves—someone who isn't afraid of bucking convention and going after what he wants. You think McKensy hasn't been entertaining them on the golf course and at the country club? You want this job? You're going to have to fight for it."

Wilson frowned. "You make a good point." He fought the urge to tug at his tie which had grown tighter by the minute. "I'll speak with Sylvia."

Bruce leaned back in the chair. "Tell her a formal event would be best. Hire a caterer—Jen will give you some names. No backyard barbeque for these people. They expect something catered and classy—something befitting a future branch manager."

"I see," Wilson said, allowing a small amount of sarcasm to slip into his voice. "I'll hire a string quartet and make sure they play only classical music."

"Excellent," Bruce said, not getting his joke at all. "In banking—like life—perception is everything."

Wilson started to argue that he should be getting this promotion based on merit, not on image, but then Jen buzzed and Bruce dismissed Wilson with a wave of his hand.

Back in his office, Wilson studied the picture of Sylvia smiling at him from a dark wood frame on his desk. She wasn't beautiful in the classic sense, but he found the smattering of freckles across her nose and cheekbones, the breadth of her smile, irresistible.

He felt bad about the morning—he hadn't realized, honestly, how traumatic telling the class about the bird would be for Tucker. And he hadn't anticipated that his boss would want to micromanage their anniversary party. She deserved better.

When all this was over, and the job was his, they'd do something really special to celebrate their anniversary. With a good bonus, he'd be in a position to give her something really nice.

Powering up his computer, he logged onto the Internet. He looked at a pair of diamond and pearl earrings, but when he tried to picture her wearing them, they seemed much too fancy.

A new car might be nice, but the minivan was in great shape, and besides, Sylvia really wasn't into cars. What would she like? She loved reading, but he couldn't very well give her a book for their anniversary.

He wanted something that would thrill her, make her realize how much he loved and appreciated her. Something romantic— that would make her think of him and not those guys on the covers of the romance books she read.

He wanted, literally, to take her breath away, and suddenly he knew exactly how to do it.

Chapter 25

On Tuesday night, Sylvia drove to Susan's house for what had become their weekly review of the Proverbs Plan. Susan lived across town, in a patio home off the back end of a golf course.

Cars already filled Susan's driveway when she arrived, so Sylvia parked on the street. She sat in the car for a moment. Her friends probably would think the whole mess-up with the anniversary dinner invitation was funny. And it was—but it was also ironic that the harder she tried to make something right, the more things seemed to go wrong. Like this possible relocation. She really needed to talk to them about it. At the same time she dreaded it.

Walking up the concrete pathway flanked with a variety of flowers and fragrant-smelling herbs—all planted and tended by Susan—Sylvia reminded herself that there would be positive things about moving. That dreading things was often worse than the actuality of them. That she should keep perspective. Plenty of people were struggling with far worse issues.

She didn't knock—Susan would lecture her if she did—and

stepped inside a cozy foyer with soft, wheat-colored wall-to-wall carpet and walls the color of honey. Sylvia smelled something warm and chocolaty and resonated with the sound of laughter coming from the kitchen.

"Hello, dear," Susan said, meeting her in the foyer. She kissed Sylvia's cheek. "How are you?"

"Dying to try whatever smells so good," Sylvia said, stepping back with a smile.

"They're chocolate cupcakes with cream filling and caramel fudge icing," Susan said, leading her deeper into the house, where Rema, Andrea, and Kelly were standing around a brown granite island. "I'm baking them for the Meals Ministry at the church—but I made extra, for us."

"And they're great," Andrea said. She looked as if she'd come straight from the courthouse, in an immaculately tailored gray dress with a black belt and cute black cardigan with ruffles. Her high heels put her just shy of six feet, and with her edgy, short haircut, Sylvia imagined her winning every case based on her impeccable style.

She greeted Rema and Kelly, and for the next thirty minutes the women sipped peach iced tea, ate cupcakes, and caught each other up on their Easter holiday.

Kelly, unfortunately, had been on call and spent Easter Sunday in the operating room where she'd taken out a ten-year-old's appendix and then assisted on a surgery repairing a fourteen-year-old's spleen.

Susan and her husband, Dan, whose children were older, had spent their holiday volunteering at a local shelter. Andrea had both sides of the family over for Easter dinner—an event, she admitted, that would not have gone over very well without the help of several bottles of wine.

When Sylvia and Rema recounted their day, the other women whooped with laughter, especially when Sylvia described giving the bird CPR, Joe's solemn eulogy in the backyard, and the grilling Wilson had taken at the elementary school.

"I'm telling you, Wilson has a whole new appreciation for how hard it is to deal with kids," Sylvia concluded, setting her glass down on a coaster.

"So your father-in-law's here," Andrea said, pouring herself more tea and looking at Sylvia with concern. "He's staying with you for how long?"

Sylvia hesitated. The question was more complicated than Andrea realized. A lot depended on whether or not Wilson got promoted and they relocated—a conversation, she admitted, they were both tiptoeing around. "I don't know. He's pretty sweet though, so it isn't a big deal."

"It's going to be very hard to put the romance back in your marriage if he's there," Andrea said flatly. She fingered the long strand of pearls at her neck. "No matter how nice he is, he's still Wilson's father, and men tend to regress whenever their parents are around."

"That's so true," Rema agreed, sitting up a little straighter. "When Skiezer is around his parents, all he wants to do is please them. He practically forgets I'm alive—unless he wants me to do something for them. 'Can you take Mom to Walgreens? Can you drop off my dad's dry cleaning?' et cetera, et cetera." She dropped a crumpled wrapper into the garbage can. "But the good news is that when his family comes, he barbeques like a fiend and we eat like kings until they're gone."

This was true. Sylvia and her family had been invited to these feasts more than once and had seen the enormous platters of meat

Skiezer grilled. Thanks to Skiezer's cookouts, the boys knew exactly what *carnivore* meant.

"I still think having your in-law around is going to put a damper on the Proverbs Plan," Andrea said. "Will he be gone by your anniversary?"

Sylvia stirred the contents of her glass. "No, but it isn't going to be a problem because there isn't going to be any romantic dinner by the pool."

"What?" Kelly frowned. "I thought you were going to talk about finances and then plan a romantic getaway weekend." She looked at Rema in confusion. "Did I miss something?"

Sylvia shook her head. "No. I messed up. Wilson's been trying to get me to use an electronic calendar, but when I tried to schedule the date on Outlook, I hit the wrong button on the computer," Sylvia said, "and a sent a request to everyone in Wilson's office."

Everyone laughed. "Couldn't Wilson just explain it?" Andrea asked. "And un-invite everyone? Ten years is a big anniversary. I'm sure everyone would understand."

"It's a long story," Sylvia said.

"Why don't we get comfortable?" Susan suggested, and steered them into the adjoining family room.

It was a small area, comfortably filled with a matching, overstuffed floral couch and love seat; two club chairs, slip-covered in a pastel pink color; and a plain pine coffee table. Family photos sat atop a plain white mantelpiece, and an older-looking bookcase held an assortment of knickknacks, books, and more photos.

The plump couch seemed to hug her as Sylvia settled into the cushions. She set her iced tea on a coaster and wondered where to begin.

"Before we start," Susan said, "I think we should pray." Everyone joined hands. Sylvia bowed her head and closed her eyes.

"Heavenly Father," Susan began, "You are good and holy and everything that is right in our lives. We praise You for Your infinite love and wisdom. As we gather here tonight, we ask that You be among us—to help us understand Your Word and enable us to help Sylvia, and also to help ourselves to have better marriages. We ask this in Jesus' name, amen."

Sylvia kept her eyes closed. She let the reminder of God's unconditional love ease her mind. How many times had her mother whispered as she kissed Sylvia good-night, *"God loves you, Sylvie, as I do."*

God has this, she thought, *so why am I worrying so much?* She opened her eyes and looked at the beautiful faces of her friends and suddenly knew exactly where to begin. The words came quickly, and it was a relief to let everything out.

"So after the anniversary, I mean business party," Sylvia concluded, "we'll probably start getting the house ready to put on the market. But you have to keep all this confidential. Wilson doesn't actually have the job."

"Well, maybe this other guy, McKenny, will get the job," Rema said.

"McKensy," Sylvia corrected gently.

"Wilson's a genius," Andrea said. "He'll get the job. I just wish you didn't have to move, Sylvia. We'll miss you so much."

"I'm not gone yet." Sylvia forced a cheerful note into her voice. "Maybe the board of directors will hate us. Wilson says that we need to put on a classy party—hire a caterer and serve pâté or something fancy." She shifted on the couch. "It doesn't sound like us at all, but

Wilson really wants us to make a good impression."

Kelly regarded her with thoughtful green eyes. "In Atlanta, my parents used to do a lot of formal entertaining. I hate to see you go, Sylvia, but I'll help you with your party, if you want."

"I know you're super busy," Sylvia said. "I couldn't impose on you."

"It won't be hard," Kelly replied. "It's mostly getting organized and hiring the right people to do the actual work. Let me talk to my mom—I'm sure she can hook us up with a good caterer. Do you have a budget in mind?"

Sylvia shook her head. She and Wilson were doing pretty well, but it wasn't like they could afford an expensive party. "I haven't gotten that far yet. Wilson is still waiting to hear back from the board of directors before we get our final numbers."

"Why does Sylvia even need to hire a caterer?" Rema asked. "We're talking, what, fifty people at the most? We could help her—just like we were planning on doing when it was just she and Wilson."

"What a great idea," Susan exclaimed. "I could easily do the desserts and the flowers."

"Skiezer could do the meat." Rema looked at Sylvia. "I know Wilson said no barbeque but even great chefs like Bobby Flay use the grill. Everybody loves Skiezer's bourbon-glazed chicken and marinated filets. We'll put him in a chef's hat and no one will know that he's really an IT manager."

As Sylvia's mind raced with the possibilities, she heard Andrea add, "I don't cook, but I can make a great fruit punch. Non-alcoholic of course. You can borrow my crystal punch bowl."

Sylvia smiled. "Thanks, Andrea." One of Wilson's best friends in college had died as a result of drinking and driving. Although Wilson hadn't been at that party, even now, more than twenty years later, it still affected him. He never wanted to be responsible for putting someone on the road who might have had a little too much.

"You guys are so sweet to even consider helping me with this party," Sylvia began, "but I'd rather have you come to the party as my friends than as caterers."

"Don't you see, Sylvia," Rema began, "that as much as you've tried to be the Proverbs 31 wife, this is an opportunity for us to be the Proverbs 31 friends. This is our 'go' time. You're our sister, Sylvia. We love you. Let us do this."

Sylvia's throat filled as Rema's words were met with murmurs of agreement from the other women. "We can make it so much more personal," Susan added. "And we'd love to help."

"I'll get my mother's recipes for some appetizers," Kelly volunteered. "Plus I've got a lot of pretty Ironstone serving dishes you can borrow." She looked at Susan. "The pattern has navy blue, orange, and white. Can you make some floral arrangements with those colors?"

"Absolutely."

Andrea turned to a fresh page in her legal pad. "Okay," she said, as if everything had been agreed upon. "We'll make a list and divide up the work."

Chapter 26

It was a little after nine o'clock when Wilson got home. Unlocking the door, he stepped into the foyer. The minute his feet hit the hardwood, he filled his lungs with a deep breath of cool, clean, *home* air. Exhaling, he could almost feel himself shrugging off the last vapors of *bank* air.

The sound of china clanging caught his attention. He spotted Sylvia partially hidden behind the dining room table. She was sitting on the rug and pulling their good china out of the sideboard.

Placing his computer bag on the ground, he walked over to her and kissed her. "Hey honey, what are you doing?"

She looked up at him and smiled. "Inventory."

He glanced at the stacks of gold-and-white serving pieces on the floor beside her. They'd used these at Easter, and he couldn't imagine why she needed to count them now. "Why?"

Sylvia reached deeper into the sideboard and began pulling out white dishes edged with a floral design. They'd never used these plates, but he recognized them as ones they'd inherited from Sylvia's family.

"We're going to need a lot of china for the anniversary party," Sylvia explained. "Here, honey, would you start stacking these on the dining room table? I need to know how many place settings we have."

He set a stack of plates on the wood surface. "I don't think you're going to have enough of either pattern."

"I know," Sylvia said, handing him more plates. "We're going to mix and match."

He hesitated, because she had said this with conviction, as if she already had some kind of plan. "But honey," he said, "shouldn't all the plates be the same pattern?"

Sylvia handed him yet another stack of heavy china. "They don't have to match, Wilson. It'll give our party more charm if we mix the patterns. Kelly has some lovely Ironstone—her parents did a lot of formal entertaining in Atlanta. She's going to show me how to pull everything together. You'll see once we get the right linens."

Wilson shifted his weight. "That's nice, Sylvia, but I don't want this party to look like we've hit a tag sale and picked up a bunch of mismatched china pieces. Bankers like things that match."

Sylvia stopped pulling things out of the sideboard and looked up at him. In her favorite denim shorts and T-shirt from a vacation in Corpus Christi, she looked exactly like the girl he'd married ten years ago. Only that girl had looked a lot happier than the one sitting here now.

"Trust me, Wilson," she said, "this is going to work. You'll like the result."

He rubbed his temples wearily. All the stresses of the day—all the meetings he'd held, all the problems and deadlines and challenges he'd addressed—seemed to return to him like a hundred homing pigeons flapping their wings in his face and fighting for space on his shoulders. He wanted to shoo them all away, shoo this conversation away.

"I don't want this party to be a lot of work for you," he said, congratulating himself for coming up with a reason she couldn't possibly object to. "Seriously, Sylvia, you have my total support to hire a caterer. That way you can enjoy the evening more."

"Don't worry," she assured him. "Andrea, Kelly, Susan, and Rema are going to help me. Susan will do the floral arrangements, Andrea will handle the beverages, Kelly will lend us china. And Skiezer is going to grill for us."

It was the last part that broke him. With his boss's warning not to let this event turn into a backyard barbeque, Wilson felt his stomach knot. "Sylvia, this party. . .it has to be right. We need to make the right impression."

"We'll make a great impression," Sylvia promised. "You look tired. Want some dinner?"

"No." He thought hard. "I think we're envisioning two different parties. I'm not talking hamburgers and hot dogs. We're entertaining some very high-level people. They're used to a certain standard."

Sylvia got to her feet slowly. Under the chandelier lights he saw the spark in her usually soft brown eyes. "What are you saying, Wilson, that our friends aren't good enough to help us throw a party?"

"Of course not," he said, backtracking rapidly. "I just think we should get professional help." When she didn't reply, he added, "I don't want it to look like we can't afford to hire a caterer and have to rely on our friends. It's an image thing, Sylvia."

"Is this how it's going to be from now on? How we look is more important than who we are? We have friends willing to help us. That's a blessing, not a liability."

He sighed. "I'm talking one evening, Sylvia. Would it be so hard to do it the way I want?"

She shook her head. "No, it wouldn't. But. . ."

"But what?"

She looked into his eyes. "You're changing, Wilson, getting swept up in work—in being someone else."

Wilson frowned. "That's just plain wrong. I'm not changing. I'm just asking for you to be conscious that my boss's bosses will be coming to our house. I'm not going to get another opportunity like this." He shook his head, increasingly convinced that he was right. "I really don't know why we're arguing about this."

"We're not. Not anymore." Shutting the door to the sideboard gently, she gave him an angry look. "I'll look into a caterer," she said. "But you are changing. You just don't see it." With her back ramrod straight, she left the room.

He'd won, but it gave him no pleasure. Wandering into the kitchen, Wilson pondered the contents of the refrigerator then closed the door. He really wasn't hungry. Maybe he had been a little too critical of Sylvia's plans, but she was definitely out of line saying that he was changing. It stung that she would think that, think the worst of him. All he wanted was to give them a better life and maybe help some other people along the way. Why couldn't she see that?

Still, he didn't like it when Sylvia was mad at him. Truthfully he didn't know a lot about parties and entertaining. He'd grown up solidly middle class, and the most formal it got was Christmas dinner.

Maybe there was a compromise. Sylvia and her friends could

handle the party with the help of a caterer. He even had one in mind. Jen had given him the name that very afternoon.

He was about to head upstairs and tell her when his cell rang. The Caller ID told him it was Bruce, and he fought the urge to pitch the phone into the garbage. These late-night calls had to stop. He punched his boss's call over to voicemail. Whatever it was could wait. Yet when the phone rang for the second time, he found himself less annoyed and more concerned. Computers failed all the time, maybe the server had crashed with the new upgrades.

Holding the cell to his ear, he ignored the voice in his head that warned him these calls would only get worse if he became branch manager.

Chapter 27

A few days later, Sylvia knelt beside Joe at the edge of the kidney-shaped flowerbed in the front yard. Digging a hole into the packed earth with her trowel, she then reached behind her for a purple-and-white pansy from one of the flats she and Joe had bought earlier at Home Depot.

"Whenever Alice and I sold a house, we always planted seasonal flowers," Joe said. "People like flowers. It makes a house look happy."

"Our house is going to look very happy." Sylvia patted dirt around the new plant and moved a few inches to her right to dig another hole. She and Joe might have gone a little overboard—they'd stuffed the minivan with flats of pansies, baby's breath, orange poppies, and ornamental grass. They'd also bought brightly colored hibiscus plants for the backyard.

"Have you given any thought to house hunting?" Joe asked.

She glanced sideways at him, but his head was bent, making his profile unreadable. "Not really," she said. "We're thinking of just getting through this party." She stuck another plant in the ground.

"What do you think of floating candles in the pool and hanging paper lanterns in the trees? Is that classy or tacky?"

"Classy," Joe instantly replied. "You know, if you want to go house hunting with Wilson, I'd be glad to mind the kids."

"Thanks, Joe, I appreciate that." She sat back on her heels. "You know that we're not saying anything to the kids about moving until we're sure we're really going, right?"

His face was as innocent as a monk's. "Oh sure," he said. "I just thought it might not hurt to look—that way when you're ready to pick a house, you'll already be familiar with the area."

It made sense, and Sylvia remembered her promise to Wilson to check out the new town. "That'd be great," she said, "but I really can't see that we'll have time before the party." She dug around a small root from one of the nearby oaks. "It might be a couple of weeks before we go."

"No problem," Joe said. "I've completely cleared my schedule— canceled my medical appointments and had my mail forwarded." He reached for another plant. "You know, I've been looking around the house, and I was sort of thinking that it could really use a new paint job. Potential buyers like neutral colors. I saw it on HGTV."

Sylvia stopped digging. She liked the granny smith green they'd painted in the kitchen and sunny yellow in the family room. Maybe the red was a little bright in the dining room, but it was cheerful.

"Thanks, Joe," she said. "But I think we'll just leave the paint for now."

"Then how about I get started on the closets? I couldn't help noticing they're really packed. I guess before we do that though, we should make some space in the attic. You've got a lot of boxes up there."

Sylvia sat back on her heels and dusted some of the dirt from her hands. The attic was jammed with stuff—she'd stored a lot of items that'd been in her parents' house that she couldn't bear to get rid of. And there were the boys' childhood things up there—boxes of artwork they'd done in preschool, old toys, their crib, and even that toy horse on springs.

"Thanks, Joe," she said at last, "but I kind of feel like I've got my hands full right now with this party."

"Then I'll definitely put caulking the bathtubs at the top of my list. You don't want to get a water leak."

"I appreciate you want to help, but you don't have to work all the time."

Joe took his time arranging a plant in the hole. "I know," he said. "But I like to feel useful. That's the worst thing about retirement, Sylvia, not feeling useful."

They worked in silence for a moment, and Sylvia thought about what he'd just said. "You still have a lot to give, but it doesn't have to be manual labor," she said. "You know that, right?"

"Oh sure," Joe said casually. "But it's best to stay busy." He stuck a plant in the ground and patted the soil around it. "So I was checking the stickers in your minivan the other day. You're due for an oil change. How about after lunch I take care of that for you?"

Sylvia noticed the shine of sweat and the color beginning to stain the top of Joe's bald head. She put down her trowel. "We'll see," she said, purposefully vague. "I could use a break. How about we go inside and have some iced tea?"

Joe stood up. He was a little wobbly so she steadied him with her arm. "Go slow," she said.

"It's the knees," he said. "They get stuck, but I'm fine now." But he patted her hand as if he liked it on his arm. "By the way," he said, "you have a few prescriptions in your medicine cabinet that have expired. You should throw them out."

Sylvia nearly stopped short. He'd been snooping! In her bathroom!

As if he read her mind, Joe smiled a little sheepishly. "I was looking for an aspirin," he said. "And you weren't around."

After lunch, Sylvia left Joe relaxing on the couch and headed for the grocery store. She was planning on making stuffed chicken breasts and salad for dinner, but as soon as she turned toward the downtown area, her brain started craving something sweet. On impulse she pulled to the shoulder of the road, pulled out her cell, and dialed Rema.

"You feel like meeting at Spoons? I'm dying for some frozen yogurt."

"Give me ten minutes to put on my face," Rema said, "and I'm there."

Something in Sylvia seemed to lighten as she neared the quaint, downtown area. Although past the lunch hour, the sidewalks were busy with shoppers, and she had to circle the square a couple of times before she was able to find a spot. It was a short walk to Spoons, and the door jingled in a welcoming sort of way as she stepped into the air-conditioning.

Rema wasn't far behind and soon swished into the store. She was wearing a short, black skirt of a stretchy material and a tunic top clenched around her middle with a skinny black belt. As usual, her heels were high, her makeup flawless, and big gold hoops dangled from her ears. "I'm so glad you called," she said, greeting Sylvia with a hug. "I was just putting away the Easter decorations and thinking of you."

"I still need to do some of that," Sylvia said, wrinkling her nose. "But I really needed to get out of the house. I'm supposed to be grocery shopping, but I had this sudden craving for something yummy."

"Skip Krogers. You can always make spaghetti," Rema said.

"That's true," Sylvia agreed. Spaghetti was always her "go-to" meal and she always kept extra sauce in the freezer. She liked that Rema knew these things about her.

They walked over to the counter and paused in front of the array of toppings. Sylvia sighed at the tubs of gummy bears, Reese's Pieces, and M&M's. "I'm getting an extra-large," she said. "How about you?"

Rema laughed. "Oh please—as if you have to ask."

They picked up their bowls and headed for the long wall with the shiny silver handles holding back containers of various flavors of homemade frozen yogurt. After circling the choices several times, Sylvia settled for the white raspberry chocolate. Rema favored the peanut butter and fudge. After piling the toppings on high, they paid for their treats and took a seat at a small table for two near the front window.

"This is amazing," Sylvia said, as the frozen yogurt melted in her mouth. "I don't even care how many calories I'm eating or if it goes immediately to my hips."

"It's too bad we can't choose where the fat goes on our bodies," Rema mused and took a bite of her frozen yogurt.

"We'd all look like Barbies."

"And eat like pigs. Somewhere I hope some female scientist is working on this rearrange-your-fat pill."

Sylvia laughed. "It's supposed to be what we look like on the inside that's most important."

"In that case, we're fine." Rema scooped out a generous portion of her dessert. "We should go back for seconds."

"It is good, isn't it?" Sylvia agreed, spooning up just the right amount of Reese's Pieces on her next mouthful. "Can you imagine working here? I would eat them out of business."

Rema smiled. "Either that or you'd get so sick of it that you wouldn't go near it." She licked her spoon clean. "So you going to make me ask you what's bothering you?"

Sylvia looked up. "Why does something have to be bothering me for us to have a yogurt together?"

"Because you always crave something sweet whenever something upsets you. Now, is it something with the boys, Wilson, or Joe?"

Sylvia smoothed the top of her yogurt. Darn her friend for always being able to see right through her. But then, wasn't that why she'd called Rema in the first place? She took another bite of yogurt and swallowed it slowly.

"Tell me it's not that bird, Sylvia."

Sylvia shook her head. "No—that's working out okay." She toyed with the yogurt. "It's nothing big, but last night Wilson and I had a fight—we're hiring caterers now to help with the party—and then this morning. . ." She sighed. "Joe started talking about all the things that needed to be done before we put the house on the market, and then he told me that I had expired aspirin in my medicine cabinet—he said he was just looking for something for a headache, but—"

"He was snooping!"

"In the closets, the attic, and apparently all the bathroom medicine cabinets." She swallowed more yogurt before it turned any mushier. "It's hard to get mad at him though. He's so sweet—honestly I think he just wants to help so we won't make him leave."

"Snooping is not helping. It's meddling. How much longer is he staying?"

Sylvia hesitated. She was pretty sure Rema was about to give her a huge lecture when she told her Joe would be moving in with them. Although outwardly Rema got along well with Skiezer's parents, she also stressed out with each visit, getting frequent headaches and escaping to Sylvia's house as often as she could. "We haven't set a date."

"Maybe you should. Better yet, have Wilson talk to him about going."

Sylvia shook her head. "He doesn't want to go home. He's so lonely there. He wants to feel useful."

"Remember last time he stayed with you? How he pretended to get sick just so he could stay longer? This is a new strategy." Rema's lips tightened. "You'd better be careful or the next thing you know he's going to want to move in with you."

Sylvia kept her gaze on the green peanut M&M melting into the volcano she'd made in her dish.

"Good grief, Sylvia. Tell me you haven't already agreed to let him move in?" When Sylvia didn't reply, Rema leaned forward. "You and Wilson will *never* have any alone time if he does."

Would that be such a bad thing? Sylvia looked up. "You know, when we started the Proverbs Plan, that's what I thought I wanted—more of Wilson. I thought if he would just love me enough, it would make everything okay." Sylvia pushed a gummy worm around in the mush in her bowl. "Now I'm beginning to wonder if it would be enough. Maybe what I want is something that Wilson can't give me."

Rema's brow furrowed. "Sylvia, what are you talking about?"

"I'm not really sure," Sylvia admitted. "It's just. Oh, I don't know. This whole move is making me look at my life a little differently." She swallowed a spoonful of melting yogurt but barely tasted it. "When we move—and even if we don't—maybe I should think about going back to work. The boys are in school full-time now, and they don't need me as much as they did when they were younger."

"If anything, I think they need you more," Rema stated firmly. "The issues they face get more complicated as they get older. Every time I talk to my sister she tells me how the classes not only get harder, but also there's always some mean kid or friend drama going on. And the whole issue of dating and drugs comes into play much earlier than you think."

"That's true," Sylvia agreed, "but even so, during the day, I can't help them. Right now I can still volunteer in the classroom, but I know that changes. Once the kids hit third or fourth grade, the teachers don't want moms in the classroom—Kelly and Andrea can vouch for that. All they want is someone to change out the bulletin boards in the hallways."

"You're on the PTO," Rema pointed out. "That's the most influential organization in the school." She pointed her spoon at Sylvia. "And that's a lot of kids, especially Simon and Tucker. Don't think your involvement doesn't factor when the school is assigning students to teachers."

Sylvia shook her head. "I don't think so," she said. "I mean, it isn't like I'm a bigwig. For Pete's sake, Rema, I go to classrooms dressed like a slice of pizza."

"And you raise money, Sylvia. Schools need money."

Deep inside Sylvia thought Rema made a good point. Mrs. Chin had been teacher of the year last year, and Simon's teacher, Mr. Powanka, had just received some kind of state award for a science project he'd done with his class. Had volunteering contributed to getting those assignments?

"Besides volunteering," Rema continued. "You're there when Simon and Tucker come home from school. You hear about their day and help with their homework."

Sylvia thought about this. That quick ride home in the minivan was an ideal time to get the boys to talk about their day. Somehow, being together, but not making eye contact, gave the boys the space they needed to open up to her. And although Simon needed no extra help from her with his homework, Tucker had to be monitored or else he'd get distracted and the assignment wouldn't get done.

"Other moms do it," Sylvia pointed out. "They have a job and they run the family and everything turns out fine."

Rema wiped her mouth with a napkin. "It can be done," she conceded. "But is that what you really want?"

Sylvia sighed. "I don't know anymore. It was boring working at the bank, but I liked the people." She'd taken maternity leave with the idea of going back after Simon had been born, but from the moment they'd placed him into her arms, she'd known that he needed her more than anybody in the world. Fortunately Wilson had punched some numbers and figured out a way for them to do it financially.

"We're a dying breed, aren't we?" Rema traced a manicured finger with bright pink polish along the top of the table. "Every day our numbers get fewer. Someday there'll be an exhibit at the museum, or the zoo, and a plaque that reads, 'STAY-AT-HOME MOM.' "

"I hope not," Sylvia said. "I mean, I respect working moms, but I'm glad I was able to be home with Simon and Tucker. It's just now—I'm in kind of a funny place. I don't want to just sit around and wait for the kids to come home from school, but I'm not sure if I'm hirable anymore; or if I am, what I'd do."

Rema fiddled with one of her hoop earrings. Her brown eyes were large and serious, and Sylvia could see that her friend knew exactly what she was talking about.

"First," Rema said, "you're not the kind of person who sits around. Think about all the work you do right now, watching the kids, chauffeuring, cooking, cleaning, et cetera, et cetera. If you worked full-time, who would do those things? Second, and most importantly, you'd miss a thousand moments with the boys that you'd never get back. Is that what you really want?"

"Of course not. I don't want to give up a moment with the boys. But now they're in school all day." She sighed. "Do you ever think about what happens when our kids get older and they don't need us to drive them to lessons or soccer games or their friend's houses? What are we supposed to do then? Everyone will have moved on, but we won't have."

Rema looked a little sad. "You don't know that," she said. "You're looking way too far into the future. For Pete's sake, Sylvia, Tucker is still in kindergarten. You have practically a lifetime with him and Simon. Why worry about this now?"

Sylvia spooned what was left of her semi-melted yogurt and then let it slide off her spoon. "Because if Wilson gets this job, everything is going to change."

Rema leaned forward. "Okay, sometimes I do think about the future. It's really scary, thinking about Skiezer retiring, being home full-time, and driving me crazy. But then I tell myself that when that time comes, something else will happen. Some other door will open. Raising a family is a good job, Sylvia, and will lead to other good things. I don't think God is going to put us out to pasture just because we focused on our kids."

"I know you're right, but I don't want to end up alone."

Both women looked up as the store door jingled and a woman with short white hair, crisp khaki slacks, and a pink sweater set walked into Spoons. She had deep, sad lines engraved in her face. Sylvia's gaze followed her to the front counter then to a table. Obviously she was alone.

The touch of Rema's hand on her arm made her jump. "Stop staring," she whispered. "She isn't you from the future."

Sylvia leaned forward. "How do you know that?"

"Because you and I are going to be little old ladies going out for frozen yogurt together and then complaining about our husbands who are either parked in front of the television or out golfing."

Sylvia sighed. "But what if I move?"

"Then we'll just have to drive farther for our ice cream. But Syl, does Wilson know how you feel about leaving?"

"Sort of," Sylvia said. "But I feel like his mind is made up. He feels like as long as our family is together then that's a home and it doesn't matter where we live."

"That's because he won't have to replicate his world. He'll go to work and come home. He won't have to deal with the million things that you'll have to figure out." She sighed. "Well, it isn't over yet, Sylvia, so don't lose hope."

Sylvia just looked at her.

"There's still the anniversary party," Rema said. "And one more chance for Wilson to see that he's got something here—something worth every bit as much as that promotion."

Chapter 28

On Saturday morning, Sylvia awoke to the smell of bacon. She blinked and looked at the clock. Eight o'clock. She hadn't slept that long in ages—why hadn't Tucker woken her up at six like he always did? She automatically glanced at Wilson's side of the bed. It was empty.

Suddenly the bedroom door cracked open, and Tucker's small face peeked around the corner. "She's awake, Dad," he whispered.

Moments later, the door swung fully open. Three Baxter males with beaming faces carried a huge tray of food into the room. She looked from Tucker to Simon to Wilson, speechless. What was going on?

"What day is today?" Wilson sang the question in a hearty baritone.

"Today is Mommy Day!" The boys sang in a much higher pitch than their father.

Sylvia sat up in bed. "Wilson, this isn't Mother's Day."

Wilson helped the boys lower the tray onto her lap. "I know, this is Mommy Day, a new holiday."

"We made you your favorite breakfast," Tucker exclaimed.

Sylvia glanced down. The tray held a huge plate of scrambled eggs and bacon. There also was a mug of coffee, orange juice, an apple, half a banana, a container of vanilla yogurt, two slices of toast, a bowl of cereal, and a doughnut. It was enough for several Sylvias, and she looked up a little suspiciously.

"You guys," Sylvia began, "what's going on?"

Wilson sank onto the edge of the bed and kissed her forehead. "We're giving you the day off—so think of something you really want to do and go do it!"

Simon bounced onto the bed. Sylvia barely lifted the coffee cup in time before it sloshed into the cereal. She couldn't save the eggs, however, from a splash of orange juice.

"I helped make the eggs," Simon informed her with a huge grin. Climbing over the hills of her legs, he finally reached the top of the bed and kissed her head. She smelled the other half of the banana on his breath.

"I made the cereal," Tucker declared.

"You can't 'make' the cereal," Simon pointed out.

"Well I poured it," Tucker said proudly.

"And you did a great job," Sylvia said. She kissed the top of each boy's head and breathed in their shampoo and little-boy smell. Was there ever a scent so pleasing to the heart?

"We all helped with the bacon," Wilson added. "It's crispy, just the way you like it."

"I still don't understand." Sylvia looked at Wilson. "This is great, but what's going on?"

Wilson's face didn't flinch under her direct gaze. "You've been doing way too much for everyone else. Today, you're supposed to relax completely. The boys and I are getting haircuts and then running some errands. We'll be home around four o'clock."

"But Wilson," Sylvia protested, "we have a lot of work to do around the house to get ready for the party."

"You can make me a list and I'll make sure everything gets done. It's time you had a day off. Boys, kiss your mommy good-bye."

"But where are you going?" Sylvia wished the tray wasn't holding her captive in the bed. "I'll go with you."

"Dad and I have this. The only thing I want you to do today is relax. Go shopping, or get a massage."

"But Wilson," Sylvia protested, "I don't need to do that." Since when was he suggesting massages? "I'll go with you and we'll run by the caterers. I want to show you the linens I picked out. . ."

Plus they'd hardly seen each other all week. Didn't he want to spend time with her?

Wilson shook his head. "You need a day off—we'll see you later."

"I love you, Mom." Tucker leaned forward to kiss her. "Can I have a piece of bacon?"

"You've already had enough." Wilson pulled the slice from the boy's hand and replaced it on Sylvia's plate. "I'll have my cell turned on if you need me."

"Simon?" Wilson prompted.

"Bye, Mom, love you."

Before Sylvia could utter another word, they ran out the door. For a moment she sat regarding her breakfast and listening to the absolute silence in the house. They really were gone, she decided, which was totally unlike Wilson. The more she thought about it, there had been something funny in his eyes when he'd looked at her—maybe he was happy to have time off from her. The boys to himself.

She picked up her fork and poked at the scrambled eggs. Unless he could grill it, Wilson wasn't very good in the kitchen, which meant that Joe probably had made the eggs.

She nibbled a bite of Cap'n Crunch cereal—Tucker's favorite. She imagined his small hands pouring the cereal and then eating the pieces he spilled.

Wilson and the boys had brought her breakfast in bed before, mostly on her birthday or on Mother's Day, but on those occasions, they'd sat on the bed and kept her company as she ate. Although she knew she should appreciate having a day off, she couldn't help but feel a little abandoned, and a little hurt that Wilson had so casually dismissed her offer to accompany them.

She pushed the tray aside and climbed out of bed. She had a million things that needed to be done before next Saturday's big party. The new flowers in front needed watering, and there were additional plants for the containers around the back deck. The outdoor furniture needed scrubbing and its cushions washed. Plus she really should go up in the attic and look for an additional punch bowl. There was menu stuff to go over, more shopping lists, and she really needed to swing by and pick up the Ironstone dishes from Kelly.

All these things, and more, needed to be done, but as Sylvia carried her tray of food back into the kitchen she found herself puttering around the room, half-heartedly clearing and cleaning while all the time wondering what Wilson, Joe, and the boys were doing.

"Frank's Dry Cleaners, Exxon, Sterling Optical," Joe read aloud. "Walgreens, Wilkerson Animal Clinic, Krogers."

Wilson tightened his grip on the steering wheel. Did his dad really have to read every store sign in sight?

"Panda Express, Exxon, CVS."

"Dad, I'm hungry," Tucker announced.

"You just ate breakfast," Wilson replied.

"Well, I'm hungry again. Can we get something to eat?"

"Sam's, PetSmart, Old Navy. . ."

"Dad." Wilson silenced his father with a quick sideways look. Thankfully Joe stopped reading aloud.

"There's the barbershop," Simon yelled from the backseat. "You just passed it!"

"Hang a U-ey," Tucker advised from the backseat. "But look for cops first."

Joe burst out laughing. "Where'd you hear that from?"

"Aunt Rema," Simon replied. "Once she and Mom made a U-turn and a cop was right there."

"And Aunt Rema said, 'Holy shooting match,' " Tucker exclaimed loudly.

"Tucker James Baxter! Watch what you say!" Wilson ordered, casting a dark glance at his father who was not even trying to hide his grin.

"Why aren't you turning around, Dad?" Simon asked. "We just passed the barbershop."

"We'll hit the barber on the way home," Wilson said. He would get the boys haircuts, but that had just been a cover story.

"So what happened when the cops pulled you over?" Joe asked.

"Oh, Aunt Rema explained we were on our way to the hospital to visit her sick aunt, so the cop let us go."

Wilson shook his head. He didn't approve of the lying, but it was a funny story. He exchanged grins with his father. "They're like Thelma and Louise."

"Who are Thelma and Louise?" Simon asked.

"It's a pop-culture reference," Wilson explained. "Maybe some-day you'll see the movie."

They drove farther down Old Elm Street. "Where are we going?" Simon asked.

"You'll see. We're working on a surprise for your mother."

"What surprise?"

"For our anniversary." Wilson glanced at him in the rearview mirror. "So everything we do today is top secret, okay?"

"Right!" The boys yelled in unison.

Wilson turned to his father. "You're up for babysitting, right?"

"Absolutely," his dad agreed.

"Why can't we come on the trip?" Simon asked.

Wilson nearly laughed. "How do you know we're going on a trip?"

"Because Poppy wouldn't have to babysit us if you weren't going somewhere."

"It could be just for a few hours." Wilson enjoyed challenging Simon's mind.

Simon was silent a moment. "If it were only for a few hours, it wouldn't be this big secret."

"You're right," Wilson said. "But that's all I'm going to tell you for now."

Something small and hard pushed into the small of Wilson's back. "Tucker, are those your feet on the back of my seat?"

The boy giggled. "Yeah."

The pressure on his back increased. "Quit it!"

Tucker's restless feet drummed against the back of Wilson's seat again. "I'm really *hungry*."

"Then you should have eaten more breakfast," Wilson said calmly. "And quit kicking the seat." Maybe it was nothing more than the power of suggestion, but suddenly Wilson's stomach began to rumble as well.

"Mason Street, Crossway Boulevard, Tannager."

"Dad," Wilson said a little impatiently, "I thought you were going to stop that."

"I'm not reading the names of stores anymore," Joe replied a little smugly. "These are street signs."

Wilson released his breath slowly. A quick check of his watch informed him he'd been on the road less than fifteen minutes. How was he going to make it all day?

His father's watch beeped. Great. Now he'd have to find someplace to stop so his dad could take his pills. Dad always insisted on taking them with orange juice and a few crackers or cookies. However, his dad merely pressed a small button on his watch to turn off the noise and said nothing.

After a moment, Wilson couldn't stand it anymore. If his dad really needed to take a vitamin or something, maybe he should say something. "Do we need to stop, Dad?"

"Not unless you want to."

"But what about your pills?"

"Oh, I'll take it later," Joe said. "Don't worry about me."

Wilson shot him a quick look to assess the validity of this statement. All he saw was the side of his father's head. The rest of his face was turned in the direction of a cluster of store signs.

"But if you need it. . ." Wilson prompted.

"I'll be fine," Joe said. "That looks like a new office building over there. Do you know what's going in it?"

"No," Wilson said. "You can't just skip taking pills, Dad. It isn't good for you."

"It was just a vitamin, Wilson, so you can relax."

Wilson wondered if his father was telling the truth or just trying not to cause trouble for him. His dad was in pretty good health, but Wilson knew he took medicine for arthritis and a thyroid condition. There might be others, too.

Ahead, the ubiquitous sight of golden arches caught his attention. "McDonald's," Wilson read aloud, sounding, he knew, exactly like his father.

"McDonald's!" three voices shouted in unison.

Without an argument, Wilson put on his blinker, and a cheer went up from the backseat. He smiled. A quick snack wouldn't hurt.

"I want a Happy Meal," Tucker yelled. "A Chicken Nugget Happy Meal."

"It's too early," Simon informed him with the air of an older brother happily imparting superior knowledge. "They're still on breakfast."

"Billions and billions served," Joe read.

"Hot cakes then," Tucker announced. "A Hot Cake Happy Meal."

Wilson pulled into the drive-through and studied the menu. A cup of coffee sounded good, hash browns, because he loved them, and a sausage biscuit because as long as he was here, he might as well.

While he waited his turn, he thought about Sylvia and hoped she was enjoying her day off. Valiantly he tried to ignore the argument in the backseat, which seemed to revolve around the existence of a Hot Cake Happy Meal. Finally, it was his turn to order.

A garbled noise came out of the order box. When it stopped, Wilson gave his order and then turned to his father. "Okay, Dad," he said, "what do you want?"

"Bacon, but ask if they have turkey bacon," his father said, "and an English muffin, but only if it's whole wheat, and butter on the side. Make sure it isn't margarine. Orange juice, with pulp if possible, and oh, and I guess I'll have one of those apple cinnamon Danishes."

Wilson dutifully repeated the instructions, wondering if his voice sounded as garbled to the operator as hers did to him. He then placed Simon's order for an Egg McMuffin meal with apple juice, and then last, but not least, he remembered Tucker's order. "And we'll have an order of flapjacks with butter and syrup. Orange juice, too." As soon as he finished, a chorus of laughter erupted from the backseat.

"What?" Wilson looked over his shoulder. "What's so funny?"

"Flapjacks," Tucker repeated, laughing.

"They're not *flapjacks,*" Simon informed him in a voice that struggled to be serious. "They're ho. . ." He tried manfully to control a laugh as Tucker hooted wildly. "Hot cakes."

"Whatever they are, you're going to be wearing them in a minute if you don't stop laughing," Wilson told them. He couldn't believe that something as simple as calling pancakes flapjacks could be so funny.

He pulled up to the cashier's window. A young lady who looked about twelve years old despite the nose piercing and heavy black mascara took his money and handed them their drinks.

"Here's your food," she said for the first time in an audible voice. "Enjoy those *flapjacks*, sir."

Simon and Tucker squealed with such delight that Wilson couldn't help but join in. Handing his father the large paper bag with their food, he swung out of the parking lot.

With a cup of hot coffee in the cup holder and the smell of a sausage biscuit wafting through the air, Wilson felt his spirits improve. He listened to the contented silence of three Baxters eating, and smiled. Hopefully there would be no more feet pummeling his back or recitation of road signs.

Sylvia's minivan purred along under him, not quite as sweetly as his Beemer, but with more than adequate acceleration and handling.

He adjusted the air-conditioning. At nine o'clock, already the temperature had reached the eighties. It'd probably go as high as ninety, and as he turned to comment on this to his father, he realized that they were about to miss the street he wanted.

Making the split-second decision, Wilson turned hard. To its credit, the van leaned into the turn. As it hugged the road, the boys shouted, "Oooooh!" and then, "Aaaahhh!"

"Sorry about that," Wilson apologized as the road straightened. He shot his father a quick look of assessment. "I didn't mean to take that corner so fast."

His dad had his cup of orange juice raised high in the air as if he were making a toast at a dinner party. Some of it had dribbled down his arm. "Are you crazy?"

As Wilson tried to come up with a reasonable explanation, his father added, "That was *great*!"

A chorus of cheers erupted from the backseat. "Yeah, Dad, that was so cool," Tucker shouted. "Can we do it again?"

"No, son," Wilson replied, knowing beyond a doubt that if Sylvia heard he'd nearly put the van on two tires, she'd kill him.

"Can we go back to McDonald's then?" Tucker asked.

"We were just there," Wilson pointed out.

"But I need more maple syrup," the five-year-old explained.

"You have plenty."

"*Had* plenty," Simon corrected with a note of unmistakable glee in his voice.

"Too much sugar is bad for you." Wilson reached for his package of hash browns. They were a little soggy from spilled coffee. "Right, Dad?"

There was a long pause, then his father laughed.

"Dad?" Wilson had a very bad feeling. A quick glance revealed his father looking over his shoulder into the backseat.

"You might want to pull over, son."

Wilson let his breath out very slowly. He knew he didn't want to know why he needed to stop the car.

Unable to contain himself a second longer, his oldest son yelled out, "Tucker's wearing his *flapjacks*, and there's maple syrup all over the backseat."

Wilson groaned.

"Mom's going to kill you," Tucker cried out happily. "She never lets us eat sticky stuff in the car."

Wilson clenched his jaw and assimilated this new information. Things weren't going as planned, but he was a man on a mission, and this mission had to be completed in a matter of hours. He couldn't let himself get discouraged by this minor setback, not when so much needed to be accomplished. Just ahead he spotted the solution and put on his blinker.

"Where are we going?" Simon asked.

"The car wash," Wilson replied.

"Are we washing the car?" Simon asked.

"Yes," Wilson agreed, "but that's not all."

Chapter 29

Sylvia spent the morning working on the pool. She emptied the strainer baskets then got into the water to scrub down the tiles and the volcano rock on the waterfall. As she worked, she knew Wilson would be mad at her—she was supposed to be taking the day off—but it seemed a waste of time to pamper herself when so much needed to be done.

At lunchtime, she made herself a peanut butter and jelly sandwich and ate it at the kitchen table, all the while trying not to imagine four Baxter men all having a great time without her.

Just get busy, she ordered herself. She did a quick vacuum, threw in another load of laundry—did it ever end?—and then looked around her somewhat clean house for something else to do. She read one of her romances until it was time to put the clothes in the dryer, but was too restless to go back to her book. She thought about what else needed to be done, and although she disliked the answer that came to her, she headed upstairs and opened the door to the storage room just off Wilson's office.

It was a room the real estate agent had told them could be converted into another bedroom if they wanted, but she and Wilson had always used it for storage. Now, looking at the piles of stuff, she realized Joe was right. They had accumulated way too much.

She'd seen enough HGTV to know the ropes—things needed to be sorted into three piles: keep, donate, and throw out. It would be a big job—but today was perfect to get started. Without the boys or Wilson home, she could sort through things at her own pace, be sentimental—even cry without anyone knowing.

Promising herself chocolate as a reward, Sylvia got started. A few hours later, she'd made some good progress—paring down the Tupperware containers of the boys' school- and artwork, donating some miscellaneous kitchen items and framed posters that she and Wilson had bought for their first apartment. She only cried once, and that was when she read Simon's handwriting in preschool. He'd filled in a blank that said, "My mother's name is. . ." and he'd written, "Sillveeah."

The boys' baby clothes were harder to give up, but Sylvia set them in the pile for the Salvation Army and traveled deeper into the room.

She ignored her mother's sewing machine and did not make eye contact with the rocker where she had spent many hours nursing the boys. Instead, she headed for some boxes that had been shipped to them from her parents' house in Ohio.

Peeling back the shipping tape, she opened a box filled with old photograph albums. Unable to resist, she took an old black one with a broken spine to the gliding rocker and settled herself on the upholstered cushions. On the first page was an old black-and-white photo of her mother grinning from her seat on a tricycle with streamers flowing from the handlebars.

Sylvia smiled at her mom's full head of dark curls, dimples, and mouth like a pink rosebud. Flipping through the pages, she traced her mother's growth—school pictures, then dance recitals, her first communion.

When she finished the album, she opened another and then another until she came to the page and the image she remembered of her mother—taken on her forty-eighth birthday, surrounded by her family and beaming at the camera. Sylvia had taken the shot just as her Uncle Calvin had threatened to moon everyone if they didn't smile like they meant it.

Sudden tears sprang to her eyes. *How did you do it, Mom? Be such a good wife and mother? You really were the Proverbs 31 woman. You made everything seem so easy.*

"Are you kidding?" The smiling woman in the photo seemed to say. *"It wasn't always easy, and I certainly wasn't the Proverbs 31 wife. But I was happy, Sylvia. I had a happy life."*

Sylvia closed the photo album. What was she doing, making up conversations with her mother? It wasn't like her mom was going to be able to help her understand what pieces of her life to hang on to and which to let go. And she didn't just mean the contents of the attic.

The quiet of the house rang in her ears, and Sylvia realized that she could either keep making up things her mother might have said to her or reach out to God. She shut her eyes, and just as she said, "Dear Lord Jesus," a door slammed, and Tucker's little-boy voice wafted into the room, "Mommy-Mommy, we're home!"

Stepping around her piles, Sylvia headed out of the room. As soon as she made it down the stairs, both boys saw her and raced into her arms.

Kissing the tops of their satiny, newly-sheared heads, Sylvia felt her heart literally expanding in her chest. "I missed you guys."

Wilson leaned over the boys to kiss the top of her head. "We missed you, too. Did you have a good day?"

"Yes," Sylvia replied. "How about you?"

Wilson nodded, but didn't quite look her in the eye. "Absolutely."

"Simon broke a glass at the flower shop," Tucker announced.

Sylvia searched Wilson's face. "Flower shop? What were you doing at the florist?"

"Tucker, it was a vase, and you weren't supposed to tell." Simon frowned fiercely at his younger brother. "After what *you* did, I wouldn't talk if I were you."

"What did you do, Tucker?" Sylvia frowned. "You smell like maple syrup." She glanced around. "And where's Joe?" Her gaze found her husband. "Wilson?"

Wilson's face froze over the way it always did when he was trying to keep something from her. "Dad's cleaning out your glove compartment for you—he says there's a bunch of expired inspection papers and insurance cards."

Sylvia relaxed slightly, but something about the look on all their faces told her they were holding something back. "You all okay?"

"We're fine. Just *fine*," Wilson said, so heartedly that Sylvia's antennas went up even higher.

"Something about the car you're not telling me?"

"Nope," Wilson said as the boys giggled.

"You got a speeding ticket?"

The boys broke out into peals of laughter even as Wilson gave her a funny look and said, "Of course not."

"Then what?" Sylvia studied all their faces. "You all look like you're bursting with a secret to tell me."

Tucker squirmed visibly; Simon's eyes blinked in a series of rapid-fire movements. "Spill it," she demanded.

"Dad hosed me off at the car wash."

"Just a little," Wilson said. "To get it off his shirt."

"He spilled maple syrup all over the backseat," Simon announced.

"It wasn't that bad," Wilson said. "We got most of it out."

"What about the glass at the flower shop?"

Wilson shifted. "Okay," he admitted, "we stopped off to order flowers, and Simon did knock over a vase by accident, but it wasn't a big deal."

"But Susan is handling the floral arrangements," Sylvia said. "I told you that."

Wilson shrugged. "The more flowers, the better."

"But what if they don't go together?"

"It'll all be fine, Sylvia. Don't worry. So what did you do while we were gone?"

"But we have a color scheme going," Sylvia said, refusing to change the subject. "You haven't seen the linens yet."

"Dad got all colors," Tucker said, and was immediately given a stern look by his father.

"It'll be fine." Wilson headed for the kitchen. "I'm really thirsty. Boys, do you want a glass of water?"

Sylvia trailed after him. "Don't you trust Susan to do a good job with the floral arrangements?"

"Of course I do," Wilson said. "Let's talk about your day. Did you go get a massage?"

"No," she said. "What else did you do while you were out? And why does Tucker smell like maple syrup?"

"Well," Wilson said, "we went to McDonald's for a snack and some syrup spilled on him."

Simon giggled. Sylvia looked at the color on his normally pale face and the sparkle in his eyes. Whatever had happened, he was highly amused. She was dying to know what it was. "So did you go anywhere else besides the car wash, the barber, and the florist?"

"We went to the mall!" Tucker cried out happily. "But I'm not supposed to tell you what we bought."

Tucker had a hard time keeping secrets and with the right prompting could probably be coaxed into telling her everything. Sylvia smiled warmly at him. "Did Daddy buy something nice for Mommy?"

Tucker looked at his father, and a big guilty smile formed on his face. "We went to the secret store," he admitted.

Sylvia looked at Wilson and felt a small thrill of excitement. He'd bought her something? "Secret store?"

"Oh, Dad saw some fancy shaving cream in the window of that beauty shop." He looked at Simon. "What's it called?"

"Trade Secrets," Simon said, straight-faced. "He bought aftershave."

"Oh," Sylvia said.

Joe walked into the kitchen. He was carrying a small shopping bag from Trade Secret that confirmed Wilson's explanation. "Hello, sweetheart," he said and gave her a kiss. "Your tires might need rotating. I don't think they did it at your last service. At least it wasn't on any of the invoices in your glove compartment."

"Thanks, Joe."

"Mom, I'm hungry," Tucker said. "Can I have a snack?"

Sylvia glanced at her watch and was surprised to see it was so late. She hadn't even thought about what to make for dinner.

"How about I spring for pizza?" Joe suggested.

The boys cheered and began to jump up and down chanting, "Pizza! Pizza!"

"You want to go with Poppy and we'll stop for a movie on the way?"

"I'll go with you, Dad," Wilson offered.

"The boys can tell me how to get there," Joe said. "You go finish up that work you were telling me about so you can watch the movie with us."

Wilson nodded. "Thanks, Dad." He bent to kiss the smooth, warm top of his father's head. "Drive carefully."

Alone in the house with Wilson, Sylvia realized it felt a little awkward. She couldn't remember the last time when it'd been just the two of them, no boys hovering around. She ran her hand through her hair and suddenly wasn't sure what to say to him at all.

He swallowed the remainder of his water and set the glass on the counter. "Well," he said at last. "Dad's right—there are a couple of things I should probably get done before dinner." He turned to leave.

"Wilson?"

"Yeah?"

She searched his face. *We're alone,* she wanted to say, *no kids. We could talk or have some private time.* She opened her mouth but hesitated. Wilson was standing in the doorway, and there was something closed off in his face. It reminded her of the expression and posture a doctor might use to nonverbally communicate the appointment was over. In his mind, she suspected, he'd already gone back to work. She felt disappointment, fear, and then acceptance pass through her.

"Nothing," she said.

Wilson closed his office door then sank wearily into his desk chair. Pushing the skin on his face hard, he sighed in relief. If he'd stayed in the kitchen with Sylvia one second longer, he'd have started spilling the beans. He was as bad as Tucker, who had blurted out the whole secret store thing. Fortunately the whole story about Trade Secrets had been believable—a plot conceived by his father who had suspected someone might crack under Sylvia's questioning. His father's aptitude for deception was becoming alarming, but Wilson had to admit it'd come in handy.

Firing up his PC, he wondered if he was going to be able to hold out for the whole week. Keeping a secret from Sylvia was torture, particularly when he knew she'd be thrilled with his gift. There were still a few things he had to pull together, but he was pleased with the progress he'd made so far.

As his computer began to synchronize, he caught glimpses of the e-mails downloading. There were a lot from Bruce, and most of them marked "urgent." He saw another few RSVPs from board members. Bruce had been right, most of them had accepted his invitation. That was a good sign. A very good sign.

He was about to open a new window and go on the Internet when he glimpsed an e-mail from Peggy Armstrong, a real estate agent he had met once briefly. They'd discussed the kind of house he might be looking for in the future.

When all the mail was downloaded, he opened the real estate agent's note first.

Dear Mr. Baxter,

I enjoyed meeting with you last week and discussing your possible relocation. Since our conversation, a house has come on the market which sounds perfect for you and your family. For your convenience, I have attached photos and the listing information. As we discussed, the housing market here is strong and houses like this one don't last long on the market. If you are interested, I would suggest that you look at it this week. This is probably ahead of your schedule, but as I stated, I felt this house was particularly suited to your needs. Please let me know as soon as possible if you are interested and I will set up a showing.

All Best,
Peggy Armstrong

Wilson clicked on the attachment. When a large redbrick colonial filled the screen, he stared at it for a long time, analyzing every inch of it, and then he went to find Sylvia.

Chapter 30

So you really don't mind watching the boys?"

It was Monday morning, and Sylvia had just called Rema, half hoping that her friend would turn her down and she wouldn't have to go out-of-town house hunting with Wilson and Joe.

"Let me see," Rema said, and Sylvia could almost picture her smiling, playing with one of the dangly earrings she preferred and pretending she had to think about it. "Of course not. My kids will be thrilled."

Sylvia pushed her hair back from her face. "Thanks," she said, and the two women quickly coordinated schedules and arrangements. "We're going to tell the boys that we're going to see where Daddy goes when he travels," Sylvia added. "Simon will be suspicious, but mostly he'll be excited at being able to hang out with Liam."

"Got it." Rema was silent for a moment. "Things are going to start happening fast, aren't they?"

"Wilson thinks they need to make a decision soon. He's got a couple more interviews this week."

"And your anniversary party is on Saturday. Speaking of which, what are you going to wear?"

Sylvia shifted her weight. "I hadn't really thought about it. Maybe that sleeveless black cocktail dress."

"That's cute," Rema said. "But something new is always perky. Macy's is having one of those take-an-extra-twenty-percent-off sales. Maybe we should take a look."

Sylvia looked at the dishes in the rack and the table topped with books, toys, and artwork. The floor probably needed mopping, and there was an entire basket of clothes to iron, especially if she wanted to wear her khaki skirt. But Joe had gone off to Walgreens to refill some prescriptions. The boys wouldn't need her until three o'clock, and besides, how many other opportunities would she have to spend time with Rema? "How about I pick you up in twenty minutes?"

"Perfect," Rema said with a smile in her voice. "I'm ready for a little retail therapy session."

Less than an hour later, Sylvia and Rema pulled into a parking spot near Macy's north entrance. Rema stepped out of the minivan. She was wearing a black leather miniskirt, an animal print tank top, high-heeled ankle boots, and long gold earrings. Sylvia smiled as Rema slung an oversized, red leather handbag over her shoulder and strode like a general toward the entrance doors.

They stepped into the handbag department where Rema was instantly distracted by the display of Fossil bags, a jungle print in particular. After deciding that it had to go home with her, she picked up a plum-colored leather bag with a cross strap. "This would look really cute with the outfit you're wearing."

Sylvia slipped the bag over her shoulder and glanced at herself in the mirror. It did go well with her black capri pants and her white

T-shirt with the bold, floral pattern, but then she glanced at the price tag and put the purse back.

Next, they wandered through the shoe department and spent about thirty minutes as Rema debated between silver and gold high heels with tuxedo ruffles down the front, and then ended up buying both. "Skiezer's going to kill me," she confessed. "I'm going to have to sneak everything into the house."

Finally they found their way to the dress department. Rema began looking over the outfits with a professional eye. "You need something classy," she said, "but it also has to be a little romantic, considering that this is an anniversary party."

"I like color, and it has to camouflage my stomach." Sylvia eyed a pretty, bright red dress on display. "Those mannequins have never birthed two children."

"You have a great figure," Rema assured her. "How about this one?" She pulled a midnight-blue dress off the rack and held it up for Sylvia's inspection.

Sylvia fingered the chiffon fabric. It had a nice float, but the neckline looked deep. "I'll try it," she said. She found her gaze going again to the bright red dress on the mannequin. Rema, following the direction of her gaze, quickly located the dress and began to sort through the rack for Sylvia's size. "They've only got an eight or a twelve."

"I could try the twelve," Sylvia said, although something in her balked at the idea of going up a dress size.

"Hold on," Rema said, "I've got another idea." The next thing Sylvia knew, her friend was checking the tag on the mannequin and then undressing it. They had to pull the mannequin's arms out of the sockets, but before long the dress was in Rema's arms.

"We can't just leave her like that," Sylvia said, pointing to the nude, armless model. "Let's put her in the twelve."

Working together, the women managed to slip the dress over the mannequin's head and stick the arms back into the body holes.

"Now she kind of looks like a Saguaro in a cocktail dress," Rema joked as they stepped back.

"At least she's covered," Sylvia said, grinning. They continued to hunt through dresses and soon Sylvia's arms were full. Heading for the changing room, Sylvia couldn't wait to feel the silken fabric on her body. It had been so long since she'd bought anything that couldn't be machine washed.

Just for one night, she thought, she'd be as romantically dressed as the women on the cover of her romance novels. Wilson and the boys would be stunned to see her in something besides denim. They might even look at her as if she were beautiful.

Dumping her purse onto the floor, Sylvia eagerly kicked off her sandals and then the capri pants and T-shirt. She reached for the midnight blue first. Lifting her arms, she let the silky material slide over her head. Straightening the twisted fabric, her eyes widened. The material exposed an alarming amount of cleavage.

"How are you doing?" Rema called from outside the door.

Sylvia tugged the neckline higher. "It's a little breezy."

"Let me see."

Sylvia stepped into the hallway. Rema took one look at her and laughed. "If you wear that one, I guarantee you'll give one of the men a heart attack, and all the wives will hate you."

Sylvia shook her head. "Not the reaction I'm going for." She stepped back into the room. The next dress, a deep pink with metallic beading around the waist was tight at the hips and a little too short. The third dress, kelly-green and short-sleeved, was too matronly. The fourth was a print that was just awful, and when Sylvia stepped out to model it, she said, "I feel like a giant candy cane. Maybe we should give up. I could wear my old, black cocktail dress."

"No way," Rema stated. "We're not leaving here until we find the perfect dress." She handed Sylvia a white dress of a chiffon material. "Try this one."

Sylvia had seen the dress on a rack but passed it up. The fitted bodice was probably going to be too tight, and besides, she wanted color. "I'm not sure I can get into this one."

"I'll help you." Rema stepped into the changing room and lifted the dress above Sylvia's head. For a moment the material caught on her shoulder, and Sylvia had the awful feeling that her arms wouldn't fit through the straps. Rema tugged hard, and the dress magically straightened. "Syl, suck it in." The cold zipper tickled against her ribs. "There," Rema announced, "look in the mirror."

Bracing herself against the prospect of seeing a middle-aged woman wearing a dress that showed only too clearly how gravity was taking its toll, Sylvia lifted her gaze.

The woman who looked back wore a white column dress that hugged the curves of her breasts and hips. Small, white spaghetti straps lay across the smooth, tanned skin of her shoulders. Her exposed arms seemed toned and youthful.

Sylvia studied herself. She hadn't known she had youthful-looking arms. Turning, Sylvia saw the way the fabric draped over her back, exposing the long, straight line of her spine. When she turned her head, her hair flashed copper highlights. *Was this her?*

"Nothing droops?" Sylvia changed angles and glanced anxiously in the mirror. Maybe she was missing something. "I don't look too fat?"

"You look like a movie star. Oh Sylvia, you're so beautiful!"

Sylvia started to reach for the price tag, but Rema slapped her hand away. "It's reasonable, and you're getting it," she stated. "Think of it as an investment in your future and Wilson's. And besides," she added, "every woman should have one dress in her closet that makes her look like a princess."

Sylvia smiled. "I do feel like a princess in this."

In the mirror, Rema beamed back at her. "Mission accomplished," she stated. "Now we celebrate."

"First you've got to get me out of this," Sylvia said, turning so Rema could unzip her. "And then where are we going?"

"Cinnabun," Rema said happily.

"If I eat one of those, I won't be able to get back into this dress. I should go home and do a hundred squats."

"One Cinnabun isn't going to make a bit of difference," Rema stated confidently. "And forget the squats." She unzipped the dress. "Who needs buns of steel when there are sticky buns instead?"

With the dress purchased and carefully placed on a hanger in a plastic case, Rema and Sylvia headed for the food court. They bought coffee and cinnamon buns and found an empty table. Sylvia eyed the creamy slab of cream cheese icing melting on the warm roll and was about to take a bite when her cell rang.

Scrambling within the depths of her purse, she managed to find the phone and answer before it rang into voice mail. Pressing the device to her ear, she heard Joe's gravelly voice say, "Sylvia?"

She felt everything inside go tense. "Is everything okay?"

"Yes," Joe replied, "but the school just called. Simon's running a fever and is in the nurse's office. They want you to come pick him up."

"I'm on my way," Sylvia said. Hanging up the cell, she looked apologetically at Rema. "Simon's sick. I've got to go."

Chapter 31

Wilson shifted the Beemer into REVERSE and carefully backed down his driveway. Next to him, his father filled the space where Sylvia would be sitting if Simon hadn't gotten sick. Although he had improved after a long night, the school policy was that kids had to be fever-free for twenty-four hours before they could return.

He felt a little guilty going without her, but if he didn't, they'd lose the chance to see the house. He was bringing the video camera so Sylvia could see it, too. But it wouldn't be the same, and he knew it.

At the same time, he was really glad that she could be there for Simon, who had looked pale as a ghost, and terribly small and fragile swaddled in blankets on the couch.

As Wilson turned onto the road, his dad opened the map, nearly blocking the right side of Wilson's vision. He didn't say a word. He figured it was better that his father read the map than all the names of the street signs they passed.

Reaching Route 240, Wilson upshifted, and the Beemer surged

forward, as if it enjoyed the chance to accelerate as much as he did.

"We go north on I-25," Joe directed, as if Wilson hadn't traveled this route multiple times.

Taking a sip of his burning hot coffee, Wilson prayed Simon felt better soon, and then found his thoughts going back to work. So much of the finance industry was a delicate balancing act, and because of this, bank services and fees were constantly changing. Customers, of course, disliked being charged for things that had been free just the week before. And yet, with federal government regulations so strict, banks couldn't operate the way they had in the past and remain in business.

"We'll stay on I-25 for about sixty miles," Joe stated. "We'll pass that big alligator place. You know, the one we went to last time I visited. Maybe we could stop there."

Wilson remembered. His dad had nearly lost his fingers feeding the alligators bits of dried fish. "I don't think we're going to have time, Dad. We're meeting the Realtor at two and it's a five-hour drive."

"Maybe on the way back, then," his father said. "I want to bring the boys back something. Especially for Simon, the poor kid. I heard him upchucking in the middle of the night."

It had been a hard, long night. "We'll make sure we bring him back something." Wilson hoped they'd have time. Along with the brick colonial, there were a few other houses the Realtor had suggested. He'd make time, Wilson promised himself.

"You think Sylvia has any idea of what you're planning for your anniversary?"

"Not yet," Wilson said. "But she has a sixth sense when it comes to things like this."

His dad laughed. "Tucker was dying to tell her. Aren't you glad I came up with the Trade Secret story?"

"Yes, but I'm beginning to wonder what else you passed off as the truth when I was growing up."

"You turned out okay," Joe said. "That's all that matters."

The scenery flashed by as Wilson considered his father's remark. He didn't agree with it, and yet he knew that his dad loved him, had always loved him, and would always love him. This was the truth of their relationship.

Miles of flat land, dotted with cows and cactus and wire fence filled his gaze. "So, Dad," he said slowly, "about you moving in with us. Are you sure?" He glanced sideways at his father. "You've lived in Sugar Hill for years—all your friends are there."

His dad put another fold in the map in his lap. "Sugar Hill has a lot of happy memories, but I would rather be with you, Sylvia, and the boys."

"What about Stephen and his family? Won't their feelings be hurt if you choose to live with my family instead of theirs?"

"I love your brother," his father said solemnly, "but I couldn't live with them. The last time I visited them, they showed me all these brochures of assisted living facilities. 'Maybe you should think about moving into one now, Dad,' his father mimicked in a falsetto voice, 'so you can still enjoy all the activities.'" His dad made a scoffing noise. "Like chair aerobics is the greatest thing since sliced bread."

Wilson's hands tightened on the steering wheel. He and Stephen, although only two years apart, had never been close. Things had gotten even worse after Stephen married.

"I'm sure they love you, Dad," he said.

"I know," he said. "But I missed a lot when you and Stephen were growing up because I was always working. I can't get those years back, but God willing, I can be a better grandfather."

Wilson was careful not to look at his father. "You were there. Remember that balsa racer we made together?"

"I sure do," his father said. "And next year, I'm going to help Simon build a faster car."

"I don't think Simon will do it," Wilson said. "But maybe Tucker will do it again."

"Simon'll change his mind," his father predicted. "He's like you. He won't be able to resist the challenge."

Wilson allowed the miles to pass in silence as he considered his father's statement. He had been a nerdy little kid and had been only too willing to take on any academic competition. He shifted on the seat. How proud he'd been to bring home another trophy or certificate.

"Next year," his dad mused, "we'll go with a silicone-based paint and more metal in the nose."

"Dad. . ."

"Don't worry. It'll all be legal."

"I'm not worrying about it being legal. I'm worrying about it being what Simon wants."

"If he doesn't want to do it, that's fine," his father assured him. "I just want to give him the chance in case he does. Sometimes people just need a little encouragement."

"I don't want Simon focusing on winning stuff," Wilson said, surprising himself with the words.

"I don't care if he wins or not either," his dad said placidly. "My best memory of building that race car with you is standing around my worktable in the basement and spending time with you."

Time together. Wilson's stomach twisted with regret. Simon had wanted him to help with his Pinewood Derby racer but Wilson had been too busy. *Busy. Busy. Busy.* The words buzzed in his ear like a telephone signal. He'd make it up to Simon, he promised himself, just as soon as this job change was settled.

He turned on the radio, effectively ending the conversation. They stopped for a brief lunch at Wendy's and then drove the remaining distance. Wilson's pulse picked up when he spotted the city limits. He felt like an arrow flying through the air, aimed directly at the center of the target, which was First Federal Bank, located in the heart of the city.

"Walgreen's, Marvelous Cleaners, Valero," his father read.

For once, his dad's habit of reading signs aloud didn't bother Wilson. In fact, he felt a wave of tenderness for the man seated next to him. Dressed in a pair of old green shorts, black socks, and his favorite brown loafers, he looked hopelessly out of fashion and endearingly oblivious to the fact.

"We'll meet the Realtor at her office," Wilson said. "But we'll drive by the bank first."

His dad laughed and slapped him on the leg. "Have I told you how proud I am of you?"

"Only about a million times," Wilson joked, "and technically it's not my bank." But he sat a little taller all the same. Old habits, apparently, died hard.

After his father had admired the bank, they drove straight to the Realtor's office. Peggy Armstrong, a short, heavyset woman with short, black hair and a firm handshake, met them in her office. After she went over a few listings, they all piled into her Lexus.

It was a short drive from the downtown area. Wilson smiled as the brick colonial he'd seen on the Internet came into sight. It was only about five years old and contained more than 4,000 square feet—significantly more than their current home. They paused at the gated entrance. The Realtor punched in a code and the black, wrought-iron gate opened with majestic slowness.

Wilson glanced at his dad. "Nice, huh?"

His dad was out of the car as soon as it'd stopped. He headed over to a basketball backboard standing just outside the three-car garage. It looked brand new, as if not one ball had ever swished through its net.

As if he'd read his thoughts, his dad turned to the agent. "Doesn't look as if anyone ever used this."

The Realtor nodded. "Well, with the country club so close, they probably play golf or tennis instead. Let's go inside."

She ushered them inside a cool, tastefully decorated house with a two-story entranceway that flanked a dining room on his right and a dark, wood-paneled room with built-in shelves that served as an office. Wilson instantly saw himself sitting behind the dark wood desk.

The kitchen was enormous, with stainless steel appliances and a six-burner gas stove that he was sure Sylvia would love. The family room featured an entire side wall of windows overlooking a multi-tiered deck that led to a kidney-shaped pool surrounded by palm trees.

"Isn't this something," his father said, admiring a stone fireplace that rose from floor to ceiling.

The bedrooms were big and spacious, and then his father positively beamed when the Realtor led them into the backyard and showed them a "casita," which was a one-room cottage with its own kitchen and bathroom.

"What do you think?" Peggy Armstrong smiled at Wilson.

"It's perfect," Wilson said. "I love it."

"I thought you would." Peggy's smile grew. "Would you like to make an offer?"

Absolutely, Wilson thought, *Sylvia would love this house.* From the research he'd already done he knew it was well worth the asking price. And yet, what came out of his mouth was, "I'd like to look around a little more."

He walked onto the grass behind the pool. The yard backed into woods, and there wasn't another home in sight. It was quiet, very quiet. Turning, Wilson gazed through the trees at the mansion behind him. It amazed him to think they could afford it, and he tried to imagine himself and Sylvia living there happily. It was much, much grander than they were used to. Well, they'd get used to having all that space in no time, he assured himself.

He walked to the front of the house and again stared at the pristine white net of the basketball hoop. Had it ever been used, or had the man who lived here been too busy to play with his sons? Would he be like that man?

Shielding his eyes, Wilson took another look at the big colonial. It gleamed in the sun like a giant-sized trophy. Was this what the promotion was all about? Climbing to the next rung of success on a ladder that stretched to infinity?

Still, he couldn't help but feel obligated to provide the best possible lifestyle for his family. And if the Lord didn't want him to accept this new job, why did Wilson want it so badly?

Still, he found himself restless, as if he were missing something that was clearly in front of him. He paced about, feeling as if his mind and heart were at war with each other, and realizing that up until now, he'd been so intent on *getting* the position that he hadn't really thought about it being the right thing for him.

Was the job worth giving up all they had?

Analytically, it was. It met the criteria in the categories of finance, career, and adventure. So what was holding him back? He could call Sylvia right now and ask her permission to make an offer.

Wilson reached the perimeter of the property. A few years ago, he'd been in a men's Bible study. One of the group members had been struggling with a decision just like the one Wilson was making. Wilson remembered the pastor advising the man to ask himself two questions.

Will taking this job help you share your faith with others? Wilson looked at the distances between the houses. They were much farther apart than in their current neighborhood. Now that he could see the other large, stately homes, there was a definite lack of close neighbors. But surely there would be other church-going families in the area. So yes, technically, he could share his faith.

Is this new job worth your life?

This question was harder. Wilson stopped in front of a large oak. He traced the lines on the bark with his finger. "Is this new job worth my life?" he asked aloud.

The selfish part of him reared up immediately, shouting inside his head that it was—and more. For once, Wilson didn't accept that voice and listened harder. Closing his eyes, he heard the leaves flutter against the touch of the wind and the far-off roar of a car. Squirrels chattered in the trees, and a car sped down the street.

It seemed idyllic here, but what would the new job do to him on the inside? Would his soul flourish, or would the very things that seemed so desirable only serve to weigh him down? He'd be making more money, but he'd also be carrying a much bigger mortgage.

Wilson leaned against a towering oak. *Heavenly Father, am I being selfish? Is this promotion what I want or what You want for me? Can our family be happy here? Will all these worries go away once I'm actually in the job?*

Wilson heard the crunch of twigs underfoot, and then his father's voice saying, "Wilson?"

He turned and automatically plastered on a smile intended to cover up these sudden doubts. He could balance the demands of the new job without sacrificing his relationships with the boys and Sylvia. It was only a matter of determination and discipline. "Hey Dad," he said. "Check out this old oak."

"Listen, this house is great," his father said, "but don't let this Realtor lady push you into anything. If it doesn't feel right, it's not."

Wilson shook his head. "I like the house," he said, "but the timing is wrong. I don't even have the job."

"So write a clause into the contract. Give yourself some time," his father urged. "But at least keep the option open. We won't find another house with a casita."

"I just wish Sylvia could see it."

"Well, you're in luck," his father said, pushing the video camera into Wilson's hands. "While you've been out here thinking, I've been filming. All you need to do is upload it."

Chapter 32

Sylvia sat perfectly still on the sofa. Simon's head was in her lap, and they had just finished watching *The Lion King*. She couldn't see her son's face, but the evenness of his breathing suggested he had already fallen asleep, or was about to, and for this she was grateful. Sleep was healing.

He'd had a hard night—they'd all had. The Motrin had brought his fever down, but he'd been achy and nauseous, clingy and unhappy. She'd managed to coax a few sips of water down his throat, but she worried about dehydration. Thankfully his fever had broken, but he'd remained lethargic with little appetite.

Simon twitched a little—Wilson tended to do exactly the same thing when he was falling asleep—and she softly stroked his arm. It was a little after one o'clock. Wilson and Joe were probably still on the road. She was due to pick up Tucker at school at three o'clock, which gave Simon time for a good, long nap.

She heard her cell chirp. Wilson probably had texted her from the road. He'd been disappointed that she couldn't accompany him on the house hunting trip, but promised to video the house and post it on the family web page he had created on the Internet. Sylvia had secretly hoped he'd simply cancel the trip.

Simon's breathing grew increasingly deep and steady. She glanced down at his pale, blond head and felt a wave of tenderness toward him. He seemed so small and fragile, so vulnerable in his bare feet and Batman pajamas. He was a complicated little boy, so full of contrasts—small for his size, and yet years ahead intellectually. So sensitive he wept in movies if anyone (or any animal) died, and yet unyielding in his sense of right and wrong. Not all his peers appreciated his better qualities, and making friends his own age had been challenging.

He stirred a little, and she stroked his hair until he quieted. When Sylvia was a little girl and got sick, her mother sat with her like this for hours, knitting, while Sylvia watched television or played endless rounds of Solitaire. Sylvia's mother brought her icy glasses of ginger ale or warm bowls of noodles and broth. Sometimes it'd felt like getting sick was a treat because everything in the world seemed to stop and her mother focused entirely on her.

Her father, however, wasn't in these memories. How could he have been, Sylvia chided herself. He'd been working—providing for his family. Being a patent attorney had been a tough job, and when he came home from work, even as a child, she'd seen his fatigue, the way he'd collapse into his leather recliner and reach for the newspaper.

He'd loved her; she knew this. But he also had been unavailable to her. Maybe she was to blame—she'd been too shy, too young to know how to talk to him and much more comfortable around her mother.

It was a different time, she reminded herself. Fathers were more involved now than when she had been growing up. Wilson wasn't like her father. Hadn't he spent last Saturday doing errands with the boys?

But Sylvia also recognized similarities. Like her mother, Sylvia was a stay-at-home mom, and like her dad, Wilson worked increasingly long hours. Wilson kept saying it was only temporary, but she knew it wasn't. Wilson essentially liked his job. Work seemed to fill some need that she couldn't.

She thought about the Proverbs Plan, how she'd hoped it would help Wilson take notice of her and rekindle the romance that had ebbed from their marriage. Obviously it hadn't worked out the way she'd hoped, but she still believed that through God all things were possible. Just when things seemed the least likely to work out was the time to hold most tightly to her faith.

She stroked Simon's hair but sensed it was more to comfort herself than him. *The Lion King* finished the last credits and Sylvia turned off the set with the remote control. She sat for a moment debating whether to move or not, and then carefully reached for a magazine on the side table. Her Bible was on top of it. She almost pushed it aside but stopped herself. She'd been promising herself to spend more time reading it, particularly Proverbs 31. She opened to the correct spot and read the verses in their entirety.

A wife of noble character who can find? She is worth far more than rubies. Her husband has full confidence in her and lacks nothing of value. She brings him good, not harm, all the days of her life. She selects wool and flax and works with eager hands. She is like the merchant ships, bringing her food from

*afar. She gets up while it is still night; she provides food for
her family and portions for her female servants. She considers
a field and buys it; out of her earnings she plants a vineyard.
She sets about her work vigorously; her arms are strong for
her tasks. She sees that her trading is profitable, and her lamp
does not go out at night. In her hand she holds the distaff and
grasps the spindle with her fingers. She opens her arms to the
poor and extends her hands to the needy. When it snows, she
has no fear for her household; for all of them are clothed in
scarlet. She makes coverings for her bed; she is clothed in fine
linen and purple. Her husband is respected at the city gate,
where he takes his seat among the elders of the land. She makes
linen garments and sells them, and supplies the merchants
with sashes. She is clothed with strength and dignity; she
can laugh at the days to come. She speaks with wisdom, and
faithful instruction is on her tongue. She watches over the
affairs of her household and does not eat the bread of idleness.
Her children arise and call her blessed; her husband also, and
he praises her: "Many women do noble things, but you surpass
them all." Charm is deceptive, and beauty is fleeting; but a
woman who fears the* Lord *is to be praised. Honor her for all
that her hands have done, and let her works bring her praise
at the city gate.*

What did these verses really mean? How could she possibly live
up to this standard? As Simon continued to sleep in her lap, Sylvia
read and reread the verses. She thought about her mother, how in
Sylvia's mind, she had embodied so many of these traits. How happy
she had seemed—and yet she recognized that her mother had been

dealing with many of the same issues she herself faced.

She closed her eyes. *Please God, help Simon feel better, and help me understand what these verses really mean because I feel like everything around me is changing, and maybe I need to change, too.*

Chapter 33

Late that evening, Sylvia was in the kitchen going over a few details for the anniversary party with Rema, Andrea, and Susan when Wilson and Joe returned from the house hunting trip.

It was a little after nine, and Rema's dog, Cookie, sleeping under the table because Rema hadn't wanted to leave him home, barked at the sound of their voices in the foyer. Rema hushed the dog then slipped him a wedge of cheese as Wilson and Joe stepped into the room.

"Hey honey." Wilson dropped his keys and wallet on the counter and crossed the room to give her a kiss. "Hi, ladies," he added, straightening.

"Nice to see you," Rema said. "But I've got to get going." Standing, she turned to Sylvia. "Skiezer will be here early on Saturday morning to start grilling. He's doing ribs and won't be happy unless they're falling off the bone. He's also smoking a turkey breast—I couldn't talk him out of it."

"Tell him thanks," Wilson said. "And please let us reimburse you for the cost of the meat." He glanced at Sylvia. "We really appreciate you all helping us out."

"Wait until you get our bill," Rema said, smiling. "We don't come cheap."

"Tell him if he needs help, I'm pretty handy on the grill," Joe added.

Sylvia thought her father-in-law's posture looked even more bent over than usual and suspected the long ride had been hard on his back. And then she remembered her manners. "Andrea and Susan, have you met my father-in-law, Joe Baxter?"

"Pleasure to meet such lovely ladies," Joe said, extending his hand.

"Nice to meet you, too," Andrea said. In her high heels, she towered above Joe. "I hear you're responsible for that lovely garden in the front of the house."

Joe beamed. "We both planted it."

"It's beautiful," Susan added. "You've got a great eye for color."

"I just look for the healthiest plants, but thank you," Joe said, inclining his head modestly.

"Well, I've got to get going," Andrea said with a sigh. "I've got an early court appearance tomorrow morning." She kissed Sylvia's cheek. "Remember, Chris and I will be here at nine o'clock Saturday morning to help you set everything up, so don't try to do everything yourself."

"Everything is going to be just perfect," Susan added, gathering her purse. "No worries."

With a few more assurances, Sylvia's friends were out the door. After waving them off, Sylvia returned to the kitchen where Wilson was peering into the refrigerator and Joe was leaning against the countertop, arms folded, eyes closed.

"Are you hungry? There's chicken-and-rice soup."

Wilson emerged from the refrigerator with packages of ham and cheese in his hands. "We ate earlier," he admitted. "How's Simon?"

"Much better. He made it through school today, but was really wiped out when he got home." She glanced at Joe whose chin was nearly on his chest. "Why don't you go sit down on the couch?"

"Thanks but I've been sitting all day," Joe said. "I think I'm just going to head upstairs for bed."

"Is he okay?" Sylvia asked after her father-in-law was out of earshot.

Wilson layered ham and cheese on the bread. "Yeah. It was a long drive. Neither of us slept well last night in the hotel either. We were right next to the elevator and it pinged all night."

Sylvia couldn't wait any longer. "Tell me about the house. Did we get it?"

Wilson shook his head. "I don't know yet—they're still considering the offer. It's a nice house, Sylvia, so even though we offered the asking price, they might get a better offer." He took a bite of his sandwich and chewed thoughtfully. "I wrote in a contingency clause so we can always back out of this deal, so don't feel pressure to buy this house if you don't like it."

"I saw the video, and the house looks like a mansion. Can we really afford it?"

Wilson smiled. "Absolutely. I like that my dad would have that little casita in the back."

"It does seem perfect." Sylvia rinsed a plate and put it in the drying rack. "What about the school?"

"That neighborhood feeds into an 'exemplary' school system."

"And what about a church?"

"Several options," Wilson said. "And we're very close to shopping and a really pretty country club with golf, swimming, and tennis."

Sylvia rinsed another plate. She was glad he couldn't see her face. Did he really want to join a country club? It seemed so vastly different—so much more upscale than the life they lived now. She wondered if he had been hiding this part of himself from her, secretly measuring his life by a different standard than the one she'd thought they shared. "That sounds great," she said, "but what happens, honey, if you don't get the job? Will you be okay?"

"I'll be disappointed," Wilson admitted. "But I don't think so many board members would be coming to our party if they weren't serious. Plus I'll have finished all my interviews by Saturday. Bruce was even hinting that they might use our party to announce me."

Sylvia stopped drying a dish. She turned slowly. "Are you sure, Wilson, that this is the right move for us?"

"I don't want to do anything that you don't want to do," Wilson replied. "We can look at other houses if you want."

She took her time setting the china platter, now dried, in the cabinet. She was pretty sure he'd deliberately misunderstood the last question. The last of her hopes that Wilson would see the value of their life here, of seeing how painful a move would be for her, died. "No," she said. "I can't imagine a better house than that one."

Wilson wiped his mouth with a napkin. "I love you, Syl. I'm glad you're up for this."

If he only knew the truth, but he either didn't see it, or else he didn't want to acknowledge it. She felt a little deflated, just like when she'd colored her hair and bought those tight capri pants and Wilson hadn't noticed. She thought about how she had tried to change herself into someone who would be more loveable, more interesting, more compelling. Someone who would inspire Wilson to turn off his computer when he got home and talk to her. Listen to her with all his mind—not just the part that wasn't still churning out something at work—and ask the kind of questions that made her feel fascinating to him.

But this was a fantasy, a pleasant one, but a fantasy all the same. No wonder so few of the romance novels she loved took up the story of what happens after the happily-ever-after. How a relationship could change so gradually it was like aging—you couldn't see it day to day but then one day you looked in the mirror and saw the wrinkles.

Maybe the whole point of Proverbs 31 was not to make Wilson love her more, but to try to be the kind of person God wanted her to be. A woman of faith and character. Maybe she couldn't do all those things in the verses, but it didn't matter how well she did them, only that she try. That's all God wanted from her.

She realized she'd been silent a long time. Putting down the dish, she came to the kitchen table and sat next to Wilson. "Tell me more about the house," she said. "I know it's beautiful, but did it have a good vibe? Or did it feel too elegant for us?"

Something in Wilson's face seemed to relax. "It did feel a little formal," he admitted. "But I think if you were there it would feel like home."

Chapter 34

Saturday morning Sylvia woke up and rolled over to say, "Happy anniversary," but Wilson's side of the bed was empty. The sheets were still warm, so she must have just missed him. She lay in bed looking up at the ceiling and thinking about her wedding day ten years ago. How she'd opened her eyes that cool May morning and felt a rush of excitement—today she was getting married!

She was going to belong to someone—not just anyone, she amended, but Wilson Baxter, who was smarter than anyone she'd ever known, not to mention tall and with those amazing blue eyes that could quite literally pull the breath right out of her.

How precious those moments had been as her mother buttoned up the back of the same white silk-and-lace dress in which she had been married. The ride to the church with her father, never one for words, but who had held her hand the entire way. And the church—walking down that aisle and seeing Wilson standing there—waiting for her—looking at her as if she were the most beautiful woman in the world.

It was a look she couldn't help but hope she'd see on his face again today when he saw her in the white dress. Oh, she knew it was a business party, but it was still their anniversary.

Climbing out of bed she threw on an old pair of denim shorts and a T-shirt. Wandering into the kitchen she looked around for Wilson. He wasn't there.

She turned on the kettle. As she waited for the water to boil, she looked out the kitchen window. It was light enough to see the folding tables and chairs stacked lying on the grass where the caterers had dropped them off the night before.

The water boiled and she dunked a teabag in a mug that the boys had decorated with markers that read, WORLD'S GREATEST MOM. She debated going upstairs to see if Wilson was in his office, but decided against it.

Andrea, Susan, Rema, and Kelly had made her promise not to try to set up the tables and chairs before they got there, and the caterers weren't due until eleven o'clock, but Sylvia restlessly set down her cup and stepped out into the cool April morning.

Reaching for the long pole of the skimmer, she decided to give the pool one last cleaning before she set the set of floating candles in it.

She'd just finished when a black-and-white Border collie charged into the backyard, circled the pool, and ran up to her with its tail wagging hard.

Cookie? Sylvia just had time to think before the dog jumped up on her and strained to lick her face.

"What are you doing here?" Sylvia dodged the long, wet tongue and patted the sides of the dog's silken head. "You get lost?"

"Cookie!" Rema yelled, striding into the backyard in a pair of red shorts and a white tank top. "Come to Mommy right now!" Rema was followed by Skiezer and the boys, who were carrying industrial-sized food trays.

With the excited dog still nearly tripping her as she tried to walk, Sylvia hurried over to help. "Let me take that," she said as Skiezer moved the tray out of her reach.

"Got it," he said in his deep voice that always reminded her of James Earl Jones.

"Sorry about the dog," Rema said, pulling Cookie away from Sylvia. "We figured we'd be here all day. I couldn't figure out anyone to take care of him."

"I told her to leave him in our backyard," Skiezer said, setting the trays down on the black metal dining table near the grill. He wiped his hands on a pair of navy shorts. "Or leave him in the crate."

Rema's eyes narrowed. "It's too long to cage a dog, and if I put him in the backyard, he'd just dig his way out. Besides"—she cast Sylvia a wide smile—"Sylvia doesn't mind."

Sylvia had a brief image of Cookie jumping up on one of the guests but quickly suppressed it. "Of course I don't."

"We'll put him up in one of the bedrooms when the guests arrive," Rema added, as if reading Sylvia's thoughts. "And the boys can watch him." She looked around for Liam and Connor, but they were already gone. Sylvia suspected they'd gone inside the house to play video games with Simon and Tucker.

The back door gave a familiar jingle and Wilson stepped onto the patio. Andrea and Susan were right behind him. "Look who I found," he said, crossing the flagstone to kiss Sylvia's cheek. "Hey," he said, smiling. "Good morning—and happy anniversary."

She smiled. At least he'd remembered. "Happy anniversary," she said. Their gazes met and Sylvia felt something happy stir in her stomach. As soon as they were alone, she'd ask him when he wanted to open the gift she'd gotten him.

"Kelly's running late, but she'll be here in about an hour," Susan said. "And I've got all the flower arrangements in the back of my Suburban."

"The punch doesn't need to be made until right before the party starts," Andrea added, "so you can put me to work on setup."

"Once I get the grill going, I'm going to need some help bringing the fryer around back," Skiezer said. He grinned at Wilson. "We're frying a turkey in a Serrano-jalapeño citrus rub that's got enough kick to jumpstart a Hummer."

Rema rolled her eyes. "You'd better make a lot of punch, Andrea. Skiezer's not kidding. I hope those bankers like spicy food, Wilson."

"I'll make a lot of punch," Andrea promised. "Don't worry."

In her denim cutoffs and ruffled yellow sleeveless top, she looked younger, less formidable, reminding Sylvia less of a highly successful lawyer and more of the woman she'd met at the women's retreat all those years ago—a woman who'd led them all for a midnight "baptismal" swim in that murky brown lake.

For the next several hours, they strung small white lights in the trees, rearranged the outdoor furniture, and ringed the pool with a series of mosquito torches. Wilson worked on the sound system, and Joe appeared midmorning with a flat of Petunias, which he squeezed into the already thick flowerbeds.

The rumble of a truck in the driveway announced the caterer's arrival. Soon the backyard was a mass of activity as the tables were rolled out and then set up on the grassy area around the pool. Although Sylvia had argued with Wilson about the need for hiring professionals, she could see that he'd been right. The caterers—a crew of four—two men and two women, obviously knew what they were doing. Effortlessly, it seemed, the snowy white linens and their deep purple accents snapped into place.

Susan anchored the tablecloths with her floral arrangements while Kelly worked on the buffet table, setting out Ironstone serving dishes. Sylvia and Rema went from table to table wrapping the back of the white wooden folding chairs in deep purple tulle.

When Sylvia and Rema tied the last bow, Sylvia stepped back to admire the backyard. Her gaze traveled from the long, rectangular buffet table beneath the shade structure to the six round tables surrounding the pool. She imagined the palms lit up with their delicate white lights and the candles flickering on the tables and in the pool. The whole effect was elegant. Tasteful. Romantic.

"It's perfect," she said to Rema. "I can't believe it's our backyard."

"It really looks great," Rema agreed. "You're going to wow everyone tonight."

"I hope so," Sylvia said. She looked around for Wilson, to see if he liked their newly transformed backyard, but he was nowhere to be seen. "Excuse me a second," she said and went to look for him.

He was in his office, and while that was no big surprise, Sylvia found the door was closed, and for a moment she stared at the silver knob then tried turning it. She hadn't imagined it; the door was locked.

"Wilson?" She knocked gently. "Are you in there?"

"Yes," he yelled back. "Do you need something?"

"Why is this door locked?"

"I'm working," he said loudly. "Is everything okay?"

"Yes, but I want you to come look at the backyard. Make sure you like everything."

"I'm sure it's fine."

She stared at the closed door and frowned. "I hate talking to you through the door. Can you please open it?"

"I'm sorry," Wilson replied, "but I'm right in the middle of something. Let me finish this. I'll be downstairs in five."

His voice was distracted. She pictured him staring into his computer, in cyberspace, a million miles away. She felt like saying, "Oh don't bother," so he would know that she was upset—that he couldn't shut her out and then think she wouldn't notice. It was a big day for him though, and she loved him enough to bite her tongue. Turning, she headed down the stairs to the kitchen to make sandwiches for lunch.

After a quick lunch, Kelly and Andrea headed home to shower and dress. The caterers chased Sylvia out of the kitchen, so she headed to the master bathroom to get cleaned up. She had just finished blow-drying her hair with the diffuser and had slipped on the white column dress when Rema knocked on the bedroom door. "Want some help with your hair and makeup?"

Two hours later, Sylvia inspected herself in the mirror of the master bedroom. Her hair was gathered at the base of her neck in a loose updo. Rema had left some strands loose and enhanced the curls, which framed Sylvia's face in a soft, romantic way.

"You like it?" In the mirror, Rema's face peered anxiously over Sylvia's shoulder.

"Love it," Sylvia said, wanting to touch the curls but knowing if she did, Rema would kill her. "You're a magician. I can't thank you enough."

"All I did was polish you up a bit. You're beautiful, Sylvia. You always were."

Only she wasn't. Her nose was a little too big, and her teeth weren't perfectly straight. She was average in looks, but somehow Rema had transformed her into someone Sylvia barely recognized. Someone with smooth, tanned skin, large brown eyes, and full, coral-colored lips. Maybe it was because she'd been looking at photos recently, but with her hair swept up like this, she could see her mother's cheekbones, and the same shape of her mouth.

Sylvia's gaze found Rema's in the mirror. "Rema, I. . ."

Rema waved her hand. "No," she said very firmly as if she knew Sylvia had been about to tell her that she loved her, but couldn't bear to hear it. "Remember," she added, "you need a face and hair check every twenty minutes, and when they pass out the appetizers, don't eat anything with onions, fish, or spinach."

Sylvia reached for Rema's hand and squeezed it tightly. "I won't," she said.

Rema squeezed Sylvia's hands. "Good luck, honey."

There was a knock on the bedroom door. When Sylvia opened it, Wilson was standing there. His jaw dropped slightly when he saw her, and for a very satisfactory moment he seemed speechless. Finally he said, "Sylvia, you look amazing."

She smiled, stepping back and drawing the door wider so he could see her better. In her high heels, she was eye level with his nose, instead of his chin, and she liked the feeling of being taller, more powerful, and someone who could still surprise him.

Sylvia turned slowly so he could admire the back of the dress. "You like it?"

He nodded tightly. "A lot." The look in his eyes confirmed this.

"Sylvia, about our anniversary. . ."

His words were interrupted by laughter, the thump of running feet on the stairs, and then four boys and a dog burst into the bedroom. Rema, coming out of the bathroom, was just in time to intercept Cookie, who had a thin line of drool hanging from his mouth and was making a beeline for Sylvia.

"Liam and Connor!" Rema said sharply. "I told you Cookie has to stay in one of the bedrooms until the party's over."

"It's okay," Sylvia said. She realized that Tucker and Simon were looking at her with big eyes. "Yes, it's me," she said, smiling.

"You look pretty," Simon said a little shyly.

"Yeah, Mom," Tucker added. "You look shiny, even shinier than Daddy's car after he waxes it."

Sylvia smiled at the look of amazement on their features. One of Rema's bobby pins ached where it scraped against her scalp, her ribs pushed hard against the dress, and her feet felt as if they'd been bound for torture in the strappy high heels. However, every bit of the pain vanished in the glow of their praise. She'd wanted to shine like a star in their eyes, and here they were, gazing up at her as if she'd just fallen from the sky. Opening her arms, Sylvia bent, smiling. "I'm still your mom."

Before either boy could step into her embrace, Rema said loudly, "Sylvia, stop! You're going to mess up your hair, and if their hands are dirty. . .you aren't exactly wearing denim."

Sylvia stiffened. Rema was right; yet part of her didn't care. What good was wearing beautiful clothes if you couldn't touch anyone? What fun was being the brightest star in the universe if her boys couldn't hug her?

"Wave Mommy good-bye." Rema took both boys firmly by the

hand. "You're going back upstairs to the game room."

She turned back to Wilson. "Was there something you wanted to tell me?"

Something unreadable flickered briefly in his eyes. "Just to have fun tonight and be yourself."

Chapter 35

The party was well into swing by six o'clock. Sylvia sipped punch by the side of the pool where she could keep an eye on the guests and still hear the doorbell.

From the stereo speakers, the strains of classical music blended with the sound of voices. There had to be at least forty people—most from the bank—filling in the open spaces of her backyard with brightly colored dresses bumping up against the dark, serious suits of the men.

The white lights outlined the palm trees and the candles in the pool flickered gently. Around her, noises of polite conversation filled the air. The caterers, dressed in black pants and white shirts discreetly moved among the guests, serving trays of stuffed mushrooms and dilled scallop puffs. She spotted Andrea, Susan, Kelly, and Rema, along with their husbands, standing near the buffet table. Her friends looked beautiful in their dresses, and Sylvia felt a wave of gratitude toward them all.

Her gaze turned to Wilson, who stood to the left of her friends talking with the two board members and their wives who had driven in from Houston. The men wore conservative, expensive-looking dark suits. Both women looked as if they'd stepped out of a fashion catalog. The tall blond was wearing a hot pink chiffon dress that Rema whispered she'd seen in a Neiman's catalog for almost a thousand dollars. The other wife had a black, sparkly cocktail dress that probably cost as much as Sylvia's dining room set. As she watched, the women detached themselves from the men and wandered over to the buffet table.

It was strange to think her whole future might be determined tonight by this very party. Wilson had said they were to be themselves, but Sylvia had seen something in his eyes when he'd said it. Maybe he meant they were supposed to be better versions of themselves, to project the executive image fitting a future branch manager.

"Lovely party," a man's voice said. Turning, Sylvia found herself face-to-face with Bruce Maddox, Wilson's boss. He was wearing a dark suit with a pink tie and pink handkerchief sticking out of his breast pocket.

"Thank you," Sylvia murmured, smiling. "It's good to see you again, Bruce."

He looked up at her. His nose was long and bony; his eyes deep set and hard to read. His suit hung more loosely than Sylvia remembered seeing at Christmas, and the hollows under his cheeks seemed more pronounced. She almost asked if he was all right and then remembered Wilson telling her that his boss disliked personal comments.

"I see Justin and Phillip talking to Wilson," Bruce said, "but where are the other two board members?"

Sylvia sipped her punch. "The Abbots said something came up, and I haven't heard from the Wallaces."

"Never mind," Bruce said. "If Wilson gets Bowers, he'll get the job."

"Wilson really appreciates your support for this promotion," Sylvia said. "I know how hard you've been campaigning for him."

"Wilson's like a son to me," Bruce said. "Besides, he's worked hard and he deserves this opportunity. Now you'll have to excuse me, but I have some business to tend to."

Sylvia's gaze followed his back as he wound his way across the crowded patio. He carried a glossy black cane, but she noticed he didn't lean much on it, merely used it to nudge people into making more room for himself—which was good because their backyard really was too small for a party like this. She held her breath as Bruce followed the curve of the pool to the other side. Jen Douglas, beautiful in a black, one-shouldered dress, caught her gaze and waved, before turning back to the group of men who had surrounded her. Sylvia watched her laugh at something one of the men said and felt a little pang. Jen looked so perfect. And while Wilson hadn't said for sure that Jen would be his new assistant, he hadn't said she wouldn't be either.

Sylvia sipped her punch. God had a plan for her—for all of them—a good plan. . .and she had to trust Him. However, it didn't mean she was going to stand idly by and let this woman work side by side with Wilson. It was time to draw the line. If Wilson wanted them to move, he was going to have to get another assistant. She looked up as Rema moved next to her.

"Who's that?" she asked, looking at Jen Douglas.

"Wilson's boss's assistant," Sylvia said. "For now."

"And later?"

"I'll have to get back to you on that."

At the edge of the pool, Wilson sipped fruit punch and offered his opinion about the new BMW series that would be released in the fall. His skin tingled in excitement that Justin Eddelman and Phillip Devall—two of the most powerful men in his company—were standing in his backyard, talking to him.

So far they had discussed cars, golf clubs, and the unlikely possibility of the Astros making the playoffs this year. He was beginning to wonder if the conversation would ever turn to business, specifically his promotion.

His shirt felt damp beneath the suit. He couldn't wait to loosen his tie. Out of the corner of his eye, he glimpsed Sylvia, her white dress nearly glowing in the fading light, talking to Lisa Eddelman and Connie Devall.

"I'm glad to see you value developing relationships outside of the office," Justin Eddelman said, drawing Wilson's full attention back to him. He was a tall, solidly built man with an enviably full head of steel-gray hair. He was probably five years younger than Wilson, and yet had three houses, including a ranch in California, and he'd been featured recently in the cover story on the *Financial Times*. "I've always felt team building was key to success."

Wilson nodded gravely. He remembered this quote from the interview in the *Times*. "Sylvia and I enjoy entertaining, and it's a great opportunity to get to meet the spouses."

Justin's heavyset features lifted into a smile. "Yes, you can learn a lot about someone when you understand their personal life."

Wilson sipped his punch. "It's just good to get to know the

people you're working with." He put a note of cheerfulness to his voice. "We're all in this together."

"But there's a downside to that," Phillip Devall said. He was a dark-skinned man with a narrow face, close-cropped dark hair, and wire-rimmed glasses. "It's a lot harder to fire someone if you're friends with them. How do you feel about that, Wilson?"

Both men smiled casually, trying to hide the intensity of the question. They were talking, of course, about the job redundancy issues that would occur as the two banks merged. Would Wilson be tough enough to handle the personnel issues?

"Well, I wouldn't feel good about it," Wilson said. "Before I let anyone go, friend or not, I'd work pretty hard to evaluate all potential solutions."

"But you'd do it if you were asked to, correct?" The glass on Phillip Devall's frames looked bulletproof, shielding a set of unyielding brown eyes. He had a reputation for being a tough boss, for firing nonperformers. Rumor had it he'd laid off more than a hundred employees.

Wilson's gaze didn't waver. "What exactly are we talking about, hypothetically of course?"

When Justin named the number, Wilson had to fight not to let his dismay show. What about his business plan which was designed to drive growth at twice the local market rate? Had it been scrapped? "I'm not a hatchet man," he said. "I believe people will perform well if we develop the right game plan. Mine drives growth at twice the local market rate."

"We've seen your plan. You're asking for some sizeable IT investments."

Wilson nodded. He realized he was frowning and forced a smile.

This evening was a test of his social skills. "If we want to improve customer satisfaction with more online banking, grow our products and services revenue streams, and be competitive, then that's what we have to do."

"If we go that direction," Phillip argued, "we'd still need to aggressively trim headcount and accelerate the timeline. We can't have the server down during business hours."

He was talking nighttime and weekends, something Wilson had anticipated but had hoped to avoid by phasing in the changes over time.

"But look, Wilson, Phil and I wouldn't be here if we didn't think you were the right person for the job," Justin said, clasping Wilson on the shoulder. "We're having brunch with Bruce tomorrow morning at the Marriot. Why don't you join us? We can go over a lot of things."

Tomorrow was Sunday. What about church? Wilson looked up as Susan approached, carrying a tray of stuffed mushrooms. Her presence was a welcome distraction. How many times, he wondered, would these men ask him to put the needs of the business before his faith? How many anniversaries, birthdays, soccer games, and cookouts would he miss?

Too many, he feared. And yet, knowing all this, he still felt the familiar pull to climb to the next level, to reach for the trophy now within his grasp.

It'll all work out, he told himself. *Once I've got the new technology and my staff in place, I'll be able to manage my work schedule better. Missing church on one Sunday isn't a big deal. God will understand.*

"What about it, Wilson?" Justin said. "The Marriott at nine?"

It was dark by the time they finished dinner. A soft breeze made the candles on the table flicker and lifted the curls around Sylvia's face. A full moon had come out, and the sight of it reminded her of when Simon and Tucker had been two and four and Wilson had been teaching them the names of the constellations. Simon had looked up at the black velvet sky and said, "The moon looks like God turned His flashlight on."

Next to her, Wilson squeezed her leg. It was his way of telling her that he was pleased with the way the evening was going. Across from her, Connie Devall was talking about a charity event she was hosting for the American Heart Association through the Junior League. It was a good cause, but the dinner tickets were expensive, and it was obviously designed for people with a lot of money. Not that being well-off was bad—and charity work was always great—it just wasn't part of Sylvia's world.

"Anyone ready for dessert and coffee?" Sylvia started to stand, but Wilson's hand on her wrist stopped her.

"Hold on," he said, and then rising to his feet, he lifted a fluted champagne glass. "May I have everyone's attention please?" At first only their table noticed, but after Wilson repeated the request several times, a hush grew over the backyard.

Wilson cleared his throat. "I'd like to thank everyone for coming," he said loudly, "to Sylvia's and my tenth anniversary. Right now I'd like to make a toast to my wife, who makes me feel like the luckiest man on earth." He looked deeply into her eyes. "Sylvia, you are a great wife and mother. You've given me ten wonderful years—the best in my life. I love you, honey." He clinked glasses with her. "Here's to many more years together." Bending, he kissed her on the lips.

Everyone applauded. Sylvia felt herself blush as Wilson pulled away and everyone stared at her. She felt like everyone was expecting her to say something nice back to Wilson, and she could barely get out an awkward, "I love you, too." And then it got very quiet. "How about that cake?" she finally managed, and everyone laughed.

Sylvia was handing out slices of vanilla frosted cake with raspberry filling (purchased at Sam's Club, which she avoided admitting when asked) when the kitchen door opened. Liam, holding Cookie on a leash, stepped onto the patio. As usual, the Border collie was full of energy.

Rearing up on his hind legs, the dog strained against the leash and began to hop, sort of like a kangaroo, in an attempt to free himself. Liam, although tall for his age and strong, had to lean his full weight to hold on to the dog. Sylvia put down the serving piece, but Rema moved faster, and with her purple chiffon dress swirling around her legs, got there first.

"I told you to keep Cookie in the bedroom," Rema hissed.

"But Mom," Liam said, "I think he has to go. Really badly. He was circling and sniffing the carpet."

Rema's lips pursed together before she handed the leash back to her son. "Then take him way in the back behind the trees," she said. "The last thing the guests need to see is a dog bent over pooping." She looked at Sylvia. "Have you got a little baggie?"

"I'll get one." The voice belonged to Simon, who along with Connor and Tucker had appeared on the patio, and they stood in a height line, tallest to shortest, looking a little self-conscious, but a little excited, too, to be part of the party. With the air of someone off to save the world, Simon dashed inside the house.

"Sorry, Sylvia," Rema said.

"Don't worry." Sylvia smiled. "Everything is going great. Boys, did you get enough to eat?"

Tucker, Liam, and Connor nodded soberly. They looked adorable in their khaki pants and a variety of colored polo shirts. Like mini-men. In Tucker, particularly, she could see not only Wilson's extraordinary blue eyes, but also the slight roundness to his face, and the shape of his mouth. Temperamentally, he might be more like her, but physically he was Wilson, minus the glasses. "You want another piece of cake? There's plenty."

Just then, Simon burst out of the back door with an empty grocery bag. The four boys and the dog quickly wound their way through the tables and disappeared into the dark areas of the backyard.

Sylvia lingered in front of the pool. She could see the reflection of her white dress wavering in the silky surface of the water. Around her, the voices of the guests mingled with the strands of classical music. And if she strained, she could hear children's laughter coming from the backyard.

She pictured them moving in a pack with Cookie leading the way, and smiled. Maybe when they moved she would get the boys a dog. She hadn't had one when she was growing up. Her mother had not been an animal person, but Sylvia thought having a dog might be good for the boys. It would teach them about caring for a pet and also be fun. It would also cushion the blow of moving.

God, she said silently, *what happens next—it's all in Your hands.*

"I haven't been to a party as nice as this one for years." The voice belonged to Lisa Eddelman, who had joined her on the flagstone. Lisa was slightly taller than Sylvia, definitely thinner, and had clear, unlined skin and large dark eyes that fixed confidently on Sylvia. "I'm on a mission," she confessed.

"A mission?" Sylvia smiled.

"To recruit you," Lisa admitted. "Justin's very keen on hiring Wilson, but we all know that it's the wife who has to be convinced."

More laughter erupted from the backyard. Tucker's voice shouted with the righteous determination of a younger sibling. "It's my turn, Simon! Give me the leash!"

"I know relocations can be hard—leaving your friends and family—but we're a very social group, Sylvia. We'd keep you busy—you golf, right? And I hear you fundraise for your elementary school. We do lots of charity work through the Junior League. I'd personally be glad to sponsor your membership, and Connie has a lot of pull."

More shouts rang from the backyard. Something was definitely going on back there. As Lisa described luncheons at the club, Sylvia tried to focus, but the snatches of the boys' conversation competed for her attention.

Suddenly Sylvia glimpsed a dog galloping along with its leash tailing behind him. Her heart sank as Liam's voice yelled, "Tucker, why did you let go?" and then, "Get him!"

"Cookie! No!" A shrill voice wailed. It sounded like Simon.

"Will you excuse me a second?" Sylvia stepped onto the grass. Her heels immediately sank into the earth, and pausing, she slipped them off and hiked up the hem of her dress. The backyard wasn't wide, but it was deep. Even so, almost immediately she spotted Cookie, running around like a maniac, trailing his leash. In hot pursuit were the boys, who were shouting at the dog to stop.

It was darker back here—but there was enough moonlight to see the trees and the fence line. Sylvia quickly changed her angle and ran to cut the dog off. It skirted around her, and as it passed, it looked right at her. She could have sworn it was laughing at her.

Great! The last thing she needed was for a big dog to run through their party. Not now, not when Wilson was so close to getting the promotion. She set her jaw. "Boys," she called, "head it off from the pool—try to herd it into the corner."

The dog was faster and more agile than any of them, but fortunately it thought they were playing a game of chase and ran circles around them, staying away from the guests and the pool. Sylvia was out of breath and definitely ready to kill the dog as it continued to evade them. Finally, the leash snagged around the trunk of a crepe myrtle.

Wrapping the leash firmly around her wrist, she led the dog— who was still fresh and full of himself—back toward the house. "You're going back to your room," she told the dog firmly, "before you cause any more trouble."

"Mrs. Baxter," Liam said, as they walked back toward the house. "We're really sorry."

"I didn't mean to let him go," Tucker wailed. "He just pulled really hard then ran away."

Sylvia retrieved her shoes. Her feet were muddy, and she didn't want to think about the hem of her dress—or what her hair was currently doing.

"Mom," Simon added, "he was digging and—"

"That's what they do, dig. Dog's dig," Lisa Eddelman interrupted. She was standing on the edge of the flagstone, and obviously had been watching the whole scene. "Well done, Sylvia," she said, smiling. "You're much faster than my last doubles partner."

Sylvia laughed. She had to tighten her grip on the dog, who began pulling her eagerly toward the board member's wife.

"You know I'm a dog person, don't you," Lisa Eddelman cooed as she bent to pat the squirming dog. Her blond hair gleamed silver beneath the pool spotlights.

"You've been a very bad doggie, haven't you?" Lisa said in a delighted tone. "And what's that in your mouth? Is it your favorite toy?" She put her hand out. "Drop it," she ordered in a commanding voice.

Cookie opened his mouth and dropped the toy into Lisa's open palm, but instead of praising the dog, the board member's wife screamed and dropped the object. Backing away rapidly, she continued to make shrill noises and flapped her hands.

"Lisa?" Sylvia's gaze went from Lisa Eddelman's horrified expression to the small, dark object lying on the flagstone. Her heart seemed to stop as she slowly registered the mothy remains of Bluebonnet.

"Bluebonnet," Tucker cried, and then he began to sob.

"We thought we stopped him in time," Liam said. "I'm so sorry, Mrs. Baxter!"

"It's okay," Sylvia said automatically. She scooped Tucker into her arms and glimpsed Lisa Eddelman kneeling by the side of the pool, splashing water over her arms.

"Simon," she said urgently. "Go get your father."

Chapter 36

After the last guest left, Sylvia turned to Wilson. "I blew it for you, didn't I?" They were standing in the foyer. It was close to midnight and even the caterers had gone. From the family room, she heard the television playing *The Lion King*, although Joe, Simon, and Tucker had long ago fallen asleep on the couch. Sylvia didn't blame them. She was so tired she ached.

Wilson loosened his tie and smiled. "You didn't blow anything for me, Sylvia. That was a great party."

She scrunched up her nose. "Are you serious? Cookie dug up Bluebonnet and dropped her into Lisa Eddelman's hand. She thought she was getting a play toy, not a dead parakeet."

Wilson laughed. "She recovered well," he said. "Although I admit, for a moment, I thought I was going to have to fish her out of the pool."

"She was just trying to wash her hands."

The party had pretty much come to a standstill as Wilson had calmly scooped up the dead bird, talked Lisa Eddelman away from the pool, and then explained to everyone what had happened.

"I don't think Mrs. Eddelman is going to be asking me to join the Junior League anymore." She studied her husband's face. "I'm sorry we didn't make the impression you were hoping for."

He smiled. "Don't say that. We did fine. And besides, what happened with the dog wasn't your fault."

"I should have told Rema to keep the dog home."

"Because of the dog and the bird, people are going to remember our party for a long time."

"But not in a good way."

"Says who? Sylvia, look at me."

She'd always loved his eyes, the intelligence mixed with kindness. "Everyone had a great time—thanks to your hard work and our friends'. I admit I had doubts, but I can't imagine how we would have done everything without them. We have a lot to be thankful for."

She braced herself, knowing she had to ask, and dreading the disappointment she'd see in his eyes. "The promotion, Wilson."

"What about it?" He tried to look nonchalant, but an excited gleam flickered in his eyes.

"Did you get it?"

Wilson grinned proudly. "You had doubts?"

"Not until Cookie dug up Bluebonnet."

"Actually that clinched it for me," Wilson informed her. "Justin liked seeing firsthand how I handled a stressful situation."

"So you seriously got it?"

The proud smile stretch wider. "Seriously."

Sylvia hugged him hard. "Oh Wilson. I'm so proud of you. Congratulations!" This was it. This was her answer. Maybe it wasn't the answer she'd wanted, but she, Wilson, and the boys were a family, and they would support each other. She'd find a way to stay close to Rema and her friends while building a new life. And she'd plaster the walls of his new office with photos of herself and the kids.

Suddenly they were kissing, and he hadn't kissed her like this in a long time, and even as this registered, her mind whirled. They would be moving. When? Was she really okay with this?

Finally he pulled back. She looked into his eyes. They were dreamy and yet fierce. Strong and gentle. That was the Wilson she had fallen in love with.

"This is so exciting, honey," Sylvia said. "But there's something we need to talk about." She paused, took a breath. "This Jen woman—I trust you completely—but I don't want her to be your assistant. It isn't a good idea."

"It's not going to be a problem."

Sylvia studied his face. "She's getting another job?"

Wilson laughed. "Not exactly."

"Then what?"

"I turned down the job."

What? Sylvia stepped backward so fast she nearly tripped on the hem of her dress. "You what?"

"I turned it down."

She was tired. Maybe she had misunderstood. Her heart began to pound and little chills ran up her arms. "You turned it down? You turned down the position of branch manager?"

"It wasn't right for me. For us."

"But you were so sure. . ."

"I know. I thought I was, too—until tonight. Sylvia, they're looking for someone to fire a lot of people and work nights and weekends. I'm not that person. I hope you're not disappointed."

"Of course not." She stared at him, stunned. "But who are you—and what did you do with my Wilson?"

"I'm still the guy who married you ten years ago and would marry you all over again."

This was something the hero in one of Sylvia's romances would say, and even as it thrilled her to hear it, she couldn't accept that Wilson had actually turned down the promotion. "But what about being passed over, becoming stagnant and all that other stuff you talked about?"

"When I turned down the job, Justin asked me why. I told him that I felt like his vision for the industry was different than mine. I didn't want to downsize and fire people—I wanted to change the fundamental business model. And I told him I didn't want to move." A look of intense satisfaction passed over Wilson's features. "He immediately assumed that I had been interviewing at other companies and said that before I made any changes, we needed to talk again—that the company needed guys like me."

"So we're staying in Sweetwater?" She could barely keep the excitement out of her voice.

"We're staying in Sweetwater." He reached for her hand. "But that's enough business talk. It's our anniversary, and I have a surprise for you."

"And I have a gift for you."

"Mine first."

They tiptoed past Joe who was snoring on the couch with Tucker and Simon sprawled on top of him, their thin limbs so entwined it was hard to separate them.

Wilson's hand gripped hers tightly as they sped up the stairs and past the framed family pictures on the walls. Sylvia had to gather the folds of her long dress in her free hand to keep from tripping over them as they hurried down the hallway.

"Wilson, slow down." But he couldn't, or wouldn't, until they reached the closed door to his office. He came to a stop, and there was a very intense look in his eyes as he swept her off her feet. He fumbled a little with the doorknob, and then it swung open and they stepped inside.

Wilson carried her over the threshold. "Happy anniversary, honey," he said.

The scent of the roses filled her senses. She saw the rose petals forming a giant heart in the middle of the room, and tealight candles flickering from small heart-shaped votives on the bookshelves, the desk, and the credenza. "Oh Wilson," she murmured as he carried her to the center of the heart then gently lowered her to her feet. "Look at the candles!"

"They're battery-operated," he informed her, "because I couldn't be sure what time the party would be over."

Sylvia stood on a carpet of red, pink, and white rose petals. It must have taken a hundred flowers to make up this heart. How soft they felt on her bare feet. How sweet they smelled. "I can't believe you did all this."

"You like it?" Wilson's voice sounded boyishly eager.

She looked into eyes. "Like it? I *love* it."

"We're just getting started," he said, looking very pleased and a little mysterious. "This is for you." He thrust a fat envelope into her hand. "I love you, Sylvia."

"What is this?" Sylvia examined the envelope from every angle. She was dying with curiosity to see what was inside. At the same time she wanted to draw out the tingle of pleasant anticipation.

"What did you do?"

"Open it," Wilson urged, "and you'll see."

She fingered the bulky envelope. There was more than just a nice card inside. But what? It seemed almost a shame to rip open the thick, cream-colored envelope, but she slid her fingernail along the seam then pulled out a fat bundle of papers inside, and her heart started to pound. She looked at him in wonder. "You're serious?"

"Very. We'll fly into Rome and rent a car. I was thinking we would head south and stay at bed-and-breakfasts—I've put some brochures in there. I thought you might want to see some of the towns your family comes from."

Sylvia's hands trembled on the pages. They seemed suddenly too fragile, too valuable to trust in her hands. Italy. She'd heard family stories of course, and she couldn't make her grandmother's marinara sauce without thinking of her. But actually going to these places, seeing them with Wilson, was a little overwhelming.

"This is an amazing gift," she said. "I don't know what to say."

Wilson smiled. "Say yes. Just like you did ten years ago."

Sylvia looked at his face, at the worry lines on his forehead that always deepened when something was very important to him. His glasses framed his amazing blue eyes and partially hid faint wrinkles around his eyes. She saw him aging, the lines deepening, the sandy-colored hair receding. And she also saw the handsome young man who had walked into the bank one day and stood staring at her, as if awestruck, and not understanding that he was that someone—that something good her mother had promised would happen in her life.

"Yes," she said. "I will."

Chapter 37

"Hi, Simon," the giant pizza slice blew him a mock kiss as it danced into the second-grade classroom.

"Hey, that doesn't sound like your mom," Will said. He was sitting next to Simon in Mr. Powonka's class, and they had just finished the spelling unit. Both he and Will had gotten one hundred on the test, plus they'd both gotten the bonus word, *aorta*, correct.

Simon shifted on his seat before turning to the boy next to him. He hoped the dancing pizza slice wouldn't do something embarrassing, like hug him in front of everyone. At the same time, he couldn't help sitting a little straighter in his chair. After all, Mr. Slice was a celebrity at their school, and he'd just singled him out.

"I know," he said. "That's my grandfather."

"Hello, everyone," Poppy said, sounding as usual as if he had gravel stuck in his throat. "Are you going to see me in the box tonight?"

"Yes, Mr. Slice!" the entire class shouted at the same time.

"What's our favorite dinner?" The slice of pizza cupped his ear, as if he couldn't hear.

The class took the hint and yelled even louder. "Pizza, Mr. Slice."

"Where's your mom?" Will whispered. Both of them knew if they got caught talking they'd get a lower grade on their weekly conduct report. Will was pretty smart, like Simon, and lately Simon had been thinking of asking him if he wanted to hang out at his house.

"In Italy," Simon replied, "with my dad."

"Remember," Poppy said, "the class that orders the most pizza gets a free pizza party delivered by Mr. Slice." He began to tap dance around the classroom.

"Your grandfather is so cool," Will said. "My grandpa lives in Ohio. I only see him in the summer."

"That's too bad," Simon said. "Poppy used to live in Sugar Hill but he moved in with us."

At first it'd been a little weird having Poppy there all the time. He talked a lot, and once Simon had caught him going through Simon's backpack. But Poppy was always doing some kind of interesting project. Poppy could take things apart then put them back together even better. He'd fixed Mom's favorite lamp and now was working on the vacuum.

"Okay, class," Mr. Powonka said. "Say good-bye to Mr. Slice, he has other classrooms to visit."

"Good-bye, Mr. Slice," Simon called along with his classmates at the top of his lungs.

Mr. Slice pretended he couldn't hear, so Simon took a deep breath and yelled even louder. Just before he left, Poppy gave him a special pat on the shoulder. Simon felt himself turn red but sat up straighter.

If anyone commented on the color in his cheeks, he'd tell them he'd just been touched by a red-hot slice of pizza, which came out of an oven that burned hotter than 700 degrees, more than 600 degrees hotter than the surface of his skin.

At the same time, he knew the facts that rolled so easily off his tongue were not what made him so special.

He was special because God loved him.

He'd prayed for his dad to spend more time with him, and just look what happened. The Lord had not only heard him, but also granted his wish. He treasured that hour in the evening when he, Tucker, Poppy, and his dad shot hoops in the driveway. It didn't matter that he was the worst shot of them all. His dad said not to worry—just have fun playing—and oh, by the way, look over there.

Simon always knew he was just trying to distract him so he could sneak a shot past him. However, Simon *never* fell for it and *always* managed to steal the ball.

Tonight, however, he planned to let his dad sneak one past him, just to make him happy, and because Simon, honestly, didn't care who won.

Kim O'Brien grew up in Bronxville, New York. She holds a bachelor's degree in psychology from Emory University in Atlanta, Georgia, and a master's degree in fine arts from Sarah Lawrence College in Bronxville, New York. She worked for many years as a writer, editor, and speechwriter for IBM. She is the author of eight romance novels and seven nonfiction children's books. She's happily married to Michael and has two fabulous daughters, Beth and Maggie. She is active in the Loft Church in The Woodlands, Texas. Kim loves to hear from readers and can be reached through her Facebook author's page.

Check out these other great
Destination Romances from
Barbour Publishing

A Wedding Transpires on
Mackinac Island
978-1-61626-535-9

A Bride's Dilemma in
Friendship, Tennessee
978-1-61626-571-7

A Wedding Song in
Lexington, Kentucky
978-1-61626-573-1

A Bride Opens Shop in
El Dorado, California
978-1-61626-583-0